"I've got a proposition for you."

Dora's eyes narrowed. Whatever it was, she didn't want to hear it.

"I'll pay you fair market value for the house and the acre of land it stands on," Grey St. Bride announced. Her jaw fell, and while he waited for her response, he went a step further. "I'll even include a bonus if you'll agree to vacate the premises within one week."

By the time she remembered to close her gaping mouth, Dora's fists were clenched at her side. Not even that could prevent the tremors that raced up and down her body.

Nor did it quell her sudden fear, her doubts.

Could Grey force her out? If he did, where could she go to start over? No matter how much he paid her, money didn't last forever. She, more than anyone, should know that.

"No, thank you," she said, her voice betraying her feelings by only a slight stiffness. "I believe I'll stay."

Blue eyes had never looked more arctic. "The devil you will."

Praise for Bronwyn Williams

Longshadow's Woman
"This is a perfect example of Western romance writing
at its very best...an exciting and satisfying read."
—*Romance Reviews Today*

The Paper Marriage
"From first page to last,
this is the way romance should be."
—*Old Book Barn Gazette*

"Creating multi-dimensional characters
in a warm-hearted story, Ms. Williams draws you
into the heart of her tale."
—*Romantic Times Magazine*

Bronwyn Williams

THE MAIL-ORDER BRIDES

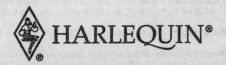

HARLEQUIN®

TORONTO • NEW YORK • LONDON
AMSTERDAM • PARIS • SYDNEY • HAMBURG
STOCKHOLM • ATHENS • TOKYO • MILAN • MADRID
PRAGUE • WARSAW • BUDAPEST • AUCKLAND

ISBN 0-373-29189-2

THE MAIL-ORDER BRIDES

Copyright © 2001 by Dixie Browning and Mary Williams

This edition published by arrangement with Harlequin Books S.A.

Visit us at www.eHarlequin.com

Printed in U.S.A.

Please address questions and book requests to:
Harlequin Reader Service
U.S.: 3010 Walden Ave., P.O. Box 1325, Buffalo, NY 14269
Canadian: P.O. Box 609, Fort Erie, Ont. L2A 5X3

To the keepers of the Cape Hatteras lighthouse,
which includes our grandfather, E. D. Burrus,
and our great-grandfather, Bateman A. Williams.

And to our sister, Sara Shoemaker,
for duties above and beyond.

Chapter One

April 1899
St. Brides Island, on the Outer Banks
of North Carolina.

Considering all she had lost over the past few months—her father, her fiancé, her friends and her reputation—it was her personal maid, Bertie, that Adora Sutton missed most at this moment. Feet spread against the rocking motion of the boat, she tried to brush out the worst creases from her gown. The travel stains would have to wait. As for her hair, which was unmanageable at the best of times, all she could do was flatten it with her hands, pin it down and hope the wind wouldn't set it free again. There was no way she could keep a hat on her head in this wind—it would be gone the moment she stepped outside.

"I'll set your bag out onto the dock, miss," said the young mate as she left the protection of the cramped passenger section. "Mr. St. Bride, he'll see to it."

"Yes, thank you very much," Dora murmured,

fumbling in her reticule for one of her few remaining coins while she scanned the bleak terrain for some sign of welcome. Merciful heaven, was *this* all there was? Aside from the bustling waterfront, she could see only sand, marsh, a few stunted trees and a scattered handful of rough cottages. A single road, roughly paved with oyster shells, crossed the island, leading directly from the waterfront to a tall weathered house perched on top of the highest dune. Before they had even reached the docks, the mate had identified it as St. Bride's house, St. Bride being the name of the man who had placed the advertisement that had brought her out to this bleak, unappealing island.

According to Captain Dozier, the man owned not only the entire island off the coast of North Carolina, but almost everything on it. Dora had murmured a noncommittal comment and silently wondered whether the king of the island was, in reality, a dragon. Hadn't some wise man once said, "Better the devil you know than the devil you don't?" Perhaps she should turn back before it was too late.

But then, another sage, she reminded herself, had said, "In for a penny, in for a pound." She hadn't come this far to allow worrisome second thoughts to send her scurrying.

However, she did wish she'd chosen to wear one of her darker gowns. While the pink lent her courage, it was rather impractical. Now, instead of looking her best, which might have bolstered her spirits, she looked rumpled and frivolous.

Perhaps, she thought with a surge of bitter amusement, she should have worn scarlet....

The advertisement had specified healthy, capable women of good character, who were seeking a mate.

The first few qualifications posed no problem. Small she might be, but she was far stronger than she looked. How else could she have survived the past six weeks? She was certainly healthy enough, if one didn't count the aftereffects of mal de mer. The brandy Captain Dozier had given her had settled her stomach, but it had done little for her equilibrium.

Capable? Oh, yes indeed. She'd been the first in her set to learn the two-step, and her voice was considered exceptional. Unfortunately, she couldn't carry a tune, but when it came to tennis, she easily outshone all her friends.

Her former friends, she amended quickly.

As to her character, that, unfortunately, was open to argument.

Behind her, men swarmed over the two-masted freighter, some bringing freight up from the hold, others carting it to a tall building that seemed to be some sort of warehouse. A redheaded man with a fistful of papers had cornered the captain, and the two men were deep in conversation.

Dora looked around helplessly. When it became obvious that no one had sent a carriage to meet her, she told herself that if this was to be the first test of her mettle, she would not be found lacking. Shifting her valise to the other hand, she approached a youth who was busily unrolling a length of stained canvas. "Where will I find Mr. St. Bride?"

Startled, the boy looked up. His face turned fiery red. "St. Bride? That's his place up there on the ridge, ma'am." Rising, he dusted off his hands and said, "Tote yer poke?"

"I beg your pardon?"

"Yer poke-sack, ma'am? Kin I tote it for ye?"

Thinking of the few coins that were all that remained between her and starvation should this venture fail, she smiled and shook her head. "Thank you, but it's really not heavy."

The boy nodded and returned to his task. Dora, stepping carefully off the weathered wharf, set out along the rough road that led to the house on the hill. She had taken for granted she'd be met on arrival, or at the very least that a conveyance of some sort would be available.

The shells were mostly crushed, but there were a few clumps here and there. Picking her way carefully, she tried to avoid the worst clumps and at the same time look around her. Merciful heavens, what a desolate place!

Stepping on something sharp, she lurched, righted herself, and wondered how long it took for the effects of a single glass of brandy to wear off. Perhaps she should have worn something sturdier than her kidskin slippers instead of packing all but a single change of clothes in her trunk to be sent out as soon as she could afford it. Which was to say, as soon as she had a husband who could afford to send for it.

Not that she even owned any serviceable shoes.

Besides, she'd wanted to make a good first impression.

Imagining every man on the waterfront staring at her the way the men had before she'd left Bath, she wished she could shrink even smaller than she was. As that was impossible, she stiffened her back, staggered once and continued her march toward what would soon be her home.

A homely yellow dog raced past her, followed by half a dozen others. After one shaggy brown creature nearly knocked her off her feet, she regained her balance and gazed around her, trying not to feel too discouraged. The house on the ridge didn't improve at closer range. Not the slightest effort had been made to adorn its uncompromising façade. Window boxes might be a nice touch. And perhaps a porch swing, or some lovely rattan furniture.

If her prospective bridegroom was anything like his house, she was beginning to feel less certain of her future. The least the man could have done was meet her when she arrived. The very *least*.

Passing a raw wooden shack halfway along the road, she wondered if it could possibly be a church. While there was no steeple, someone had erected a cross over the doorway. She tried and failed to imagine being married in such a place.

It was no easier than picturing herself marrying a total stranger.

Numerous sandy footpaths cut away from the main road, leading to what appeared to be several one-room cabins. Off in the distance she saw a long wooden structure with a shed jutting off the back. The few trees she saw were stunted, bent low as if by a constant wind.

Not a single shop in sight. She sighed, thinking perhaps she should have waited to be met. Then, at least, she could have asked questions before committing herself completely. If only she hadn't been so determined to demonstrate just how strong, capable and sensible she was. To prove that she met every single qualification Mr. St. Bride had specified in his advertisement for a wife.

A shaft of sunlight broke through the dark, racing clouds. She told herself it was a good omen after a

stormy crossing. *You listen here to me, Dora Sutton—*
whatever he's like, the man would never have adver-
tised for a wife if he hadn't wanted one.

That in itself was encouraging…wasn't it?

Nor, she reminded herself, would she have responded if she hadn't been desperate. A husband was
the last thing in the world she wanted, but at that point
she'd had little recourse. Which was why, professing
to be a widow, she had written her qualifications, and
Mr. St. Bride had arranged her passage, and now here
she was, for better or worse.

It could hardly be worse than what she had left behind.

Stepping on another broken shell, she hopped on
one foot and steadied herself on the picket fence she
happened to be passing. Beyond the fence stood a
cozy-looking cottage, far smaller than the house on the
ridge, but larger than any she had seen so far. Behind
the house, an elderly man on a ladder appeared to be
repairing the roof of an outbuilding of some sort. As
the entire contraption was leaning, it hardly seemed
worth the effort, but then, that was the least of Dora's
concerns.

Waving away a cloud of midges, she trudged on,
setting her sights hopefully on the gaunt structure
ahead. The brisk, salt-scented breeze helped to clear
her head but did little to steady her legs. She still felt
as if she were on a rolling deck, although the captain
had assured her that the effects would pass quickly.

Evidently she was no better a drinker than she was
a sailor.

The closer she came, the more she dreaded the coming interview. To think that not long ago she'd been
celebrating her engagement. Henry Carpenter Smythe,

a young man her father had met on a business trip to Richmond and brought home with him, had seemed to be everything any woman could want. Handsome, with lovely manners and a delightful sense of humor, he had quietly let it be known, without actually boasting, that he was more than comfortably situated.

Dora had been smitten at first glance. Intent on impressing him, she had arranged a dinner party and invited a dozen of her closest friends, praying that Henry wouldn't fall instantly in love with her best friend, Selma, who was easily the most beautiful woman in their set.

He'd been polite to all her friends, but no more than that. At her father's invitation, he had extended his stay at Sutton Hall, and two weeks later, after a whirlwind courtship that had been encouraged by her father, Henry had asked her to marry him.

On St. Valentine's Day he had given her a handsome diamond ring and they'd begun making plans for the wedding. They had talked of June weddings and bridesmaid gowns and flowers, and who Henry's best man would be.

"If I'd seen him first," Selma had declared, "he would have been mine." She'd said it in jest, but there'd been something about the way she'd persisted in hanging on to Henry's arm at every meeting, quizzing him about his friends and asking if he had a brother, that had made Dora rather uncomfortable.

But then, at the time, Dora had been increasingly concerned over her father's health. He'd lost weight and seemed distraught. Even if she hadn't fallen in love with Henry, she would have encouraged him to stay because her father seemed to perk up in the younger man's company.

When Henry had asked for her hand, her father had beamed, offered his blessing and urged them not to wait. "I'm looking forward to seeing my first grandson before I die," he kept saying, and each time, Dora would hasten to assure him that he would soon be teaching a raft of grandsons to ride, to hunt and fish.

One or two, she'd thought privately. After a few years. First she wanted time alone with her husband who, seemingly every bit as eager to wed, had talked about the trips they would take together, the home they would build, the children they would eventually have...

That had been in February. Now here she was, barely two months later—orphaned, seasick, tipsy and penniless—about to face a future as the mail-order bride of a man she had yet to meet, in the most godforsaken place she had ever seen in her entire life.

Well...not quite godforsaken, she amended. There was the tiny, steepleless church.

Standing on his wide front porch, a tall, dark-haired man slid a pair of leather-palmed hands into the hip pockets of his lean canvas trousers as he gazed with satisfaction over his windswept island. He'd watched as Dozier's bugeye, the *Bessie Mae & Annie,* pulled alongside the dock. Watched the men swarm aboard, lift the hatches and begin unloading freight. Still others tackled a deck cargo of lumber, swinging bundles off onto the wharf. Clarence's crew of warehousemen began logging in and transferring crates to the warehouse for future shipment, setting aside a few small parcels to be brought up to the house.

Grey nodded in satisfaction. They knew what they were about, the men of St. Brides. A bit rough but, for the most part, good men, deserving of all he had done for them. All he planned to do.

Today's woman, however, couldn't have come at a more awkward time. He needed to leave within the hour if he wanted to reach Edenton by tomorrow morning. His brother, Jocephus, after setting up a meeting with another ship owner with a view to consolidating their two businesses, had asked Grey to take part in the negotiations, even though Grey had no direct interest. While his brother might be better at reading fine print, Grey was the acknowledged expert when it came to reading men.

Circumstances had made Grey St. Bride what he was. Some called him arrogant because he made laws as he saw fit and expected those laws to be obeyed. Grey didn't see it as arrogance, but simply as the only way to keep peace among the tough, independent men who lived and worked on St. Brides Island.

He'd been seventeen, Jocephus nineteen, when their father's health had begun to fail. Calling his two sons to his bedside, the old man had given them their choice of his various and scattered properties. Jocephus, then a student at Chapel Hill, had chosen the family's two small schooners and the warehouse in Edenton; Grey had chosen the island that had been granted by the state of North Carolina to his great-grandfather more than a hundred years earlier.

By the time Grey had actually inherited the island that bore his name, there'd been little left but a single storm-ravaged house and a few dilapidated wharves and warehouses. More valuable was the dependable deepwater inlet on the north side, between St. Brides and Ocracoke Island, as well as a less dependable one to the south between St. Brides and Portsmouth.

He remembered standing on this very spot—gazing out over the free-ranging livestock that had eaten down the vegetation to the point where blowing sand had covered half the maritime forest—and thinking something had to be done if the island was to survive, much less thrive.

Left to the meager population of transient seamen, inlet pilots and seasonal fishermen who came late in the summer for the mullet, residing in bulrush-thatched huts bordering the North End, the entire island might have washed away before anyone could take measures to secure it. As it was there were tree stumps visible at low tide in both the sound and the ocean, a mark of the constant erosion.

The first thing he'd done was to bring in a few stockmen to pen up the livestock so the scrubby vegetation could recover. Next, he'd brought in carpenters to rebuild the docks and warehouses and provide sturdier housing for the permanent men. Three years ago, it had occurred to him that something was still missing.

Women.

Actually, he hadn't thought of it until Emmet Meeks had led a delegation up the ridge to ask what he could do about bringing out a few women.

"Thing is, Cap'n—" the men gave him the courtesy title, saying damned if they were going to call him Saint. "—see, the thing is, it takes so long to go over to the mainland and meet up with a woman and court her, and then, when she finds out where we hail from, they don't want nothing to do with us."

Not to mention the fact, Grey had told himself, that most of the men, as decent and hardworking as they were, lacked certain social graces, shyness being the least of their problems.

It was Almy Dole, boatbuilder and general carpenter, who had expressed it best. "Maybe once we get 'em stranded out here for a spell, it won't be long before we start looking right good to 'em."

That had planted the seed—because the men were right. In order to thrive, a community needed stability, and that meant creating families. To that end he had tracked down the circuit preacher who served the nearby islands of Portsmouth and Ocracoke, and convinced him to add St. Brides to his charge. Then he'd set about building a church and a parsonage. Next, he'd composed a carefully worded advertisement and sent it off to the newspapers in three different coastal towns on a rotating basis, as he lacked the amenities to deal with more than one or two women at a time.

Some called him hard as pig iron. Grey preferred to think of himself as a visionary. Generous but firm. According to the terms of the old land grant, no St. Bride could sell so much as a grain of sand, but there was nothing to say he couldn't give it away. So as an added inducement, part of the marriage bargain was to deed each married man an acre of land and the material to build a house.

His plan included an initial exchange of letters with any applicant before he arranged for her outward passage. Those who didn't pass muster would be sent back with enough funds to support them until they could make other arrangements. He hated to send any woman back, knowing she had to be desperate to even answer such an advertisement, but if his plan was to work at all, he had to maintain standards. It took a special kind of woman to survive on a barrier island like St. Brides. Rejecting those he deemed unsuitable was actually a kindness.

But it also meant that his plan was progressing far slower than he had hoped.

As a shaft of sun glinted on the head of golden hair a few hundred yards down the road, Grey eased his hands from his pockets and crossed his arms over his broad chest. He could easily have met the woman at the landing and interviewed her there, as he'd be leaving within the hour. It would have saved time. But experience had taught him that distance lent him the perspective he needed to make a judgment. Gave him time to watch a prospective bride and size her up. By the time she reached him, he would likely have made up his mind whether or not she would do.

From what he'd seen so far, this one looked none too promising. A man needed good stock if he hoped to breed up a passel of strong St. Bridians. The woman coming up the road looked as if a stiff breeze would send her tumbling tip over toenails.

Eyes narrowed against the sudden glare of the sun, Grey studied the yellow-haired woman who was trying to hold down her skirts with one hand, hang on to her valise with the other, and still keep her hair out of her face as she staggered up the road toward him.

Staggered?

A fair man, he gave her the benefit of doubt. Walking in sand and shell took some getting used to when a woman was accustomed to sidewalks or hard clay roads. Then, too, she'd just crossed the Pamlico Sound. With a thirty-knot breeze out of the northeast, the waters might be a bit choppy. The effects took a while to wear off.

On the other hand, he needed women who were

sound of wind and limb. Even with his inspection hampered by layers of billowing skirts, it was plain to see there wasn't much in the way of flesh on this one. Maybe he should have specified a minimum weight. No runts need apply.

Grey made every effort to evaluate the woman objectively, but something in the way she moved distracted him. Such as the way her arms would fly out for balance when her foot caught the edge of a deep rut or a clump of uncrushed shell. When a gust of wind caught her skirt and she swatted it down again, offering him a clear view of the shape underneath, he barely managed to hang on to his objectivity. Shifting uncomfortably, he found himself reacting in a way that was not only inappropriate but damned embarrassing.

Waiting until she was close enough to see the set of her features—he firmly believed that given the right circumstances, a woman's disposition could be read in her face—he descended the worn wooden steps. Obviously, she was tired and irritated. Only to be expected. Other than that, he couldn't quite decide. She was a real beauty, though, and beauty was definitely not an asset on an island where men were men and women were rare.

He'd intended her for James Calvin, his chief carpenter. Thank God he hadn't told him she was due in today, because he was going to have to send this one back and try again. Whatever else she might be, a woman with her looks was trouble just waiting to happen. The last thing he needed was to set the men fighting over her like a pack of mangy hounds.

At the foot of the dune, Dora stopped and watched the man striding toward her. *This* was Grey St. Bride? *This* was the man who had advertised for a wife?

There must be something terribly wrong with him—something that didn't show from the outside. Either that or the brandy had affected her eyesight, because even from this distance he appeared to be strikingly handsome. Tall, with a rangy sort of leanness that reminded her of the live oak stumps she'd noticed along the shore, worn down to heartwood by centuries of wind and water.

"Mrs. Sutton?"

Dora remembered just in time that on her application she'd claimed to be a widow. "Mr. St. Bride?"

Warily, silently, they sized each other up. Dora, still reeling from the long crossing, swayed on her feet. Forcing back a lingering queasiness, she managed a parody of a smile. "What a—an interesting place," she said. It was the best she could come up with. *Bleak. Stark. Inhospitable. Definitely the ends of the earth.* "I'm sure it must be quite lovely in the summertime." *It's the middle of April, for heaven's sake. If ever a place is going to be lovely, surely it would be by now.*

Grey took in everything about the woman, then wished he hadn't. Seeing her at close range only confirmed his decision. Skin that pale, that soft, would never survive the harsh climate. As for her hands, if they'd ever done a lick of work it couldn't have been anything more strenuous than wielding one of those fancy feather fans society ladies used for flirting.

Her eyes were the color of Spanish moss, shifting from gray to green. A man could lose his wits trying to figure out exactly which color they were.

"Not got your land legs under you yet, Mrs. Sutton? The trouble with living on an island is that there's only one way to travel. I'll be glad to pay for your time, but I'm afraid—'' His keen senses picked up the smell of brandy. And while he wasn't one to hold the occasional drink against anyone, man or woman, it was just one more thing he could chalk up against this particular woman. She was too frail, too pretty, and evidently prone to drink.

She'd never last out a month. If the hard work expected of a St. Bridian woman didn't defeat her, the solitude surely would. Pretty soon she'd insist on leaving, and then, there would go his best carpenter. It had happened before. What man, offered a choice between work on a desolate island and a woman like this, would choose the job?

"Darling, you can't possibly expect me to move out to that wretched island of yours. I'd wither and die within a week."

Echoes of the past. Grey blocked them out and studied this small butterfly of a woman before him. The women who replied to the advertisements he'd been placing monthly were inclined to be plain, verging onto outright homely. If they could have found a husband at home, they would never have applied to his advertisement. It didn't take a Solomon to know that whatever she was doing here, this one would be nothing but trouble, setting the men against one another.

Besides which, he wasn't altogether immune to her himself. If he'd had no other reason to reject her, that would be enough.

"Mrs. Sutton, I'm afraid you won't do. I mean this purely as a kindness, for you'd never survive. For the most part the men here are decent enough, but they're a rough sort. Their wives will have to be tough as nails to stake a claim and hang on to it."

Grey found it all but impossible to meet her eyes, though he was commonly known as a direct man. Shifting his weight on his big, booted feet, he tried to think of some compelling reason that might convince her to leave. He could hardly tell her that he hadn't been this tempted by a woman in years, especially not one who reeked of brandy and looked as if she'd just been tipped head over heels out of a handcart.

"I'm tough," she said, meeting his gaze with surprising directness.

"The nearest doctor is almost a day's sail from here."

"I'm healthy as a horse," she said calmly.

"We've no amenities—no shops or tearooms—the kind of places ladies like to spend time."

"I can do without those." One by one, she continued to swat down his arguments, as if daring him to send her away.

"Dammit—begging your pardon, ma'am, but you're too pretty! If I let you stay, the other men will never be satisfied with plainer women, and you must know, those who come out here are mostly ones who can't find a husband anywhere else."

She blinked those incredible eyes of hers. At least she didn't simper. Finally she said, "I can be plain. I am, honestly, it's just this gown—pink is—it's so flattering."

The air left his lungs in a hefty, hopeless sigh. Dammit, he felt like a dog, but for her own sake—for the sake of his peaceable community—for the sake of his own peace of mind, she had to go. "Your return passage won't cost you a penny. The *Bessie Mae & Annie* belongs to me, her captain is in my employ. Naturally I'll pay for your time…." He reached for his wallet.

Pay for her time? Dora thought wildly. Time was not a problem. Time, she had aplenty. What she *didn't* have was another place to go. She had burned all her bridges—or rather they'd been burned for her. After coming all the way out to the ends of the earth, where could she go from here? Off the edge?

Pride fought with anger and desperation. After an exchange of letters—two on her part, one on his—her passage had been arranged. It had never once occurred to her that after all that, she would be rejected.

Fighting the urge to batter him with her fists, she forced back her anger and reached for pride. Head held high, she glanced disdainfully at the bills fluttering in his hand and turned away before the tears could overflow. She might have to crawl behind a sand dune to bawl her eyes out on the way back to the boat, but she would die before she would let him see her shed a single tear.

"Mrs. Sutton?" he called after her.

"I don't need your money," she pronounced clearly without turning around. "As you said, there are no shops here, no tearoom—why on earth would I even want to stay?"

"But Mrs. Sutton—"

She kept on walking as fast as she could, hoping to be well out of range when the dam broke. As it would. She was just too tired, too empty—too totally without hope, to hold back much longer.

The church. If she could just make it as far as the church...

But before she even reached the church, someone called out in a wavering, pain-filled voice. "Miss? Could I bother you for a hand up?"

Blinking away the moisture, she glanced over the neat picket fence and saw that the man who'd been standing on a ladder when she'd passed by the first time was now lying on the ground.

Without a second thought, she swung open the gate and hurried to his side. "What happened? Are you hurt?"

Obviously he was hurt. "My ankle," he said with an apologetic look. "It's not as young as I thought it was."

It took her a moment to realize he was attempting a joke. In spite of her own situation, she was touched. "Let me help you sit up, and then we'll see what needs to be done."

He was not a large man. Pain clouded his eyes, but he managed a smile that cut through her defenses. Her own tears would have to wait.

Obviously embarrassed at having to ask for help, he attempted to lean forward to unlace his boots. With a soft, impatient murmur, Dora brushed his hands away and carefully removed his boot.

"Oh, dear."

"Would you mind fetching St. Bride before he gets away? If he'll help me into the house, I'll be fine in no time at all."

"It could be broken," she said.

Fetch St. Bride? She'd sooner fetch the devil himself.

"Wrenched it good, that's all. I've broke enough bones to know the difference." His weathered face had paled noticeably. Dora could only hope he was right. Hadn't the dragon king mentioned that there was no doctor on the island?

"If you'll lean on me, I can help you inside. My father sprained his ankle once. They had to cut his boot off, it swelled so quickly."

The injured man twisted around, peering hopefully at the house on the ridge of dunes while Dora looked for something to help her get him inside. A crutch, or even a walking stick would be perfect, but she was going to have to improvise. Scanning the tidy yard, she looked past the fallen ladder, past a sagging net pen holding a goose and several chickens to a handcart filled with gardening tools and a small wooden crate. Perhaps she could wheel him up to his porch and...

Perhaps not. It would have to be the crate. Dragging it closer, she managed to get him up off the ground and seated. Sweat beaded his furrowed face, but he thanked her as politely as if she'd offered him milk and sugar for his tea.

"As soon as you catch your breath, we'll take the next step," she said firmly. She might not measure up to his lordship's lofty standards, but at least this much she could do before she left. "There now, if you'll just take my hands..."

He was only a few inches taller than she was, and frail for a man who looked as if he might once have been far more robust. The steps up onto the porch were a problem, but patiently, she supported him until, hobbling beside her, he managed to get inside.

"There now, if you'll just steer me to the settee I'll rest a spell until the swelling goes down. I thank you kindly, that I do."

"Who lives here with you?" Surely he had someone to look after him. The almighty St. Bride would have seen to that.

"Buried my wife two years ago, out by the fig trees. I've managed on my own since then. Can't say I'm not glad you come along when you did, though. If that old gander of Sal's was to get out again, we'd have had us a real set-to, with me down on his level."

Hating her feelings of inadequacy, Dora located a towel, dipped it in a basin of cold water and applied it to his swollen ankle. In other circumstances she might have been embarrassed at such an intimacy, but the man was obviously in pain. She could hardly leave him here alone.

Besides, it wasn't as if she had anywhere else to go. The boat that had brought her to the island would probably be returning to Bath as soon as it finished its business here. She could hardly go back there.

"I have a few minutes before I have to leave. What else can I do to make you comfortable before I leave?" she asked brightly.

He appeared to consider the offer. And then he said, "You're one of St. Bride's women, aren't you?"

One of St. Bride's women? How many did the man have, for heaven's sake?

"You know about that? About the advertisement?" Fighting to keep despair from her voice, Dora managed to smile.

Ignoring her question, Emmet Meeks said, "'Pears to me we could both use a cup of strong tea, missy."

"Dora," she murmured. "Dora Sutton." She had left Adora behind. The only good thing about being rejected was not having to go on with a lie. Or face the shame of admitting how gullible she'd been to believe Henry when he'd said he loved her. Of allowing him to—

Yes, well…from now on out, she was simply Dora.

"Emmet Meeks," the man replied, still pale, still obviously in pain, but determined to hide it. It occurred to her that they were two of a kind in that respect. "My wife, rest her soul, swore by tea. Said coffee rotted a man's bones. Reckon maybe that might be what ails mine?" His smile was more of a grimace, but it occurred to her that he must once have been a handsome man.

It also occurred to her that he was not in the best of health, sprained ankle notwithstanding.

The cottage was scrupulously neat. The walls had been whitewashed, the effect being warm and bright, with a faint pattern of wood grain showing through. There were hand-crocheted rugs on the floors and a basket of onions and withered apples on the kitchen table. Homely touches one would expect of a woman, but hardly of a man.

While Dora filled the kettle, her host told her where to find the teapot. "I can't stay long," she reminded him, almost wishing she could. Wishing she could linger in this unlikely sanctuary until she could think of what to do next, where to go. With no money, no family and no friends—with her reputation irredeemably shattered—perhaps she could just stay right here in this warm, friendly room and sip tea forever.

That old woman? Oh, that's Dora Sutton. Ruined herself over on the mainland, don't you know. Couldn't go back, couldn't go forward, so she just sat there and drank tea until she withered up like a dried plum.

Chapter Two

Once she had brewed a pot of strong tea, which more or less exhausted her culinary talents, Dora looked about for her valise and remembered that she'd left it out in the yard. She would tell someone at the docks—that nice red-haired man, perhaps—about Mr. Meeks's ankle. Surely he would see to sending someone along to do whatever needed doing.

"So you're one of Grey's brides," Meeks repeated. "Who're you going to marry?"

Who? Well, no one, it seemed. Dora sat back down and stared at the man reclining on an old-fashioned settee in the tiny parlor. Pride alone kept her from telling him she'd been found wanting. He'd thought she was too pretty? Absurd, she told herself, feeling a rising inner heat that had to be anger. "Well...that remains to be seen, doesn't it?"

"My Sal was the first," Emmet confided wistfully. "Grey ordered her out special for me. Couldn't have done better if I'd picked her out myself, and that's the Lord's truth. St. Bride deeded me an acre of land and the lumber to build us this home. Helped build it with his own hands, he did." It was as if once the man began to talk, he couldn't seem to stem the flow. "He builds one-room cabins for the single men, but he don't deed 'em over until six months after they marry. So far, none of 'em that's married has stayed that long. That makes me the only man on the island besides St. Bride to own so much as a grain of sand." Pride was evident in his pale face.

But beneath the pride, there was loneliness. Dora understood grief and loneliness all too well. Somewhat to her surprise, she was tempted to pour out her own tale. What would it matter? He was a stranger, someone she would never meet again after today.

But telling wouldn't change anything, it would only open the wounds again. The time for grieving was past. She had her future to secure now.

"Mr. Meeks, I really do need to leave now if I'm to catch the boat. I promise, though, I'll send someone back to look after you."

In a younger man, his smile might have been called teasing. "Call me Emmet. Been a while since I heard a lady speak my name."

"Then, Emmet, I'd better hurry. It's been—well, of course, the circumstances weren't the best, but I'm truly glad I met you. Perhaps one of these days…"

What could she offer? Not friendship—there wasn't time. "Perhaps Mr. St. Bride will find you another wife. Not to take the place of your first wife," she added hurriedly. "I know no one could do that, but someone—a companion…"

"A companion," he echoed wistfully. "Should've thought to tell him before he left."

Before he left?

"Is Mr. St. Bride leaving, too?" If his high-and-mightiness was sailing on the same boat she was, she just might end up shoving him overboard to see if he could walk on water.

"Gone a'ready. Saw him set off across the ridge while you were helpin' me to the house. Probably all the way out past Pelican Shoal by now, with the wind where it is."

"He's gone?" Dora didn't know whether to rejoice or despair. At least he wouldn't be sharing the cramped passenger cabin with her all the way across the Sound.

"Then I'd better—"

"Settle down, child. If you were fixin' to sail with Cap'n Dozier you're too late. He's halfway out the channel by now, won't come about for nobody, so you might's well settle yourself in for a spell of waiting. Mail boat's due in day after tomorrow. You could catch a ride out then if you're still set on leaving. Dozier'll be back the day after that."

Settle herself in how? Where? She would like to think she'd begun to mature in spite of her father's indulgences—the events of the past six weeks had surely hastened the process. But panic was her first reaction. What was she supposed to do, build herself a sand castle? Throw herself on the mercy of the first friendly face she came across?

Hardly. Foremost among the hard lessons she'd been forced to learn was that the world did not revolve around the Suttons. If she was to survive, it would be up to her to find a way.

"The—Mr. St. Bride, that is—um, happened to mention that my passage was paid on the *Bessie Mae & Annie*. What about the mail boat? Is it very expensive? Where would be her next port of call?"

"Well now, as to that, Grey owns the *Bessie Mae.*

Mail boat's a different matter—she don't have much room for passengers. Won't cost you much for deck space, but if I was you, I'd wait.''

Wait for what? Dora thought with the first fine edge of panic. Wait to be sent back to Bath, where women she'd known all her life would turn away and even cross the street to avoid embarrassment when they saw her coming? Where the men would look her up and down with a certain speculative gleam in their eyes that made her feel as if she'd wandered outside in her drawers and corselet?

No, thank you.

Where she would have too much pride to beg and too few resources to keep from starving?

No, thank you indeed!

''I don't suppose there's a—um, a boardinghouse here?'' Where she could wash dishes to earn her keep until she could think of something better to do.

Emmet shook his head. ''No need for one. There's a longhouse for the pilots up at North End. Been inlet pilots here long's there's been a good inlet, ready to go out and meet incoming traffic, guide 'em across the shoals. Come August, there's mullet fishermen, but now we got more of a permanent population. Like I said, St. Bride built cabins for them that don't stay in the barracks.''

''What about the—the women? Where do they stay?'' Surely she could find someplace to shelter until she could get off St. Bride's blasted island.

''When Sal was here, we took one of 'em in. Didn't stay long, poor woman. Lit out on the mail boat two days after she come. Since then, if the circuit preacher's not here, they stay at the parsonage. If he's here, he moves up to Grey's house, let's 'em have his place until things is settled one way or the other. Like I said, so far none of 'em's stuck more'n a month or two, 'ceptin' for my Sal.''

"Do you suppose—?" She hardly dared voice the question. If it involved the cooperation of Grey St. Bride, she knew in advance the answer. Having ordered her to leave, he would expect her to be gone. Instead she'd stopped to help someone in need and missed the boat. He could hardly blame her for that…could he?

"Now, if you was to want to stay here until the *Bessie Mae* gets back" Emmet said thoughtfully, "reckon there's not much Grey could say about it, seein's he deeded this place to me, fair and square."

Dora looked about the small cottage. There appeared to be several rooms, including the kitchen off the back. There was also a narrow, steep stairway leading to what must be more rooms or an attic. Altogether, compared to Sutton Hall, Emmet's cottage was scarcely larger than the servants' quarters out behind their carriage house.

Odd that it should feel so…safe. Did she dare stay here long enough to plan her next move? No matter how despotic he might be, St. Bride could hardly chase her off his island as long as she remained on the part of it that Emmet owned.

Stalling for time until she could weigh her options, Dora said, "Would you like more tea? Perhaps I could—" Cook his dinner?

Hardly. She wouldn't know how to start. She'd been no more truthful in her application when she had claimed to be a capable woman than she had when she'd called herself a widow.

Heaven help her if she had actually married St.

Bride, as she had naively expected to, and he'd discovered the extent of her lies.

Fortunately, Emmet seemed more interested in talking than in dining. "Did I tell you about Sal? I buried her out by the fig trees. Sal used to race out there of a morning to beat the mockingbirds to the ripe figs." His smile was for another woman, another time. Dora started to speak, but he continued, and so she leaned back in the uncomfortable spindle-backed chair, determined to be the audience he so obviously needed. She might be shockingly inadequate in most respects, but she could certainly listen for as long as he wanted to talk.

"Now'n again I haul a chair out there by her grave and study on the way things turn out in a man's life. Planning don't do much good, not when there's a Master Planner up there with his own notions of how things is going to turn out."

"Fate," Dora murmured. She knew all about the way life's chessboard could tilt with no warning, sending all the pieces crashing to the floor.

He nodded. "Some calls it luck—some might call it fate when a young woman happens by an old man's house just when his sand's about to run out. Does she stop and help when the old fool climbs up a ladder and takes a fall, or does she walk on by?"

Inside her flimsy kid slippers, Dora's toes curled. What was he trying to say? That fate had directed her to his gate just as another door slammed shut in her face? Whatever it was he suggesting, could she afford not to listen? If she'd already missed the boat, what choice did she have?

"St. Bride, he signed up the circuit preacher before he sent for the first brace o'women. My Sal was one

of 'em. With our own preacher on the line, we could
send for him whenever there was any splicin' that
needed doing without having to sail o'er and hitch up
on the mainland.''

Dora waited. She had a feeling he was leading up
to something, only she couldn't imagine what it could
be. Surely he wasn't about to ask her to marry him.

"Works out real good. Course, there's not a lot for
a preacher to do here less'n there's a marrying. Not
much sinnin' to preach at, not like some of his other
charges where they have saloons and wild women.
Grey won't tolerate sinnin' on St. Brides—says if he
allows sinnin', first thing you know he'll have to bring
in a sawbones and a sheriff.''

Most of the color had returned to his weathered
face. Dora murmured something to the effect that a
doctor might be useful, but Emmet, now that his initial
discomfort had lessened, seemed more inclined to talk
than to listen.

"Now, Preacher Filmore, he's a good man. Give
you the shirt off'n his back if you need it. The Lord
sort of slowed up his talking so folks wouldn't miss
any of his words. Trouble is, I listen a whole lot faster
than he talks, and besides that, he don't even play
checkers. Not even for black-eyed peas. Calls it gambling, and gambling's a sin in his book. So you can
see the fix I'm in.''

She couldn't, but she was beginning to see where
the conversation might be headed. Evidently, the slow-
talking minister would be expected to take care of Mr.
Meeks and keep him entertained until he was on his
feet again.

And just as evidently, Mr. Meeks's patience would
be sorely tested.

"Now Grey, he's a meddler, for all he means well. Long as they're living here on his island, a man don't have no choice but to go 'long with his notions, 'specially since they generally turn out right good. I reckon he told you about the plans he has to pair up the single men with wives and start raising younguns?"

She wasn't about to admit that she'd come here believing St. Bride meant to marry her himself.

"Used to be families living out here back in his pa's day. Storms run most of 'em off. Shoreside washed in near half a mile. Since then, sand covered up just about everything left standing. He tell you about that?"

She shook her head. The man had told her little except that life on his island was hard, and that she would never be able to survive here. He could hardly know she had survived far worse than wild winds and raging seas.

He had also told her she was pretty. No one had ever told her that before—at least, not without wanting something from her.

"Won't be easy, finding a schoolteacher. Finding the preacher and getting him to take on another charge was hard enough. Poor man can't hardly keep up with things as it is. Like I said, he talks so slow it takes him two hours to get through a one-hour sermon." He chuckled, and Dora felt some of the tension that had gripped her ever since she had recklessly answered the advertisement begin to ease.

"Licensed to marry folks, though, that's mainly what he's here for. Married Sal and me, right and proper. We was older than some, but when Sal came out, St. Bride, he thought we'd suit, set a good example, he said.'' Nodding, he added, ''Said words over her grave when I buried her.'' He paused as if, satisfied with his summary, he was searching for his next topic. He had told her several times over about his wonderful Sal. The poor man was obviously starved for companionship.

So much for the wonderful Mr. St. Bride.

Dora leaned to one side to peer through a window, wishing she could see the docks from where she sat. What if Emmet was wrong and the *Bessie Mae & Annie* hadn't actually sailed yet?

But even if by some miracle she mananged to catch the boat before it left, would she be any better off? There were few jobs available for women who'd been coddled all their lives. When the time came, no matter what their personal inclinations, they were expected to marry men of their fathers' choosing—men who would continue to pamper them. As far as Dora was concerned, even that door had been closed.

From her rocking chair—Sal's rocker, according to Emmet—all she could see was that towering monstrosity of a house on the dunes. Castle St. Bride.

Fortress St. Bride, she amended bitterly.

''So I said to myself,'' Emmet Meeks went on, and Dora turned her attention back to her elderly host, wondering if she'd missed something. ''Either she will or she won't. Don't do no harm to ask.''

''To ask?''

''Don't take offense, Miss Sutton, but the fact that you come here in answer to St. Bride's piece in the paper means you've run plumb out of luck over on the mainland.'' She opened her mouth and closed it again. It was no less than the truth. ''Happens, I'm alone in the world but for a dog that lives with me,'' he went on. "After my wife died I went over to the mainland for a spell. Saw a doctor, thinking maybe I could get me a pair of spectacles—it was getting so I couldn't even see the channel markers, let alone the shoals. Doc said I had clouds in my eyes—said the best specs in the world couldn't clear 'em away." He stirred his tea, sipped it and continued to speak, thoughtfully peering into his teacup. "Saw another doc while I was there. Told me my heart was tired."

"Oh, no…" she murmured.

"Said if I was lucky, I still had a few good years left before it gave up the ghost." His clouded blue eyes captured and held her clear gray-green ones. "What I'm trying to say, Miss Dora, is that I'd as soon not live 'em alone. I've got my dog, but Salty, she's not much of a one for conversation."

Dora was aghast. What could she say under the circumstances? Was he asking her to *marry* him? Was he daft?

More to the point, was she?

Because she actually found herself considering it. Seriously considering marriage to a man she'd known less than an hour.

Yet, was it any worse than marrying one she'd never even met? That was what she'd been prepared to do until she'd been rejected.

"I'd not ask much of you, Miss Dora. If you'll agree to stay on as my companion—as my friend—I can't pay you much, but I promise to deed you my house and my land and bless you with my dying breath for your kindness."

Grey made it as far north as Long Point and dropped anchor in Wysocking Bay. He'd have liked to get farther, but sailing alone in his 30 foot sloop, he preferred to lay over until daylight. Too much was depending on him to take any foolish risks.

Damn it all, why had the woman showed up just as he had to leave? It would be several days—possibly as much as a week—before he could get back, and then he'd have to start all over again.

There had to be a way to word his advertisements so that only the right sort of woman would apply. Not too young, not too old, like poor Sal. Not too pretty, but not plain as a mud fence, either. Sturdy women, not given to fancy pink dresses and flimsy pink slippers.

Going below, he unwrapped the supper his housekeeper, a giant of a man named Mouse, had provided. Cheese, cold cornbread and smoked fish, with a handful of dried apples to follow. Back up on deck, he consumed the lot without tasting any of it and thought about the woman. Dora Sutton.

Who the devil was she? Why would a woman with her looks bother to answer his advertisement? While he might not be up on the latest fashions, he knew quality when he saw it. That fancy pink frock of hers, in spite of the stains and wrinkles, was quality.

She hadn't taken his money, which meant she was not entirely without resources. Otherwise his conscience would never let him rest until he'd tracked her down and seen to his own satisfaction that she was all right. He'd been called a martinet—his own brother had once jokingly called him a tinhorn dictator—but he would never willingly allow anyone to suffer as long as he had the means to prevent it.

Thank God she was no longer his problem. She was the kind of woman who set a man's sap to rising—his own, included. Being married wouldn't change that fact. All she would have to do was stroll down to the landing on a busy day and every tongue between North End and Shallow Gut would be dragging on the ground. Next thing, there'd be fights among his men, demands that he find them a pretty, yellow-haired wife with high breasts and a hand-span waist.

Did they think he could simply sail across the sound, pick out a few likely candidates, knock them over the head with a club and drag them back to the island? Matchmaking required patience and careful planning. It took guts, tact and finesse, not to mention the ability to handle large amounts of frustration.

Any way you looked at it, turning a rough crew of transients and watermen into a settled, civilized community was damned hard work.

Thank God he had what it took to do the job.

With a million stars reflected in the black water all around him and Dora Sutton stuck in his mind like a peck of sandspurs, Grey allowed himself the rare indulgence of reliving a chapter from his past. Back when he'd first fallen in love with her, Evelyn had been almost as beautiful as the widow Sutton. A tall woman, she'd had auburn hair and an imperious way he'd found amusing…at least for the first few months.

The years that had given her more generous proportions and darkened her hair had done little to lessen her loveliness. Lately, though, he'd noticed a few lines of dissatisfaction on her face. Come to think of it, even her voice was beginning to sound more querulous than melodious.

But that was Jocephus's problem, not his. Thank God. One thing about having once fallen hard for the wrong woman, Grey told himself—it lent a man insulation. Taught him what qualities to look for in a wife, as well as which ones to avoid like the plague.

Back on St. Brides, Miss Adora Sutton, the once-popular but now-disgraced daughter of one of Beaufort County's most prominent citizens, challenged her host to a game of checkers after a modest supper of cold biscuits and molasses, served with dried fruit and tinned tomatoes. Not too long ago she would have turned up her nose at such a crude repast, but having had nothing at all to eat since the ship's biscuit and brandy Captain Dozier had offered to settle her stomach, she'd scraped her plate clean, going so far as to lick the molasses from her fingertips.

When the last rays of daylight dimmed, she lit a lamp and plumped a pillow to support Emmet's ankle. They had played a game of checkers, and fading vision or not, the man was a wizard. "One more game?" he teased.

"All right, one more," she agreed, "but only if you promise to keep your foot up on that stool." Dora tried to imagine what it must be like to be alone in the world, with both a failing heart and blindness a distinct possibility. The poor man was so lonely he was reduced to talking to a dog, a pen full of chickens and one old gander. He insisted that his ankle wasn't bothering him, but she knew the swelling alone must be uncomfortable.

They played two more games, and then she insisted on helping him to his bedroom. It had been decided after she had agreed to stay on as his companion that she would sleep in the parlor for now, on a pallet made up of quilts his wife had brought with her. Tomorrow, with Emmet's permission, she might clear away the clutter in the back. If he objected, she could always see if the attic was at all habitable. It would be hot as blazes, but at least it would be private.

I'll do my best to look after him for you, Sal, she thought as she snuggled down on her hard bed and stared up at the ceiling. *He's really a dear man. He misses you terribly.*

The snug frame house was a far cry from Sutton Hall, but for the first time since her world had come crashing down, Dora felt a measure of peace. Of hope. And oddly enough, of security.

Sooner or later she would have to face Grey St. Bride again, but not tomorrow. Emmet assured her that whenever he sailed north to Edenton to visit his brother, he was usually gone for several days.

Meanwhile, she had much to learn, and Emmet promised to begin teaching her first thing tomorrow. She had confessed when she'd agreed to stay on that she was willing to learn—eager, in fact—but that at the moment, her domestic skills were limited to making tea and boiling eggs.

Emmet had smiled in a way that hinted at the handsome, charming scamp he must have been in his youth. He was only fifty-eight, but looked much older. "I reckon until I'm steady on my pins again, I'll have to take my chances."

"Do you really think you can teach me to cook?" The playful challenge was not without a degree of desperation. She had her work cut out for her if she ever intended to be self-sufficient.

"I'm a right fair hand at plain cooking. Sal left a book of recipes. I made out a few things, but like I said, my eyes aren't what they used to be."

"Then I'll read and you can interpret," she said,

hoping he wouldn't ask why a woman who lacked even the most basic skills had come here to marry a simple workingman.

The last thought on her mind as she closed her eyes, rolled onto her side and tucked her fist against her chin was of a tall, dark-haired man with an incongruous dimple in his chin. A man who had told her she wasn't suitable—that she was neither wanted nor needed here. That she was, of all things, too pretty!

You and your blooming island can go take a flying leap, Lord St. Bride. I'm here, and I'm staying, and that's the end of that!

Chapter Three

Among the nicest features of Emmet's house were the two porches. From the front she could look out past the garden, down toward the landing and watch the activity as ships lined up waiting to come alongside and unload or take on their cargo.

The back porch looked out over a chicken house, three enormous fig trees and one lonely grave, a sagging net-fenced pen and the outhouse. Beyond those there was only sand, a bit of marsh, some scrubby woods and more water. Both front and back porches were sheltered under the deeply sloping roof, which made them good for both sitting and hanging clothes out to air.

When it came to laundry—to drying her most intimate garments, however, Dora chose the attic. Someone—Sal, perhaps—had strung a line across from rafter to rafter. According to Emmet they had planned to turn the space into another bedroom, so as to house St. Bride's women until they could make other arrangements. With a small window in each end, it would have served well enough.

She tried to visualize what could be done with the

small space. Now that she no longer had to live up to anyone's expectations but her own, she was beginning to discover not only new interests but new talents.

For instance, she was quite good at planning. Better at planning than at the actual doing, but that would come in time. The important thing was that she had a perfectly good brain and a pair of capable—marginally capable—hands.

For no reason at all, she thought of the man who had sent for her, only to reject her. "Here's one in your eye, St. Bride."

Her friend Selma Blunt used to announce her serves that way when she meant to zing one across the net. But then, Selma had always been fiercely competitive. She'd always had to be the best at anything she attempted. More often than not she'd succeeded.

Selma had wanted Henry. So far as Dora knew, she hadn't succeeded there. She did know, however, that both Selma and her personal maid, Polly, had done their best to spread the gossip. Her own maid, Bertola, had told her so.

Well, Selma could have Henry Carpenter Smythe with her blessings. The two of them deserved each other. Personally, Dora found the position of companion far preferable to marriage. If she ever did marry, the truth would have to come out, because she simply wasn't capable of living a lie.

But then, neither was she ready to confess to the truth.

Sighing, Dora thought of what an utter ruin the Suttons had made of their lives. Her poor father had been unable to accept failure. She, at least, was trying to recover and make a new start. Whether or not it was what Emmet called fate, she happened to have stumbled onto the ideal solution. Instead of being forced to marry for the sake of security, as she had resigned herself to do, she had found the perfect position with a man who was content with what she could offer. Best of all, she had found a friend.

The early morning sun came streaming through the window, striking her face with blinding brilliance the next morning. She had her pallet rolled up and hidden behind the settee by the time Emmet emerged from the bedroom.

"You shouldn't be up," she scolded. He had up-ended a broom and was using it as a crutch.

"I'll be dancing a fandango before you know it."

"Fandango, indeed. You're a scamp, Emmet Meeks, do you know that?"

His eyes, clouded though they were, had a decided twinkle. "Been called it a time or two. I reckon we'd best see to clearing out the back room. After Sal died I shoved everything inside and shut the door. There's a bed under there somewhere. I built it. Didn't do as good a job as James Calvin would've done, but I reckon it'll hold a small woman."

"Emmet, are you sure? I don't want to—hurt your feelings."

"Go to it, gal. Can't have you sleeping on the floor."

"I don't mind at all," Dora assured him. Although as long as she was going to live here, she would really prefer an arrangement that would afford her a bit more privacy, not to mention comfort.

After a leisurely breakfast of scorched sausage, overcooked eggs and embarrassed apologies, she helped Emmet out onto the front porch where he could watch the goings-on at the landing, arranging a stool for his ankle. The swelling had gone down, but he was still unable to pull on his boot.

Washing dishes involved bringing in water from the rain barrel, heating it on the woodstove, pouring it over a chunk of brown soap and scrubbing until the plates came clean, then heating more water to rinse them and drying them with a towel made of a flour sack.

In the process she managed to burn her fingers, drop a cup, which was thankfully thick enough that it didn't break—and splash water all over her bodice.

"Well, that's done," she announced proudly, joining her employer on the front porch just as the red-headed warehouseman passed by.

"Morning, Clarence," Emmet called out.

"Morning, Emmet. Miz Sutton." It was the same man she'd seen yesterday when she'd stumbled off the boat. Evidently word had spread, as he obviously knew who she was. If he was surprised to see her still here, he hid it well. "Looks like rain tomorrow," he declared.

Salty, Emmet's yellow dog, who appeared to be a mixture of retriever and shepherd, yapped once and then curled back into her spot of sun on the corner of the porch.

"On his way up to fetch Grey's ledger, I reckon," Emmet said when the man walked on by. "With the way business is picking up, it don't pay to let things slide." Emmet's rheumy gaze followed the lanky young man walking along the shell-paved road to Castle St. Bride, as Dora had come to think of it.

"Mercy, it's warm." She discreetly plucked her damp petticoat away from her body, wishing she had more than a single change. So far, she'd learned to wash drawers, stockings and dishes. Her education was progressing by leaps and bounds, but with every leap forward, she was aware of many more shortcomings.

Really, she thought, something should be done about women's education. What good was knowing the proper seating at a dinner party for twenty-four when one could barely manage a simple meal for two?

Emmet eased into a more comfortable position. "If Grey had in mind to marry you to one of his key men, there's Clarence, or James Calvin or Almy. You got any particular leanings?"

"If you mean do I favor any particular man, I've spoken only briefly to Clarence. I've never even met the others."

Dora, who had already decided that she would far rather stay on as a companion than marry any man, asked, "What would have happened if I'd been accepted, but then my prospective bridegroom and I hadn't suited?" Now that marriage was no longer a possibility, she could allow herself to wonder.

"I reckon you'd have suited any man with eyes in his head. St. Bride must've figured you wouldn't thrive in a place like this. One thing I'll say for the boy—when he makes a mistake, he's not too proud to admit it. He's hard, but he's not heartless."

The boy. Grey St. Bride had to be at least thirty years old, but then, coastal men, like farmers, tended to age earlier than men like Henry and her father. Although one would never have known it from his soft white hands, Tranquil Sutton had come from a long line of Beaufort County farmers. Sutton Hall had once been centered in more than two thousand acres of rich, productive farmland before it had been sold off, a few hundred acres at the time, to enable her father to go into what he called "investments."

As it turned out, he'd have done better to lease out his land and live on the proceeds.

"You're going to need a pair of real shoes. Pity Sal's things won't fit you. She was a sturdy woman." He fell silent, and Dora completed the thought. *But evidently not sturdy enough.*

Looks could be deceiving. "I left my trunk in storage over on the mainland." While it wasn't a hint that he might offer to send for it, she could hardly stay on with only two dresses and a single change of undergarments.

"I'll have Clarence send for it when he comes down the ridge again."

"How much do you suppose it would cost to ship it out?"

"Cap'n Dozier'll see to it. He brings out supplies two, three times a week."

Grateful but embarrassed at having to accept charity, Dora reached down and scratched the ears of the dog sleeping beside her chair. Things were moving almost too quickly. Having her trunk shipped out— moving into Emmet's house... There was still one big obstacle to be faced before she felt truly secure.

St. Bride.

"Well. I suppose I should—should go and find something useful to do." Rising, she turned to go inside.

"Easy, girl, you'll come about just fine."

Dora was proud of each small accomplishment. Better yet, Emmet seemed just as pleased. Using her eyes and hands along with Emmet's encouragement and Sal's recipe book, she cooked another meal. After fanning the smoke out the window, they dined on underdone biscuits, scorched bacon and what was supposed to have been sauce made from dried apples, but ended up a tasteless, lumpy mush.

Emmet praised it all and Dora swelled with pride. If she could do this much now, she could do even better with enough practice. She wasn't stupid, after all—only inexperienced.

The next day she accomplished two things. First she mastered the art of cooking beans, then she worked up her courage to slide a hand under Emmet's hens and remove the eggs.

Unfortunately, the gander chose that morning to escape from his pen, which was separated from the chicken's side only by a length of fishnet. The wretched bird chased her back to the porch, hissing and clacking his beak. She ended up throwing six of the seven eggs she'd collected at the vicious creature.

Emmet had laughed until she almost felt like throwing the last egg at him, but then, she'd had to laugh, herself.

After that had come the crucial test. Fish. "Filleted and fried?" she asked dubiously, thinking of the heavy cast-iron frying pan and the hot bacon drippings their old cook had always used, and the way the grease had always spattered. Could she do it without burning down the house?

"If you don't mind, I believe I'd as soon have it stewed." Evidently Emmet picked up on her uncertainty.

"Then stewed it is," she said, covering her relief. "Sal says potatoes, onions, corn dumplings and salt pork." She had read the book from cover to cover, trying to absorb in a matter of days the lessons of a lifetime.

"And fish," Emmet said dryly, and they both laughed again.

That was something they did frequently. Laugh together. For the life of her, Dora couldn't imagine why, because nothing either of them said was particularly funny. The best she could come up with was that they were comfortable together. Here in their safe little world, where there were no real threats, the smallest things brought pleasure.

More than once she warned herself not to look back, for the past held little but pain. Instead she focused on the future. After only a few days, when nothing disastrous happened, she felt secure enough to lower her guard.

Emmet would have probably listened if she had gone on and on about the latest fashions, or even the latest gossip about who was courting whom. Somewhere between then and now—between Bath and St. Brides, those topics seemed to have lost their appeal. With the perspective of time and distance, her entire life seemed incredibly shallow compared to that of a man who had once guided big ships through a treacherous inlet—a man who had finally found love, only to lose it so suddenly.

At Emmet's urging, however, she related a few stories from her childhood. Small things. Like hanging around the kitchen hoping to get a taste of frosting before it went on the cake. Like dressing up on rainy days in gowns she found in a trunk in the attic.

Nothing at all about her father's losing everything, including the home that had been in their family for more than a hundred years. Certainly nothing about his suicide, or her shame in allowing Henry to seduce her.

Dora talked and Emmet listened, and then Emmet would talk while Dora listened. More often than not they ended up laughing together over some trivial incident from either her past or his. They played checkers—clouded eyes or not, he was a wicked competitor.

And then, Emmet suggested she marry him.

It wasn't a proposal so much as a business proposition. Dora was sitting in one of the two parlor chairs, rubbing her foot through her lisle stockings, as the sole had finally worn through her left slipper.

"I beg your pardon?"

"Now, don't jump ship before you hear me out." Emmet had buttoned his blue shirt up to his neck and put on his best denim trousers. His ankle had healed enough that he was able to get around quite well. "I'm an old man. Like I said, my sand's running out. While I'm still able to get about, I'd like to see things settled between us. Now, Grey, he means well, but he might take a notion to send you on your way once he gets back—ought to be showing up most any day now. If I remember correctly—and I gen'ally do," he added with a familiar twinkle—"this house is mine for my lifetime, then it goes to my widow and any issue I might have. Otherwise, it turns back to St. Bride."

Frantically thinking of all the reasons why such a match was absurd, Dora hardly heard what he was saying about his house. St Bride was on his way home. He would find her and…what?

Emmet waited patiently for her reaction. Having presented his case, he left the decision to her.

Could she stay on as his companion if she said no?

If not, where could she go? Could she even afford to leave the island? She had no desire to marry. On the other hand, such an arrangement would benefit both and harm neither.

Dora took a deep breath. Then, suppressing second thoughts, she accepted.

The wedding was held the next day, before St. Bride could return and object. It was quite small. Clarence was there, his smile bright enough to light up the whole church. And the two carpenters, James Calvin and Almy Dole. By then Dora had met several of the local men. She couldn't help but feel relief at not being thrust into a stranger's arms by Lord St. Bride.

Clarence was nice. Red-haired and freckled, he had an engaging smile. She rather thought he was an intelligent man, but on the few occasions when they'd met, she hadn't been able to think of a single thing to say to him.

As for the boat-building carpenters, James Calvin and Almy Dole, who were cousins, according to Emmet, they both seemed equally decent. Both were dark haired, dark eyed, really quite attractive men, but painfully shy. If Emmet was right and St. Bride had picked out one of those to be her husband, what on earth would they ever have found to talk about?

She sighed, waiting for the minister to stop clearing his throat and get on with the marriage service. Emmet didn't need to be standing for any length of time. Besides, St. Bride was expected at any time.

Somewhat surprisingly, the church was filled, all three rows. Most of the men appeared to have made an effort at grooming for the occasion. Hats in hand, hair slicked back, each one bowed gravely as Emmet introduced them to his bride-to-be. Instead of flowers, the church was beginning to smell distinctly like fish.

Suddenly struck by the absurdity of the situation, Dora managed to swallow her mirth just as the preacher said sonorously, "Friends…we are… gathered here…"

He did, indeed, speak slowly, just as Emmet had warned. It wasn't so much a drawl as an emphasis on each word spoken. Halfway through the proceedings Dora was ready to scream, "Get on with it, do, before I lose my courage!"

But she gripped Emmet's arm and they supported each other until they were finally pronounced man and wife.

On the way back to the cottage, having been showered with shy smiles, a few mumbled blessings and even a bow by a courtly old gentleman wearing faded denim and rubber boots—Dora walked slowly, aware that Emmet was tiring. His ankle was largely mended, but he still had a limited amount of strength.

She'd been able to take most of his daily tasks on herself, even if she didn't do them particularly well. After nearly a week she was still discovering strengths and weaknesses, as well as abilities she might never have known about if her life hadn't taken such a sudden turn.

They had almost reached the front gate when Grey St. Bride came riding over the dunes on a big, shaggy bay horse. "Oh, dear, he's back, she murmured.

"Heard he was due in," replied Emmet equably.

Suddenly the animal reared. Silhouetted against the sunset, the man appeared to Dora almost like a centaur. Her mouth went dry and her heart began to pound until she could hardly breathe.

Shading his eyes against the lowering sun, Emmet said cheerfully, "Good evening, to you, St. Bride. I reckon you've met my wife. Sorry you missed the wedding."

Protectively gripping her husband's arm, Dora heard with amazement the cocky note in his voice. Weak or not, he suddenly sounded far younger than he had only moments ago.

St. Bride looked from one to the other before his gaze settled on Dora. "The devil, you say."

Chapter Four

"Aren't you going to congratulate me, Cap'n?" Emmet asked, grinning broadly by now. "I reckon you had in mind marrying her off to James or Clarence, but I need her more than them two does."

Slowly, his eyes never once leaving Dora's, Grey St. Bride swung down from his horse. "Madam, I told you—"

"You told me I wouldn't do. That I was too weak. Well, you don't know me at all. I'll do just fine!" Pain from all the wounds that had been inflicted over the past few months suddenly coalesced into raw anger.

Emmet patted her arm and stepped between them. "I've enough laid by to see to her care and feeding," he told the other man, quiet pride lending him stature. "You'll not be inconvenienced."

Though his intent was clear, there was a tremor in his voice that warned Dora he was overreaching his limited resources. Fearing that he might actually challenge the younger man, she stepped forward and tucked her arm through his again. "If you'll excuse us now, Mr. St. Bride," she said firmly, "I'd best get started cooking our marriage dinner."

Not waiting to see the effect of her words, she tugged Emmet toward the gate and ushered him through, wondering if she had taken leave of her senses, deliberately taunting the man that way. Among several qualities she had recently developed was a rather alarming strain of recklessness.

However, she couldn't resist glancing over her shoulder just before she closed the front door behind them. Grey was still standing in the middle of the road, threat implicit in every inch of his tall, powerful body.

The bigger they come, the harder they fall.

Had she heard that somewhere, or only read it?

Never mind, just so long as it was true.

Emmet headed for his favorite chair and collapsed, fanning his face with his straw hat. "I reckon we set the boy in his place," he said, looking smug despite his flushed face. "Don't fret, Doree, Grey won't give you a speck of trouble. He's a fair man. Gets his dander up when things don't go his way, but you have to remember, the boy owns near about the whole island. Him, and his father and grandfather before him."

Which went a long way toward explaining his arrogance, she allowed grudgingly. Even so, he was too tall, too strong and entirely too male. "I don't like him," Dora said flatly. "I don't care if he owns every twisted tree and every grain of sand in sight, he doesn't own me. And he doesn't own you—and he doesn't own our home."

Emmet smiled, but it seemed somewhat forced. He's tired, Dora thought ruefully. Walking to the church, then having to stand there until that tedious, slow-talking minister finally pronounced them man and wife—it was enough to test the strength of a much younger man. And then, to be challenged on the way home by the St. Bride...!

"Let me slide your stool closer, then I'll see what I can do about dinner."

"To tell the truth, wife, I'm used to eating dinner in the middle of the day."

"Oh, I know—it's supper. I keep forgetting. You wait right here and I'll bring you a glass of your blackberry wine."

She brought two. Gravely they saluted their union with a silent toast, totally unaware of the brooding man gazing down at their cottage from his vantage point on the highest ridge on the island. Dora made a silent vow that Emmet would never regret marrying her and giving her a home. She would be the best wife any man could wish for, as long as she didn't have to...

Well. At least she could see that their wedding supper was neither scorched nor underdone. She was beginning to get the hang of cooking, thanks to Sal's recipe book and Emmet's patient translations.

Emmet was ready for bed by the time the first few stars emerged. Dora waited until she could hear his soft snores through the closed door, then she heated water and bathed in the kitchen, put on her nightgown, blew out the lamp and sought her own narrow bed. Her last waking thought was that no matter what St. Bride had said—no matter what he thought of her, she was safe here.

In his house on the hill, Grey stared morosely at Meeks's cottage. She was down there, laughing up her sleeve for making a fool of him. What kind of a woman would take advantage of an old man whose health was so precarious that Grey had actually been meaning to send his own housekeeper down once a day to see to the necessary?

Dammit, he should have made arrangements before he'd left for Edenton. If the woman hadn't shown up just when she did—if he hadn't allowed her to distract him—none of this would have happened. Mouse could have gone down each morning to see to the old man's meals and make sure he hadn't died of heart failure in the middle of the night. He could have brought his laundry up to the house to be done along with Grey's.

A wife. Godalmighty, he thought as he watched the last light go off in the cottage below—if there was one thing the man didn't need, it was a wife. He'd kill himself trying to satisfy the gold-digging little witch.

She'd done it purely out of spite, Grey thought bitterly. Because he'd told her in effect that she wasn't worthy of being a St. Bridian. Why else would a beautiful young widow who wore fancy pink gowns and flimsy kid slippers marry a man more than twice her age? A stranger, at that.

For his property?

Hell, it was only a cottage, and not even on a fashionable resort beach like Nags Head or Cape May. However, if she thought she could talk Emmet into selling it, she was in for a surprise.

"Damned female," he muttered. One last glance down at the dark cottage set his imagination off on a pointless and decidedly unwelcome course. Honeymoon dinner, be damned!

Just before the lights went out he'd caught a glimpse of her pink skirts swishing back and forth. From his higher vantage point he could only see the lower half of the room. But the windows were open and he'd heard drifts of laughter. Heard them and wondered what the two of them found to laugh about.

And admitted to himself that any man with a shred of decency would be glad Meeks could laugh again after so long.

"Damned woman," he muttered. Turning away, he reached for the mail that had come in on the boat that morning. He had better things to do than visualize what was going on down the ridge. One thing for certain, though—if Emmet turned up dead after his wedding night there'd be hell to pay. Grey had made it his business to look after the old man's health after finding him halfway to John Luther's place back in December, his lips blue and a look of panic on his face.

He'd carried him home, called in the preacher, and between them they had stayed at his bedside until Grey could get a physician over from Portsmouth Island.

That was when he'd learned the truth—that the poor old man was not only half blind, he had a failing heart. The doctor had given him some pills for his heart, a tonic for his general health, and warned him against hard physical labor. Nothing could be done for his eyes. A lifetime spent on the water, according to the eminent Dr. Skinner, could do that to a man.

But tonic or no tonic, the last thing a man in Emmet's condition needed was a woman like Dora Sutton, ripe for trouble and not above marrying for spite. Unfortunately, he could hardly crate her up and ship her back to where she came from now, not without upsetting Meeks.

However he would make a point of keeping a close

eye on what went on down the ridge. At the first sign of any shenanigans, the lady would find herself hustled onto an outward-bound schooner before she could even slap a bonnet on her head.

The mail. He'd come back fully intending to go through the week's mail. Already the blasted female was interfering in his business.

The first letter was from Jocephus, written before Grey had arrived for his last visit. He took some small comfort in the fact that occasionally, even with the U.S. Postal Service, things didn't go according to plan.

"Evan, your nephew and sole heir, continues to do well at his studies. The boy takes his intelligence from me, quite obviously. Ha-ha. Evelyn mails him cookies each week, which I suspect he raffles off for spending money. She spoils the boy something fierce, but then, I suppose all mothers are the same."

Grey was not in a position to know about all mothers, having lost his own when he was a mere lad. He did know, however, that Evelyn had doted on her only child from the day he'd come into the world, red faced and squalling fit to bust a gut.

Smiling, he refolded the letter and set it aside to be answered in the coming week. He had long since gotten over having fallen in love at the age of nineteen with the toast of Edenton, a beautiful young woman who'd been horrified at the thought of trading her comfortable life for the rugged island of St. Brides.

She had married his brother, instead, and Grey had forced himself to stand as Jo's best man. He had returned to the island the very next morning, nursing a broken heart and a hangover. Both had quickly mended, and he'd thrown himself into planning the rebuilding of his island community. In the back of his mind there might have been some idea of showing Evelyn just what she had passed up, but somewhere along the way, his motivation had changed.

His determination, however, had not.

Over the next few weeks the pattern the newlyweds had established early on continued. The bride and bridegroom talked together, laughed together and shared tasks, with Dora taking on all those she could manage and watching carefully to see that Emmet didn't overextend himself.

Emmet talked about places he'd been, people he'd known, triumphs and mishaps in which he'd been involved. At first Dora listened because she owed him that much and more. And then she listened because she was quickly coming to care for this frail, gentle man she had married in such haste. She listened, too, because while he was relating his own story, he couldn't ask her about hers.

But then, one evening shortly after their wedding, Emmet paused in the middle of one of his hurricane stories. "Whatever's troubling you, girl," he said quietly, "I'm almost as good a listener as I am a talker."

And perhaps because she needed to talk about it—or perhaps because not to confide would have indicated a lack of trust—Dora began hesitantly to speak of her past. Small things—games she'd played as a child. Pets she remembered. Nothing that would give rise to questions as to why she was here, married to a man she would never have considered marrying if her life hadn't suddenly fallen apart.

"Well, you see, there was this man..."

When he simply nodded, she searched for the best

way to explain what her life had once been like. Oddly enough, her past no longer seemed quite so relevant.

While it was true that her father had lost a fortune that included their very home, then shot himself rather than face ruin, Emmet had lost the wife he adored.

"I don't suppose his name really matters," she said wistfully.

Emmet watched the sparkle fade from her eyes, the smile from her face. He nodded for her to continue, and she did. "Henry and I were already engaged by the time my father—lost everything—and killed himself." There, she'd gotten over the first hurdle.

As if to give her time, Emmet pushed himself up from his chair and went out to the kitchen to bring her a tumbler of water. "I take it your young man didn't stand by you."

"Stand by me?" Her eyes threatened to overflow, but she managed to laugh. Henry had completed the task her father had only begun, destroying any possible chance she might have had of happiness. "Hardly. You see, Henry had lost all his money by investing in the same stock scheme my father had, only neither of them realized it at the time. They'd both been told that by keeping the deal private, they stood to recoup a fortune beyond their wildest dreams—something to do with South American oil and diamonds, I think." She spoke rapidly, as if by skating fast enough on thin ice, she could reach the other side without plunging into the freezing depths. "Evidently Henry got wind of trouble first and decided to insure his future by marrying me, Daddy's only heir. What he didn't realize until too late was that Daddy had mortgaged our home and invested everything he could scrape up in the same risky scheme. And then he—" She swallowed hard before she was able to continue. "Once he realized what he had done, Daddy decided that the only way to look after me was to find me a wealthy husband."

Ironically, she had found herself a far better husband than the one her father had chosen.

"Henry was somewhere up north when the *Wall Street Journal* broke the news. When it came out, Daddy shot himself."

Dora breathed deeply, like a winded runner. Somewhere nearby a whippoorwill called softly to its mate, the melancholy cry almost an intrusion. The constant sound of water lapping against the shore was like music heard from a distance, while beside her, Emmet rocked slowly in the slat-back rocker, offering her time to recover.

Now that she had put herself back in that time, that place, Dora found herself unable to go on, yet unable to stem the flow of memories.

It was the night after her father's funeral. Everyone in town had attended, even the servants, even though, with no money to pay them, some had already left to find other positions.

Needing to be alone to make sense of all that had happened, Dora had wandered out to the summerhouse, with its chintz-covered settees and rattan tables and chairs—the place where Henry had proposed to her barely a month earlier.

Henry had not returned in time for the funeral, yet she hadn't been particularly surprised when she'd seen him that evening, following the winding path through the magnolias and cypress trees. She'd known, of course, that he would come as quickly as he could.

She opened the door, needing more than anything

in the world the undemanding comfort of his strong arms, the healing balm of his love. As if her father's suicide hadn't been enough of a shock, the reading of the will had left her stunned, wondering how on earth a man who had inherited wealth and accrued still more could have lost it all in less than a week.

"He's gone," she'd said, her voice rising to a thin wail as she rushed into the arms of her fiancé. "Oh, Henry, Daddy's gone—everything is gone. Tell me I'll wake up and it will all have been a dream."

The vultures hadn't even waited until after the funeral to descend. Strangers brought in by her father's lawyers had been taking inventory for the past two days while the lawyer himself met with creditors in her father's study. That was when she'd learned that her father had even sold her pearls, her diamond-and-sapphire bracelet and the gold-and-emerald broach he'd insisted on keeping in his office safe.

"Henry, tell me what to do," she'd wept in her fiancé's arms.

"Shh, it'll be all right," he'd murmured. "You still have me, sweetheart. Let me make you forget all this."

Feeling as if her whole world had collapsed, she'd been in desperate need of comfort and security. Several times they had come close to making love, because Henry's kisses had been so very exciting. This time when he tossed several cushions onto the floor, eased her down and began unbuttoning her bodice, she hadn't tried to stop him.

It had ended far too quickly. She remembered the pain—remembered feeling chilled and oddly disappointed. As if she had reached for a rainbow that hadn't been there. Henry had rolled over onto his back, his clothing awry, and stared up at the ceiling. Feeling bereft, she had waited for him to reassure her that their wedding would take place quietly, as soon as decently possible, because she needed him now more than ever.

Only he hadn't.

When she'd asked what she should do now that her home was going to be sold out from under her, he'd looked at her as if she were a stranger.

"What to do?" Rising to stand over her, he began tucking his shirt back into his pants. "My advice to you, dear Dora, is to find yourself a paying position. There must be something you're good at. God knows, the last thing I need if I'm going to have to start all over again is a spoiled, whining wife hanging around my neck."

She remembered thinking it must be some horrible, tasteless joke. Only how could he possibly make jokes at such a time, when her whole world had crumbled around her? When she'd needed him more than ever?

When they had done what they had just done.

"Henry—"

"Goddammit, Dora, I'm ruined, don't you understand? I lost every damned cent I could beg, borrow or steal! Why do you think I asked you to marry me? Because you're so damned irresistible? Come, girl, even you can't be that stupid. Once I got wind that things might be headed for trouble, I started looking around for a backup plan. And there you were, daddy's precious darling, ripe for the plucking." In the rapidly fading light, his features had twisted into those of a stranger. "So I thought, why not? The old man can't live forever, and once he dies, I'll be set for life."

They were standing stiffly apart by then. Dora, her gaping gown held together by only a few buttons, felt behind her for a chair. "Th-that's not true. You—you've been drinking. Besides, if you thought something was wrong, why didn't you tell my father? Why didn't you warn him before he—before he—?"

"Before he blew his brains all over your fancy French wallpaper? Because I didn't know the old bastard had gone out on a limb to put everything he could scrape together into the same lousy deal I had, that's why! It was supposed to be a private, limited opportunity!" By that time he'd been yelling, patting his pockets as if to be sure he hadn't lost anything. "Five investors, one in each state, I was told. All names kept secret, they said. Once it paid off, we'd all be rich beyond our wildest dreams. God, I can't believe I was so *stupid!* They must've rounded up every idiot who could scrape together a few thousand dollars and sold them the same bill of goods!"

She had stared up at him, dazed, struggling to make sense of what she was hearing after the absolute worst three days of her life. "But—but then, why did you—"

"Allow you to seduce me?" His bark of laughter had made her flesh crawl. "Why not? You landed-gentry types sure as hell owe me something for all the time I wasted in this crummy little backwater town."

He'd started to leave, turned back and said, "Oh, yeah—I forgot this." Lifting her limp hand, he'd kissed her fingers and then removed the diamond engagement ring she had scarcely had time to get used to wearing.

She'd still been there, numb with shame and disbelief, when her maid, one of the few servants who had stayed on, had found her. Bertola had taken one look at her face, then at the condition of her clothes, and said, "He done it to ye, didn't he?"

The little maid was hardly more than a child, but Dora had turned to her and burst into tears. "He—he doesn't want me," she'd wept. "He said he—said I—we owed him…"

"Hush, honey, you come on back to the house now." And Dora had allowed herself to be led back to the house that would soon no longer be hers. "I'll run warm water in the tub. You might want to smear some salve down there, where—you know. So it won't burn so much. I know it don't seem like it now, but you'll feel better by an' by, Miss Dora. I'll bring you some hot whiskey and sugar, it'll help you sleep."

Such wisdom and understanding from a sixteen-year-old maid. Dora had been in no condition to wonder about it at the time, and now that it occurred to her, it was too late.

She had slept that night…eventually. Slept and woken in time to say goodbye to the last of the servants. Head aching, heart numb, she had waited for her three best friends to call, as they'd promised to do after the funeral. She'd been told she could stay on until the house was sold and the new owner took possession, but she would rather not stay alone and there was no money to pay anyone to stay with her. She was warned not to think of selling any of the furnishings—as if she would.

Bertola had offered to stay on, but Dora knew she would need to find other work as quickly as possible. It was just beginning to dawn on her that without a home—without funds—people might actually starve.

Surely one of her friends, Dora had told herself, would invite her to stay with them until she could think more clearly about the future. They had all visited back and forth, she in their homes, they in hers.

So she'd continued to wait in the big old house with its familiar polished woodwork, its familiar faded murals, its tall, arch-topped windows draped in black. She'd blamed the rain when no one came to call the next day.

Then, too, she'd told herself, they were probably embarrassed for her. First, losing her father in such a shocking way, and then losing her home—practically everything she possessed. Granted, she was now poor while they were still wealthy, but surely their friendship had been based on more than a shared social position. They couldn't possibly know what had happened in the summerhouse. Henry certainly wouldn't brag about it, not after breaking their engagement the very same night. Gentlemen didn't break engagements, much less…the other. If he even hinted at what had happened, he would quickly find himself run out of town—or worse.

It was Bertola, as the two of them were packing Dora's trunk a few days later, who finally told her the truth. Not content to take her virginity—although she'd been a willing partner, to her everlasting shame—Henry had deliberately destroyed her reputation. The scoundrel had put it about that when he'd hurried back to town to offer her his condolences, Dora had seduced him, intent on making sure he married her as quickly as possible.

That's when he'd discovered, to his astonishment, that far from being a virgin, his fiancée was a bold, experienced adventuress. His heart, of course, had been shattered beyond repair, but how could he possibly accept damaged goods? How could he possibly bestow his honorable name on a woman half the men in town must have known intimately?

Bertola claimed tearfully that she'd done her best to refute the wicked tale, for hadn't she known Miss Dora ever since she'd first come to work at Sutton Hall as a scullery maid? But who would take the word of a servant over a fancy gentleman from up north?

"That Polly," she'd exclaimed indignantly, Polly being the personal maid of Dora's best friend, Selma Blunt. "She's the worst. It ain't enough she steals and then brags about it, but to lie about something she knows ain't the truth, the devil's gonna take her right down to the bad place!"

Dear, faithful Bertie. Dora had given her a coat, three dresses and a lace collar, but she had refused to take any money. Of all she'd left behind, it was Bertie she missed the most. Riches could be lost. True friendship was invaluable.

Now, months later and many miles away, Dora sat in companionable silence with the man she had married in desperation and silently closed the door on the past. Somewhat surprisingly, the pain had lessened with time. Someday perhaps even the scars would fade.

"Thank you, Emmet, for listening. I feel better for having told you." She had told about her father, and about the fiancé who had broken their engagement because she hadn't, after all, been an heiress. But she'd held back her most shameful secret of all. That she was damaged goods, as Henry had called her.

It no longer mattered, because Emmet didn't expect *that* of her. One of the advantages of moving to the ends of the earth, even though it was only some fifty-odd miles away by water, was that no one here knew about her past. Here there were no friends to snub her, to huddle in corners and whisper about her, or cross the street when they saw her coming. No expectations to live up to, no reputation to guard as if it were the crown jewels. From here on out, the slate was clean. Her future was what she made of it.

"Don't forget to take your bedtime pill," she reminded her husband as he got to his feet and reached for the cane he still used, even though his ankle was completely healed. Pills at night, tonic in the morning. Reminding him made her feel better, as if she were doing something in return for his patience in hearing her without comment, question or criticism.

And for giving her a home when she'd had nowhere else to turn.

Tomorrow she would store the last of Sal's things in the attic. She had finally uncovered the bed. It was small, but not at all uncomfortable as long as she didn't turn over in her sleep and fall off onto the floor.

From his castle on the hill, as some jokingly called the weathered old structure that had first been built nearly a hundred years earlier and added onto by succeeding generations, Grey watched for some indication that the woman was up to no good. Watched as they sat in the two porch rockers with their morning coffee, talking together, gesturing occasionally, seemingly content. He watched as Sal's old gander chased Dora around the backyard.

Sal had rescued the bird from the dogs and nursed him back to health. The creature was mean as a three-legged weasel. Emmet claimed he was too tough to cook, but Grey had a feeling the old man kept him for sentimental reasons. And so the bird stayed on, escaping every few days to chase after Dora whenever she stepped outside.

Grey continued to watch her, waiting for her to show her true colors. At the first misstep, he vowed, she'd be gone, set aboard the next boat out. If he had to, he'd go with her and find some decent middle-aged widow to come out in her place to look after Emmet. Marriage in his condition, wouldn't matter. What he needed was someone capable of keeping him company and seeing to his needs.

Instead, the poor fool had gotten tangled up with a haughty baggage who managed to get herself talked about by half the men on the island. He was damned sick and tired of hearing Miss Dorree this, and Miss Doree that. Just let her pick up her pan and walk down to the landing for fish, and every man on the island started panting.

She damned well had to go before his whole plan came unraveled.

Chapter Five

Seated at his desk the following day, Grey tried to concentrate on rewording his advertisement. What with all the distractions, concentration was becoming more and more difficult. "Young women with farm experience."

To do what? Milk the cows? St. Brides boasted one poor old bull, whose duty it was to service the dozen or so cows descended from those that had been brought out generations ago by some misguided stockman, or had since escaped from a cattle barge and swum ashore. There hadn't been a calf produced in the past four years—which meant no fresh cows. Which meant no fresh milk. It was all the stockmen could do to keep the poor creatures supplied with hay. There were no pastures to graze on, only the wild sedge; not even Grey St. Bride could command grass to grow in windswept, tide-prone sand.

He had a choice of having the cows butchered and salted down, the meat to be distributed among the men, or he could have a young bull shipped out. Making a note on the order he was working up for Captain Dozier, Grey went back to his advertisement.

"Wives needed. Must be young, strong, healthy."

Not for the first time, he asked himself why any young woman in her right mind would agree to move to a place that lacked even the most basic amenities, to marry a man who worked from sunup to sundown and bathed only on rare occasions. The younger men might even take a notion to ship out whenever a ship came in that was shorthanded, and be gone for months, if not years. For the most part they were decent, hard-working men. Still, what did they have to offer a woman?

More to the point, why had he ever thought he could turn this place into a settled, civilized community, one where children could grow up and learn a trade, or be taught their letters until they were old enough to go off to school? Once grown, some would move on—a few always did. But of those few, some would eventually marry and return to the island with their families.

Of course, if he followed his plan to deed each married man an acre of land and supply lumber to build him a house, St. Brides Island would one day no longer belong solely to a St. Bride.

So be it. By that time it would be up to his nephew Evan to take on the responsibility of doing whatever was best for the island's inhabitants. Grey would have done his best.

His attention strayed, as it did all too often lately, to the neatly fenced cottage, clearly visible through the window of the room where he worked. "Damned female," he muttered. Shifting uncomfortably, he thought about the way she had looked when he'd confronted her that first day, all light and bright in her pink gown, with the gray skies behind her and a shaft of sunlight picking out the gold in her hair. With her flashing green eyes and her stubborn little chin.

Wrenching his attention back to the task at hand, he finished writing out his requirements, wording them as tactfully as he possibly could and still get his meaning across, then set the letter aside to go out on the next mail boat. He was reaching for his daily ledger when he saw Dora step out onto the front porch, peer around the corner of the house, then scurry to the road, closing the gate behind her.

Emmet's dog crawled under the fence and trotted along beside her as she turned toward the landing. She was carrying a pan, which probably meant she was after fish.

Which meant that every man in sight would drop what he was doing to watch her. The woman was a distraction, pure and simple. The first time she caused an accident by waltzing down there while his men were hoisting a heavy load onto the dock from the cargo hold of a ship, was the day she'd be gone.

Damned disruption, that's what she was, he fumed. A man couldn't even concentrate on his work!

Dora was worried. Even from her own room, through two closed doors, she could hear her husband coughing. Just that morning he'd complained of aching muscles. Actually, it was more an apology than a complaint, for Emmet was not a complaining man.

Her first impulse was to send for the doctor, but the only one she knew was in Bath. She wasn't at all certain he would come, even if he happened to be free. If St. Bride thought so blooming much of the welfare of his people, then why wasn't there a full-time physician living here? Or even a part-time one?

She could try her hand at doctoring if only she could remember a few of the remedies her old family doctor had used on her childhood sniffles and upsets. Whatever the dose, it had always tasted perfectly terrible. Trouble was, she didn't have a single dose of anything available. Nor did Emmet have anything other than his tonic and his heart pills.

She would simply have to face St. Bride and insist that he send for someone immediately. Why in the world hadn't he hired himself a doctor instead of a preacher? The minister who had married them was no doubt a worthy man, but useful he was not.

"Don't you dare get up, you've been coughing all night," she scolded as she brought Emmet his morning coffee in bed, with an extra spoonful of sugar. Hadn't her mother given her a spoonful of sugar with something that tasted like turpentine dribbled on it for a cough?

She had no idea whether it was the sugar or the smelly red liquid that had soothed her throat—or simply the fact that she was being taken care of. Even as a child, she'd seldom been ill.

"Stay right there and cover up," she warned. "I'll be back in plenty of time to gather the eggs and boil them for breakfast, and then we'll see about letting you get up."

Not until she was halfway up the ridge did it occur to her that she'd marched into his bedroom without a second thought. Not long ago, she would never have dared to do such a thing.

But Emmet was different. He was her friend.

He was also her husband, but she thought of him first as her friend. With a kind providence and a healthy young wife to care for him, they would have many good years ahead. Playing checkers. Talking over old times. Threatening what they were going to do to that old gander if he didn't stay in his pen.

The castle was even more formidable at close range, but no more so than the creature who opened the door. With his gleaming dome of a head and his eye patch, he reminded her of one of the illustrations in a book of pirate stories she'd had as a child.

"Is Mr. St. Bride at home?"

"Yes."

"Well?" she said when the man didn't seem inclined to move. "May I speak with him?"

"No."

Deep breath. Patience. The creature is obviously lacking in wit. "Then perhaps you'll tell him that my husband, Mr. Meeks, is ailing and needs a physician." Her foot was beating an impatient tattoo on the gritty porch floor.

Before the one-eyed butler—if that's what he was—could answer, St. Bride came quietly up behind him and placed a hand on his massive shoulder. "It's all right, Mouse. This lady is our new neighbor."

With an anxious look over his shoulder, the huge man called Mouse disappeared into the gloomy interior, and Dora was left to deal with St. Bride. "Don't mind my friend, Mrs. Meeks. He's inclined to be a bit overprotective."

"Yes...well." Dora braced herself and said, "Emmet's not well."

"More than usual?"

"I don't know what you mean."

"Come now, Mrs. Meeks, you knew very well when you talked him into marrying you that Emmet was a propertied man with a weak heart. Why else would a woman like you tie herself to a man of his age?''

Her immediate impulse, so foreign to her nature that it shocked even her, was to claw his eyes out. It wasn't true. It *wasn't!* It might be true that she'd had no place to go and no means to get there, but she certainly hadn't chosen to marry Emmet for material reasons. Not *solely* for material reasons. That would have made her no better than Henry Smythe.

"Yes, well—think what you like, but my husband needs help.''

"Oh, I'm sure he does,'' Grey said silkily.

Dora bit back her temper. This was about Emmet, not about her. "He's been taking his pills and his tonic—I think it's mostly alcohol, but it seems to make him feel better. I don't think the coughing has anything to do with his—his heart, but last night he complained of aching muscles, and I don't want to take any chances.''

He appeared to be weighing the situation. Finally he nodded. "I'll walk down the hill and look in on him.''

"Are you a doctor, along with everything else?''

"Everything else?'' He appeared to be amused, and Dora, who had never—at least not until recently—been prone to violence, wanted to beat him with her fists until he recognized the truth—that she was not what he thought her.

She was worse.

"You know what I mean,'' she snapped.

"Do I? Suppose you tell me what you mean, Mrs. Meeks.'' They were halfway down the boardwalk that led from his porch to the shelled road by then. Face flaming, Dora did her best to stride out in front, but the wretched, long-legged man had no trouble keeping up with her.

"Mrs. Meeks? Dora. What is this *everything else* I'm accused of being?"

By the time she could come up with an appropriate response, they had reached her own gate. When Grey reached past her to lift the latch, she turned and said, "You know very well what I'm talking about. The way you order people about as though they were your subjects. Even if your business is marriage brokering, that's no reason to set yourself up as some sort of minor deity."

She was wound up and going strong, and all he could do was stand there, looking amused. "Well, let me assure you, you don't own me and you don't own my husband, so I'll thank you to—to kindly mind your own business!"

You're dragging the man to your house, practically begging him to do something for Emmet, and at the same time you're telling him to leave you alone? He must think you've lost your mind.

"Yes, ma'am." He sounded entirely too subdued. Besides that, he was grinning. Unable to think of a single annihilating thing to say, Dora swept past him into the house.

"Emmet? I'm back. I've brought his lordship to visit you."

When Grey burst out laughing as he crossed the room toward Emmet's bedroom door, Dora grabbed the egg basket and let herself out the back. If she had to spend another moment with the maddening man, she might do him irreparable harm.

A few minutes later, having collected three eggs and one pecked hand, she let herself back into the house.

Grey met her at the door of Emmet's bedroom. "I believe he's suffering from nothing more than a bad cold," he said. "His color's good. His pulse is steady."

Dora wanted to say something biting, but as the man was only doing what she'd asked him to do, she could hardly complain. It wasn't his fault he affected her the way he did.

"I was pretty sure that's all it was, but I didn't want to take any chances. Thank you for coming," she added grudgingly. She tried to edge past him, eager to see for herself, but Grey continued to bar the way. Nor did she care for the smug look on his face. "Yes, well…thank you. I'm sure Emmet appreciates your concern."

In other words, go! Go before I do or say something wildly inappropriate.

"I'll send Mouse down with a bottle of brandy. A small dose now and one later. Meanwhile, you might cook him a hearty fish broth. I'll stop in this evening to see how he's faring."

He didn't budge. Stood there like a blasted tree, but at least Dora could see past him enough to tell that Emmet was all right. Actually, he was grinning. Amused, no doubt, because she didn't share his lofty opinion of Lord St. Bride.

Irritated with both men for no real reason, she plopped her basket on the table, endangering the eggs, and said, "I'd sooner make a broth of that blasted gander."

Emmet laughed then, but his laughter ended up in a fit of coughing.

"I'll come by later, as I said, and send Mouse down

with something for that cough. Behave yourself, Em," Grey said, and then let himself out the door.

Dora watched him stride away, still fuming. Even the way he walked irritated her. As if he owned the ground he walked on.

Which, she reminded herself, he did.

"Fish broth," she muttered, trying to recall if Sal's book had a recipe for anything that sounded so dismal. Why not chicken broth? Chicken broth with noodles. Chicken broth with rice…neither of which she had the least idea how to prepare.

They had chickens, but until she could find someone to kill and pluck one of the poor creatures, it would have to be fish. At least fish came scaled and dressed. She had learned that the first time she'd gone, pan in hand, to the landing.

"John Luther just come in," Clarence had told her the first time she'd gone seeking fish. "Got some nice flounder today." He'd indicated a small pier farther down the shore, where nearby, several men were tarring nets.

"Do I just go and ask?" She'd had no idea what fish cost. Emmet hadn't given her any money—she hadn't wanted to ask, but she had very few coins left.

"Yes, ma'am, you just go give him your pan and he'll give you enough for dinner. If you want some to salt down, he might charge you a penny or two, but for eating, he'll not charge you. We take care of our own here on St. Brides, ma'am," the warehouseman had told her.

They took care of their own. She remembered the warm feeling the words had given her at the time. Regardless of what Lord St. Bride said, she was now one of their own.

"Emmet? Are you still awake? I'm going to walk down to John Luther's. We'll have a nice fish broth for dinner."

No response. He was asleep. Just as well. Rest was the only cure for a cold.

Some twenty minutes later, she approached John Luther, a weathered man with the bluest eyes she had ever seen, with her request. Hands black with tar from the nearby barrel, he insisted on dressing her fish for her. "Me and Emmet, we have an understanding," he said gravely, wielding a wicked-looking blade. "He grows collards and onions, I take him a mess of fish from time to time."

After thanking him profusely and asking after his two sons, Dora and the dog headed home with a dish-pan filled with small dressed flounder. She had just passed the church when she saw St. Bride striding toward her. Salty, the disloyal creature, trotted to meet him, her tongue lolling out and a blissful expression on her wide face.

St. Bride scratched her ears, his gaze never leaving Dora. "Been down to the landing?"

"As you can plainly see."

"Who dressed your fish?"

She started to tell him, then thought better of it. "I don't believe that's any concern of yours. You told me to make fish broth—I intend to do it."

He was impossible to understand. Either he was angry with her for daring to disobey his orders, or laughing at her for no reason at all. Every single time she saw the man, or even thought about him, her heart commenced to pound and she could feel her face turning red. One of these days he would push her too far and she would say something she would regret.

Heaven help her if that happened. She had a feeling that, given enough provocation, his temper would be utterly devastating.

He certainly brought out the worst in her, and she'd always been known for her sunny disposition. "I appreciate your coming to see Emmet this morning," she said, forcing a smiling. "We won't bother you again. As you can see—" she held up her pan of fish "—I'm perfectly capable of looking after my husband."

His eyes glinted dangerously, whether from anger or amusement, she couldn't have said. "See that you do, madam. And keep this in mind—Emmet has friends on this island. Friends who would take it amiss if anything were to happen to him." With that, he strode on past her, leaving her to stare after him. She was tempted to throw the flounder at him, but she would probably miss the target. Then she'd have nothing for Emmet's supper and Grey would have something else to hold against her.

If anything amiss were to happen to Emmet? Her husband was suffering from a cold. Everyone caught a cold now and then. And while it might be miserable for a few days, she could hardly be blamed for that. She hadn't suffered so much as a single sneeze in years.

Why did St. Bride suspect her of marrying Emmet for his money? She wasn't even aware that he had anything more than the simple cottage. Even if he did, there was nothing here to spend it on. No place to wear her pretty gowns, if her trunk ever arrived. Not so much as a tearoom where one could go for a bit of gossip, a plate of cookies and cheese, and a cup of oolong.

Staring after him, Dora couldn't help but compare

him to all the other men she'd known. St. Bride was not only taller, but broader across the shoulders, narrowing dramatically about the nether regions. The man looked as if he could balance a keg on each shoulder with room to spare. He had long, muscular limbs and large hands—square palms with surprisingly long fingers. His feet, encased in salt-stained leather boots, were in scale with the rest of him.

By comparison, Henry had been hardly more than a pretty little boy, his features small and even. Too small and too even, it occurred to her now, yet she'd thought when she'd first met him that he was wonderful and handsome beyond compare. Being the envy of all her friends had only heightened the romance of it all.

No point in looking back, Dora reminded herself. She called out to Emmet as soon as she entered the house. "I'm back. I'm going to put the fish on to cook, and then I'll bring you a cup of tea."

She could hear him chuckling, and even though it ended in another bout of coughing, the sound of his laughter warmed her heart. She knew he was amused at her awkward attempts at cooking. Not a day passed that she didn't learn something new—such as rinsing the clothes twice before she hung them out to dry so they wouldn't be stiff with soap. Or tossing a handful of corn into the gander's side of the pen to keep him from flying against the net when she went to gather the eggs.

And which hens wouldn't peck when she slid her hand beneath them and which to chase off the nest before stealing their eggs.

Despite her many failures, Emmet never complained. He might gently tease her a bit, but then he

would show her or tell her where she'd gone wrong.
If she was proud of her modest accomplishments, Emmet was even prouder. It was a lovely relationship,
one she was coming to value more with each passing
day. It was almost as if she'd been born again into a
world that was completely different from anything she
had ever known. Best of all was an increasing sense
of her own worth.

Emmet's catarrh improved daily. By the third day
his coughing had ceased altogether, his throat was no
longer inflamed, and he was ready to get out of bed.
Dora, using Sal's book of recipes, set out to prepare
a feast to celebrate. There was a cistern near the back
of the house to catch the rainwater that guttered off
the roof. On the cistern was Emmet's cool-house, a
latticed affair in which he hung bacon and ham.

She chose the smallest ham, carried it into the
kitchen, plopped it down on the table and stared at it,
totally perplexed.

Emmet shuffled into the room—three days in bed
seemed to have aged him rather than restored his
strength. "Been a spell since I had ham. Don't reckon
there's any sweet potatoes to go with it?"

Slowly Dora shook her head. "I thought ham was
supposed to be pink. With pineapple and cloves and a
lovely brown sugar glaze."

Well, of course she knew better—she wasn't quite
that stupid, only she didn't know how to go about
affecting the transformation.

Behind her, Emmet began to laugh.

And then, she did, too. They were still laughing like
two silly schoolchildren, when St. Bride rapped on the
door frame and let himself inside.

"Am I interrupting something?" he asked, eyes narrowed suspiciously. "Em, are you supposed to be out of bed yet?"

So then Emmet had to explain about the ham, and Dora's remarks, which, of course, St. Bride took seriously. "I'll take it up to the house. Mouse can cook it and bring it back down when it's done."

"You'll do no such thing," Dora declared, immediately on the defensive. "I know very well how to bake a ham." At least she would when she found the recipe in Sal's wonderful book, which, according to Emmet, had been passed down from her own mother.

Grey continued to watch her as she set about making a fresh pot of coffee. Emmet preferred it boiled the way Sal had done it, with a dribble of cold water and bit of eggshell to settle the grounds. Dora humored him in that, as in most other things.

"Beats me at checkers, she does," Emmet was bragging. "Danged if she lets me win a single game. Sal used to let me win every other game, just to humor me."

Dora plopped the pot of water on the stove. Some sloshed over, sizzling when it spilled on the hot iron top.

"I haven't had a good game of checkers since the last time Jocephus was here. Maybe you'll allow me to come over after supper and play you a game or two," Grey said, pulling up a chair to the kitchen table.

Dora's lips tightened. The man was up to something. Why would he come sniffing around now, when he had never even bothered to congratulate Emmet on his marriage?

Most of the others had been at the church, even

though they hadn't actually been invited. But of course, she reminded herself, Grey had been visiting on the mainland. Otherwise, the wedding might never have taken place. It was his church, after all.

She removed a pan of biscuits from the oven, relieved to see that they were round and golden brown, not flat and black on the bottom as so many of her attempts turned out. While the two men sat at the table and talked about plans for dredging a channel into one of the ponds in the marsh to provide sheltered harbor for the fishermen's boats, Dora proudly took up her biscuits and placed them in a napkin-covered basket. *So the dont swet,* Sal had written.

So they wouldn't sweat?

It was just one of many lessons she had learned from her husband's first wife. She was coming to feel as if the woman hovered nearby, watching to see that she took good care of Emmet.

With a sense of satisfaction bordering on smugness, Dora placed two mugs of coffee, a pitcher of tinned milk and one of molasses, and the basket of beautiful biscuits on the table before her husband and his guest.

The look on St. Bride's face told her she had in no way redeemed herself. No matter how long she stayed or how hard she worked, she would never be able to please the man. Which was just as well, because she had no desire to please him.

"Looks good, Doree," Emmet said. He never failed to thank her for her efforts, even when those efforts were all but inedible.

Grey said nothing. Breaking open one of her flaky creations, he dribbled on a swirl of golden molasses and lifted it to his mouth, holding a napkin up to catch any drips. Dora watched every movement, barely able to breathe.

Capable? Yes, indeed, your high-and-mightiness. And growing more capable with every day that passes.

Emmet winked at her. Bless his dear heart, he knew how she felt about St. Bride. Instead of dribbling molasses on his biscuit, he dunked it in his coffee, leaning over so as not to drip on his clean shirt.

Dora's gaze returned to the younger man. He was too large for the small chair, too tall for the low ceiling—and far too handsome, even with his strong, angular features, for any woman's peace of mind.

No wonder she couldn't stand him.

She waited for his compliments. Emmet claimed he was a fair man. We'd see just how fair he was.

Not by so much as a flicker did his expression change, yet Dora knew. Her heart sank. Snatching a biscuit from the basket, she bit into it without bothering to split it apart first.

Tasteless. Utterly tasteless. She had forgotten the salt.

"I'd better be getting on back, Em—Mrs. Meeks. I'll send Mouse down for the ham."

"Please don't bother," Dora said airily. "I won't be cooking it right away because—because of the salt. I'm sure you've read the latest medical theory—that too much salt is bad for the heart. Emmet and I have stopped using salt, haven't we, Emmet, dear?"

One of Grey's winged black brows rose slowly. "Then I'll see you both later. Emmet, get out the board. I feel a winning streak coming on."

Chapter Six

Dora was certain it was deliberate. The maddening man began showing up every evening after supper for a game of checkers. He seldom stayed for more than a single game, but it seemed to Dora that that one game took an eternity. First Grey would lean back in his chair and stroke his jaw, drawing her reluctant attention to the dimple that centered his square chin. Then he'd stretch out his legs, first one, then the other, and then he would lean forward, chin in hand, elbow on his thigh, and study the board some more.

Emmet mostly sat and waited, an odd, almost secretive smile on his face, as if he were planning his next move. Watching them, Dora wished she knew more about men. Wished someone would write an instruction book. She'd thought she knew her father, and he had done the unthinkable.

And then, of course, there was Henry....

Now, she was even beginning to have doubts about Emmet. If she hadn't known better, she would have thought he was up to something. *It's only a game, silly. Men are like little boys when they're playing games. It's their nature—trying to best one another.*

Her father had played chess. Played it rather badly, though he'd be the last to admit it. He always made some excuse when he lost—which was almost always. The pork roast he'd had for dinner hadn't sat right. Or he was worried about the low price for cotton.

He'd called checkers a child's game and refused to play with her, no matter how many times she would beg him on rainy days when she couldn't go outside and was bored with reading. Knowing how he always sulked after losing a chess match, she suspected he was afraid of being bested at a child's game by his own daughter.

It had been Bertola, her maid, who'd been her favorite opponent on days when the weather closed in and Dora had read every book she possessed thrice over. Bertola could barely read and write, but she was a whiz at cards and checkers. Now, in a fit of nostalgia, Dora thought back to those rainy days in the small back parlor before a roaring fire, sharing the pocketful of sweets Bertie would sneak from the kitchen.

Another world, she mused. Sighing, she put the past behind her and studied the gentle man she had married. Emmet loved the challenge of playing with St. Bride. Dora was adequate, but she'd never been particularly competitive when it came to board games. Unlike tennis and croquet, those had been simply a means of whiling away a few hours until the weather improved. Once she'd grown older and her social life had expanded, she hadn't had time for such pastimes.

Now she wondered if Bertie had missed their games these past few years, if she'd felt somehow deserted. It wasn't as if they'd been exactly friends—and yet, Bertie had been the only one to stand by her when those she had considered her friends had deserted her.

"Sorry, mate," Grey said, grinning with satisfaction as he blockaded Emmet's move and removed his last king, thus winning the game.

Rising, he flexed his shoulders, drawing Dora's eyes to his magnificent body. She'd been sitting in the corner, quiet as a mouse, with a basket of mending beside her. And while she'd been diligently plying Sal's needle, a closer look would have assured even the most casual viewer that instead of mending Emmet's stocking, she was creating a ragged lump where the hole had been.

"Wife, why don't you offer Grey a slice of that apple cake you baked this morning?"

Emmet had taken to calling her "Wife" whenever Grey dropped in. She'd been puzzled at first, until he'd told her he was staking her claim to his property, should Grey ever decide to contest her rights. She'd scolded, "Hush! Don't even talk about such a thing. You're going to live forever, because I'm going to take such good care of you!"

Grey, the wicked man, was smiling at her now in a way that told her quite clearly he expected her cake to be no better than her biscuits had been. "Don't let me take you away from your darning, Mrs. Meeks."

Thus challenged, she carefully placed the sock in her mending basket so that the lumpy mend wouldn't show, then stood and brushed the loose threads from her skirt. "It's no trouble at all, Mr. St. Bride. Would you care for a cup of coffee as well?"

Both men watched her leave the room, shoulders squared as if she were marching off to battle. Grey said quietly, "How do you think she'll stand up if we have a bad storm season? I have a feeling we're about due for one."

"Plenty of storms back in Bath—reckon they strike rich and poor alike. She'll surprise you though, boy. For all she's not got much heft to her, there's grit in her craw."

"For your sake, I hope so."

"You say there's another woman on the way out?" Grey had mentioned the possibility when they'd first settled down to play. "Doree'll like having another female to talk to. Won't admit it, but she's lonesome." They spoke quietly while Emmet folded the board, bagged the checkers and replaced the game on a shelf under the table.

"First one should be showing up most any time now. Name of Mattie Blades. From her letter, I think she'll suit Jim Calvin just fine, but if she doesn't, there's another one coming out from Little Washington in a week or so. Widow, a few years older. I'm thinking to pair her up with Clarence, seeing's how you stole his first woman right out from under his nose."

Grey smiled. Emmet nodded thoughtfully. Both men were aware of the unspoken words lying just beneath the surface.

"I reckon it's a lot like checkers," the older man observed. "Moving folks around and matching 'em up. Never know who's going to come out a winner."

Before Grey could follow up on the analogy, Dora was back with two plates of cake. At least, Grey presumed it was cake. It was brown, coarse and crumbly. "Thank you, Mrs. Meeks."

Dora had never seen a shark, but she imagined that if the creatures smiled, it would look something like Grey St. Bride at that moment. "I'm boiling more coffee.'' She tossed the words over her shoulder belligerently as she whisked out of the room again.

''It's the stove, most likely,'' Emmet said after she'd gone. ''Even Sal said different stoves takes some getting used to, and mine weren't new even when I got it, if you'll remember.''

Both men applied themselves to the cake, which tasted better than it looked. Emmet could make all the excuses in the world, but Grey knew the truth. If the woman had ever done a day's work before she'd arrived on his island, he'd be very much surprised. Everything about her had shouted privilege, from the way she'd presented herself to the way she'd been dressed, to those pale, smooth hands of hers. For the life of him, he couldn't figure out why she'd stayed on. She had to have been desperate to have married a man so much older. Not that Em wasn't as fine a man as ever lived, but a woman like Dora...

Hell, she was beautiful. Spunky, funny, kind...he was even coming to like her, and that he could ill afford to do.

Moments later, when she brought in two mugs of coffee, Grey couldn't help but notice her hands. Still small and shapely, they were now red and rough, the fingernails either broken off or pared short.

''Thank you, Mrs. Meeks,'' he said gravely. Em seemed content with the match, and that, he told himself, counted for a lot.

''You're welcome, Mr. St. Bride.''

Grey wasn't fooled by her demure response. If ever a woman wanted to do him bodily harm—and there'd been a few who'd been tempted—it was Dora Sutton. Dora Meeks, he amended. For Emmet's sake, she was holding her tongue, but it was plain she'd like nothing better than to feed him to the hogs.

"I'll stop in tomorrow," he said, carefully placing his mug on the table beside Sal's mending basket. She'd tried to hide the mess she was making of Em's stocking, but not much escaped Grey's notice. He'd always been a noticing man. For a man in his position, it was mandatory.

He only hoped poor Emmet didn't try to wear the thing, else he'd have to cut a hole in his boot to make room for the knots.

Her trunk arrived the next day, a mere three weeks delayed due to the fact that she'd lacked the nerve to ask Emmet to pay storage and then pay to have it sent out. She'd told the clerk back in Bath that she'd send word where to ship it once she was settled. With her future hanging on the promise of a newspaper advertisement and a single exchange of letters, she'd been wary of pushing her luck by arriving, bag and baggage, before she was certain she'd be staying.

Dora was overjoyed to see Clarence wheeling it up the road in a handcart. Salty barked, Emmet came to the door, and Dora, after one glance through the kitchen window, fairly flew out to meet him.

"I am so *awfully* tired of pink," she declared breathlessly, and Clarence grinned as if he knew just what she was talking about. "Not having enough clothes," she explained. "Salty, stop sniffing and move out of the way. Do you think you could carry it through to the back room? Oh, mercy, everything will have to be aired out, and it looks like rain."

"Not before tomorrow. Morning, Em. John Luther

says to tell you he's saving you a nice mess of spot. Wants to know if your collards has gone to seed yet.''

"Pulled 'em up last week. Tell 'im he'll have to make do with poke salet.''

"Right over there in the corner," Dora instructed. "Well, I guess this makes me an official resident of St. Brides. Bag and baggage, isn't that what they say?''

Clarence stood up, flexed his back and smiled again. Really, she thought, for such a plain man he had a truly infectious smile. A body couldn't help but smile back at him. "You'll stay for a taste of my apple cake, won't you. To tell the truth, it's really Sal's cake—at least, it's her recipe, but I'm working on it. This time I almost got it right, didn't I, Emmet?''

And so the three of them finished the last of the cake, which was drier than ever, but at least the raisins were good, for she'd soaked them in Emmet's medicinal brandy. They discussed the woman St. Bride had ordered, who was due to arrive soon.

"I hear this one's intended for James Calvin," Emmet opined. "If she don't take, might be another one out in a week or so. Takes some longer than others to work up nerve enough to come out here.''

It had taken Dora exactly half a day. She'd seen the advertisement, made up her mind and acted on it before she could lose her courage. At the time she'd been so distraught that she'd assumed it was St. Bride himself who had advertised for a wife.

"If they take to one another, I reck'n James'll get started building another room onto his cabin." The warehouse manager went on to confess shyly that he was next on the list.

"I'm sure either of you could have found your own

bride," said Dora. And then curiosity overcame her and she blurted, "Why don't you just go and find your own wives instead of letting that man pick them out for you?"

Clarence's blush was a partial answer. The man was painfully shy. Most of the men she'd met so far were shy, although she'd never seen the others actually blush. "It's not all that easy, Miss Doree. A man can't just up and quit work one day, sail across the sound, walk ashore and pick him out a woman. Most women want to be courted, and courting takes time. Truth is, I wouldn't even know how to start. Then, even if you do it right and she says yes, you got to go ask her father for his daughter's hand, and like as not, he won't want her going off to a place like this. Truth to tell, it's a whole lot easier when a woman comes out here, knowing what to expect. All we have to do is tote our bed over to the parsonage for her to sleep in till she makes up her mind. Then we put on a clean shirt to go calling."

Dora had already learned of the practice letting the prospective brides sleep in the parsonage in a bed provided by their intended. She'd considered it a quaint custom but knew better than to question it. St. Bride was a law unto himself.

Clarence went on to say shyly, "I've heard tell that after a woman's been out here a few days, the men start looking better to 'em."

Once past his initial shyness, Clarence Burrus seemed inclined to talk. And because Emmet appeared to be enjoying the company, Dora encouraged him to linger. "But what if you don't like each other?"

"Oh, Grey don't force you to go through with nothing," Clarence confided. "James, he'll set with her of an evening while they get acquainted. If they hit it off, Grey, he'll send for the preacher, and by the time he gets here, James'll have a new room built onto his cabin. All the men pitch in to help.''

"If the plan works so well, why aren't any of the other men married?"

Emmet looked at Clarence. Clarence looked at Emmet. It was the younger man who spoke up. "Most of 'em take one look and go back to where they come from. Them that stay on might get homesick. Even if they marry, first thing you know they'll up and leave, taking their husbands with 'em. Happened more than once.''

Emmet said with quiet pride, "My Sal took to the place right off. Most don't. Something about the island just don't seem to set well with womenfolk.''

Dora could certainly see why—it was a man's world. Then, too, if every prospective bride was offered the same treatment on arrival that she'd been given, it was no wonder they all fled.

After Clarence left, she hurried to open her trunk, then gazed in dismay at the crushed contents. Bertie had folded each gown so carefully, but no amount of care could make up for weeks of being crammed tightly in a small trunk. She would simply have to heat up the flatirons, set up the cumbersome ironing table and see if she could press out the worst wrinkles without burning a hole in the delicate fabrics. This time there was no Bertie to help her.

On the other hand, she would soon have another woman to visit with. They could sip tea and talk about...

Talk about what?

It occurred to Dora that not a single one of the

things that had once engaged her interest was of the slightest importance to her now. To think she'd wasted hours—years, in keeping up with the latest dances, the latest fashions and the latest songs, perfectly content to idle away her life in frivolous pursuits.

She'd do better to try and learn how to darn a stocking so that the resulting lump didn't wear a blister on a toe. Or how to keep a cake from cracking open across the top. Those were the things she needed to discuss with another woman, not the latest fashions and who was courting whom. The craft of housework she might learn from a book, but the art involved— that was the part that continued to escape her.

Poor Emmet didn't have a single pair of hose that didn't need darning. She had tried to help until he had gently asked her not to bother.

Methodically she began shaking out the gowns, winter things on top, summer clothes on the bottom. Her shoes would be in the very bottom.

While she worked, she thought about the woman who was shortly to arrive. According to Emmet, St. Bride kept a list of the men he wanted to anchor down by finding them suitable wives. Carpenters were valuable, as was his warehouse manager and the men who handled freight. The inlet pilots and fishermen figured somewhere lower on the list, as they were inclined to move to wherever the fish and the greatest inlet traffic could be found.

Obviously, she hadn't been considered a suitable candidate for any of those, as he'd tried his best to send her back.

Well, she was here for keeps now, she told herself, shaking out a musty-smelling gray sateen. Here and married to a man who had quickly become her good friend. And whether or not it suited St. Bride's famous plan, things could not have turned out any better as far as she was concerned.

Hands on her hips, she pondered the heap of wrinkled gowns piled across her bed. They would have to go somewhere. Emmet's house, obviously designed and built by a man, with a man's lack of practicality, made no accommodation for a woman's wardrobe. His few shirts and trousers hung from wooden hooks on the bedroom wall.

Her own gowns would hardly benefit from such treatment, and as they would probably have to last her a lifetime, she'd do well to take care of them. She thought of the roomy back porch with its sloping roof—considered what it would take to enclose it, then shook her head. It was Emmet's house. If he wanted another room added on, it was up to him to suggest it. She was grateful to have her own bedroom; a dressing room was a bit too much to ask.

Separating her summer things from her dark woolens, she repacked the winter garments. If the moths got into her trunk, she would simply have to darn the holes. Perhaps with enough practice, she would learn to do it without making lumps.

Shoes, she thought, her toes curling in anticipation. She'd been wearing the same miserable kid slippers ever since she'd arrived, nearly a month ago. Emmet had cut a strip of leather to lay inside them, which helped immensely, but nothing could take the place of a pair of well-fitted high-tops when a woman was on her feet all day.

Pausing in the middle of the day for luncheon—she was still trying to learn to call it dinner, she chattered on about her clothes, and whether or not there would be moths in the attic.

"Oh, listen to me, I'm gabbing on and on about things you can't possibly be interested in."

"Fair's fair. Many's the time you've sat there while I rambled on about one thing and another. Reckon I owe you some listening time." His eyes twinkled. "Leastwise, even if I don't understand lady-talk, I like watching the way you color up when you get all excited."

So Dora chattered on and, occasionally, Emmet would break in with a question. By mutual consent they avoided talking about her past, while he talked freely about his own. Mostly about his life as an inlet pilot and how he had taken one look at Sal and realized why he had waited so long to find himself a wife. He loved talking about Sal, and Dora enjoyed seeing the sparkle come back to his clouded eyes, the unconscious lift of his thin shoulders.

The next day, having fully recovered, Emmet replenished the woodpile. Next, he killed, plucked and dressed one of the oldest hens. Faced with a limp, warm carcass, Dora nearly lost her breakfast, but she swallowed hard, opened Sal's book, read what must be done and dutifully proceeded to do it.

The results were…edible, at least. As usual, they chatted about this and that, and then, at Dora's insistence, Emmet lay down to "rest his eyes."

"You've done more than enough today," she began, "if you're going to beat St. Bride at checkers after supper, you'd best rest up."

Within minutes, he was snoring. Dora, with a tender smile, pulled a spread up over his slight form. It was warm, even for mid-May, but she was so afraid he would catch a chill and fall ill again.

Shopping list in hand, she set out for the landing. According to Emmet, a list handed to Captain Dozier would be filled often on the return trip, whether he was bound for Little Washington, Bath or Edenton, his usual ports of call. They were running short of coffee beans. And flour—she had wasted so much of it in her efforts to learn to bake.

Salty stirred herself to waddle along beside her. Dora appreciated the company. She often found herself talking to the dog, for as patient as Emmet was, she hated to bore him with too much frivolous chatter.

"Just wait until you see my new Swiss muslin with the green-and-white-striped sateen underskirt," she said, striding along the shell-paved road in her second best high-top shoes. "I have a hat with a band to match, and green slippers, too."

None of which, she thought wryly, was at all suitable for her new role in life. She'd have done better to give all her clothes to Bertie in exchange for a few sturdy dark cottons that wouldn't show soil, and a pair of thick-soled leather boots. Bertie could have supported herself until she found another position by selling them.

Still, she hadn't been able to resist putting on her favorite blue-sprigged muslin that morning. Amazing what a change of clothing could do for a woman's spirits. If hers were any higher, she'd be flying.

It had rained in the night, but now that the clouds had blown away, the sun glistened on every blade of wild grass. The air smelled of salt and horse manure and some spicy shrub that grew along the shoreside. Brushing her hair from her forehead, she reminded herself that she was going to have to start wearing a hat or else end up with a face full of freckles.

Salty, who had recently gained a remarkable amount of weight, was forced to trot to keep up with Dora's spirited pace. "You've been eating too many of my mistakes, girl. From now on I'm feeding them to the chickens."

"Morning, Miz Doree," someone called out as she neared the harbor. Smiling, she looked around and waved. Several men had stopped work, some were leaning on shovels. All waved back.

Most of the men she now recognized by sight, if not by name. James Calvin, the boatbuilder who was considered the island's best carpenter, had helped build Emmet's house, the church and the parsonage. He respectfully doffed his cap as she approached, then reached down to scratch Salty behind the ear.

"I'll take one of the pups when they're done," he said. "My old dog up and died on me last week. Big, brown fellow—you might've seen him around. He was a wanderer, all right. Called him Rover."

"One of what pups?" Mercy, the man had finally found his tongue! Did that mean she was officially accepted as a St. Bridian?

"Salty's pups. I reckon it's only fittin', seeing as how Rover was probably the papa." His smile was slow in coming, but surprisingly appealing. It occurred to Dora that he was really quite an attractive man. She hoped St. Bride had chosen him a lovely wife.

"I should have guessed. I thought it was because I'd been feeding her so many scraps."

James chuckled, and Dora thought, if it had been Clarence speaking of such matters, his face would have flared up hot enough to blister. According to Emmet, James Calvin was a plainspoken man. She decided she rather liked the quality.

It never occurred to her that it was the same quality that she disliked so intensely in Grey St. Bride.

From the office above the warehouse, Grey watched the arrival of Emmet's wife. The way she was lollygagging about, keeping the men from their work, you'd think this was one of the fancy afternoon socials Evelyn used to love so much. These men had better things to do than to stand around making fools of themselves over a mop of yellow curls, a pair of green eyes and a shapely female body.

He made a mental note to sail over to Portsmouth one day soon for a visit with a certain obliging widow.

Clarence loped down the steep stairs from the second-floor office and met her at the door. "Mornin', Miz Doree. You need something I can order for you?"

"This—" She handed him the short list. "And I just thought of camphor. I shook out all my winter woolens, then dragged the trunk up to the attic and repacked them, but I'm afraid the moths might get in and ruin them."

"That they will, ma'am. John Luther was saying just this morning that it was going to be a bad year for storms and a worse year for bugs. Want me to ask Grey if he can spare you some camphor balls? He's up in the office. Mouse always keeps a stock on hand in the summertime."

"Oh, no, please. I can wait until the boat comes out again."

"Ask Jim to give you some cedar shavings. That ought to keep 'em away till Cap'n Dozier gets back."

Dora thanked him and lingered to watch as the men resumed their various tasks. Emmet had explained that being situated on a deepwater inlet that led into a shallow sound, St. Brides was the ideal interim port for deeper draft vessels to transfer their freight to smaller boats, called lighters. The lighters transported it inland, returning with outward-bound shipments which were stored in St. Bride's warehouse until they were taken aboard outward-bound ships.

Evidently the day she had arrived had been a slow day, lending her the impression that St. Brides was the ends of the earth. Today, it looked more like the hub.

Turning away, she was greeted by a second chorus of smiles, waves and friendly remarks. Her heart swelled with a warm sense of belonging.

If St. Bride was in the warehouse office upstairs, and if he happened to be watching from the window, it might interest him to know that the men liked her, even if he didn't. *I'll do just fine,* she vowed, not for the first time—if only to spite the man.

Chapter Seven

St. Bride was indeed watching from the office above the warehouse. How was it possible, he wondered irritably, for the pesky woman to attract every man on the island? Maybe she was a witch—a golden-haired sorceress, working her magic on an island full of vulnerable victims.

The trouble was, getting rid of her now would not be an easy task. Emmet wasn't going to take kindly to losing her, even if Grey could have managed to buy her off. He could have sworn she would never be satisfied in a place like this, and dissatisfied women, as he knew to his sorrow, were the devil's own handmaidens. Just look at the brides who had come and gone, taking with them some of his best men.

If Dora left and took Emmet with her, that might not be a bad thing. At least he'd be near medical help if his heart acted up. But for reasons Grey had yet to fathom, she seemed determined to stick it out. As witness all those fancy frocks she'd had shipped out. Why the devil hadn't she simply brought them with her?

While Grey didn't profess to be an expert on women's fashions, he'd heard Jocephus complaining more than once about how much Evelyn spent on gowns alone, not including the jewelry she considered a necessary part of any outfit. Judging from what he'd seen so far, Meeks's bride had equally expensive tastes.

Not the jewelry. She hadn't worn a wedding ring when she'd arrived, nor did she wear one now. Not that she needed the adornment. In that outfit she had on today she looked fresh as a spring rain, fragile as a rainbow.

Nor was he the only man who couldn't take his eyes off her.

At least, he thought with wry amusement, she had changed the men's attitude toward finding wives. Even the most hardened bachelors were seriously interested now. Two of them had shaved their beards. A few had even cleaned their fingernails, although tarring nets was a messy business.

Grey warned himself, not for the first time, to let her be. She was Emmet's problem now, not his. Trouble was, his own house looked directly down on the Meeks Cottage, and with the windows open and the wind from the right quarter, he could hear the sound of their laughter, hear them calling back and forth from the house to the yard.

And hearing it, his imagination never failed to create images he could have done without. Especially after Emmet had confided his worry of running out of water, as Dora liked to drag the washtub out onto the back porch for her nightly bath.

Once the lamps were lit, if he happened to glance that way, he could see her parading back and forth between the kitchen and the front room. Not that he wasted time watching, because he had far better things to do. All the same, he couldn't help but be aware of what was going on down there.

What the devil *was* going on down there? Surely she wasn't sleeping with the old guy—his heart would never stand it. It was a wonder she hadn't poisoned him with her cooking.

Come to think of it he did seem to have lost some weight lately.

Was that her game? Find herself an ailing, elderly husband and wait for him to kick off so that she could inherit his property?

In that case she was in for a hell of a shock. While she might end up with a roof over her head, unless she was a better fisherman or stevedore than she was a cook, she wouldn't last out a week. There were no jobs to be had on the island, not for a woman. If something happened to Em, she might look around for a replacement.

He dismissed the thought. It wasn't going to happen. She might inherit the house and property, but she could never sell it—that was written into the deed. After marrying Sal, Emmet had managed to accumulate a small savings account in a mainland bank. Inlet pilots were well paid. But that would have long since disappeared had not Grey made small, regular deposits. Unable to read his bank statements once his eyesight went bad, Emmet had never known the difference.

Grey was still standing at the office window some five minutes later when he caught sight of her again. He told himself he should be pleased that the old man had found pleasure after grieving for so long over his first wife. If having someone else step into Sal's shoes made him happy, then that was between the pair of them.

He would, however, make a point of keeping an eye on her. The nightly checker games were an excellent opportunity to let her know, without making an issue of it, that Emmet was not without friends.

"What's the matter, don't the figures add up?" Clarence had come upstairs, a sheaf of papers in hand.

"Figures? Oh, yeah—the figures." The figure he'd been picturing had nothing to do with the bills of lading he'd been studying when he'd been interrupted by the clamor below. Erasing his frown, Grey said, "They tally up just fine. At the rate we're going, we should be ready to add on to the lumber shed in another few months."

Grey believed in operating on a pay-as-you-go basis. He had his plans, and he had his methods. When it came to building his transshipping business, he was right on schedule.

When it came to building his community, he was a few years behind, but he was working on a remedy. All he had to do was discover a method of winnowing out the women who answered his advertisement, making certain they were suitable for his purposes before they arrived. It was damned difficult to do through an exchange of letters, especially when some of them could barely write. The letter from the Blades woman had obviously been written by someone else.

"Tell me, Clarence, if you were me, how would you go about selecting the kind of people we need out here?"

The warehouseman appeared to ponder the problem. "I reckon we could use us a doctor. Maybe a drink house, like them over to Portsmouth, and a—well, you know—women. For them that don't find wives." He reddened painfully and, sighing, Grey laid his papers on the scarred oak desk.

"Women. It always comes back to women, doesn't it? Without 'em, nothing seems to work right, yet the minute they set foot on the island, we've got nothing but trouble."

Clarence grinned, not at all shy with the man he'd known practically all his life. "Might be better if we gave up on wives and settled for widows over on Portsmouth."

Grey had to chuckle. His own arrangement was no secret, but then, any man who cared to was free to make his own arrangements. Most settled for a night or two with one of the willing "widows" over on Portsmouth Island.

"You know, if I were St. Bride," Dora mused as she worked lard into the bread flour, using the quick finger movements Sal had described in the recipe book, "I'd arrange to meet the women over on the mainland instead of bringing them all the way out here first. That way it would save trouble and disappointment if things didn't work out."

"Then I'd still be lying out in the backyard with my leg swole up like a puffing toad, and you'd be married to some young blade over on the mainland," Emmet retorted.

She laughed, as she'd been meant to do. "All the same, for someone who claims to be so smart, his lordship doesn't appear to have much luck with his matchmaking, does he?"

Emmet went on snapping beans, some of the first to come over from the inland farms. His own vines were blooming but not yet bearing. "He ever come right out and say he was smart?"

"Well, isn't it obvious that he thinks he's some sort of genius? The way he pushes people around saying, 'You can live here in one room,' and 'You can live there in two,' and telling people who they can marry and who they can't?"

Dora pinched off a bit of dough and tasted it to be sure she'd remembered to add salt. They continued to discuss Grey's plans for turning a barren island with an all-male population into a settled community.

"If you ask me, he's taking entirely too much on himself. I'm not saying he's arrogant—" He was, of course, but she wouldn't say it aloud to Emmet, who invariably defended the man. "But he's nowhere near as smart as he thinks he is."

"Boy's only acting sensible. Took what his pappy handed down and set to work making it better. Can't blame him for that."

She began to roll the dough and stamp out rounds with a jar lid. "Oh, yes I can," she said calmly. She could blame him for any number of things, most of all for allowing her to come all this way and then trying to send her back. For not approving of her, not liking her, and telling her as much to her face. Oh, he'd told her she was too pretty, which was certainly not true, but without knowing the first thing about her, he had found her wanting. The least he could have done was to give her a chance to prove her worth.

It was more than vanity, she assured herself. Any vanity she might once have possessed had died a painful death by the time she'd been reduced to answering an appeal for brides who were willing to remove to an isolated barrier island. At the time it had seemed the only solution for a woman who had lost everything she possessed, including her reputation.

Any vanity she now possessed was based on more than her average looks and her once privileged position in Beaufort County society. Here, she was learning to cook, her recent successes almost matching in number her spectacular failures. Given two or three sunny days in a row, she could wash, dry and iron a load of laundry without scorching, shrinking or over-bleaching anything too badly. She could sew up a split seam, a relatively easy task for someone who'd been forced to embroider countless samplers as a child. One of these days she might even get the hang of darning a stocking without making an unholy mess of it. French knots and satin stitches obviously weren't the answer.

Now *that* would be a true cause for vanity.

And if it pleased her to wear her prettiest gowns while she worked, it was nobody's business but her own. She might as well have some use from all the finery she had accumulated for her honeymoon and never got to wear.

"Hats, gloves and all," she muttered, mopping perspiration from her brow with a forearm before sliding the pan of biscuits into the oven and slamming the door. She'd had only to burn herself once before learning never to touch any part of the ugly iron monster without first swathing her hand with a towel.

With the beans snapped and ready to boil, Emmet rose to go outside. He had taken to spending hours each day in his garden attacking bugs and weeds and lingering to admire his vegetables. "They lag behind them on the mainland, but they're acoming right along," he'd said proudly. Having nailed strips across the legs of an old chair so that it wouldn't sink up in the sand, he sat outside in the sun with his shirt buttoned up, while Dora, sweltering in the early June heat, went about her household chores, her shirtwaist unbuttoned down to her camisole.

They would call back and forth through the open window whenever she had a question—and questions came up frequently.

If she happened to be outside hanging clothes or tending the chickens, which she still didn't quite trust not to peck her hand, she would wander over to the garden and they would talk about this and that. She tried not to think about her mother's old rose garden, and the way of life she had left behind.

Her present life was more than enough. She'd been fortunate beyond belief to find someone who demanded nothing of her but companionship. Truly, she told herself, she was perfectly content.

As days passed, with a new woman expected almost daily, Dora speculated on what she would be like and whether or not she would stay. Evidently, not all of them did. Having met St. Bride and seen his island, she could well understand how any woman might take one look and change her mind about staying.

"Didn't Grey say another bride might be coming any day now? It's been almost a week."

"Mmm-hmm. Reckon it takes women more time to make up their minds. Not my Sal, but most."

"All the same, I'd like to be there to meet her. It's frightening, arriving all alone without knowing a single soul."

Emmet nodded in agreement, but Dora knew that being a man he could never fully understand how a woman felt in such circumstances. Alone, totally dependent on strangers, without even knowing where she was to sleep.

"She'll likely show up today or tomorrow," he predicted. "Dozier, he don't much like hauling passengers. He'll put it off till Grey gets onto him about it, then he'll load 'em up and haul 'em on out. Like as not, have to haul 'em back again if Grey takes a notion they won't do." He winked, knowing that Dora had been placed in that category. It was only one of several small jokes they shared.

He might not be young or handsome or wildly successful, Dora told herself, but she gave thanks every day for having married Emmet Meeks, and did her best to repay him for giving her a home.

Emmet was fascinated by all her pretty things. Sal, she happened to know, had possessed very few dresses, and those in calico or gingham. Even her winter coat had been made from an old quilt.

Never less than respectful, he loved to see her all dressed up, loved to feel all the silks and satins, and she loved seeing his innocent pleasure. Today she was wearing a simple peach-colored dimity with a sprigged overskirt to do her chores. Before heading outside she'd put on a white pancake straw hat with matching ribbons to shade her nose.

Emmet chuckled, seeing her sweep outside dressed up, as he put it, like the Queen of England. Now and then she would even dress for supper in one of the newer gowns she'd had made for her trousseau. She would parade back and forth across the parlor, swishing her skirts, delighted at his reaction. It took so very little to please him.

"Land sakes, I never in my whole life seen the likes of that," he would exclaim. "What do you call it?"

"It's called a resort dress," she would say. Or a ball gown. Or a morning frock. "This one's taffeta. Listen closely and you can hear it whisper when I turn around quickly." And then she would swish her skirts, perhaps waltz a few steps, and Emmet would chortle and clap his hands.

Like a little girl playing dress up, Dora went through her wardrobe, touched at the way he responded to even the simplest effort to bring him enjoyment. You'd think the man was starved for entertainment. Once when she lifted her ruffled petticoat to show him her matching striped cotton stockings, he went into a coughing fit until she had to slap him on the back.

Each day they found things to laugh over, and that pleased her enormously. Emmet thought her hats were absurd, and so she tied a ribbon around his old straw hat one evening and pranced around the parlor wearing that, a layered chiffon negligee and a pair of his old boots. They had both collapsed, laughing. He'd still been smiling when he'd risen to say good-night.

Somewhat to her amazement, so had she. "You know what? You're good for me, Emmet Meeks. I've learned more in these past few months than I learned in all the twenty-three years before."

Up on the windswept dunes in his weathered castle, Grey sat at his desk working on plans for the future and trying not to look through the darkness to the brightly lit windows below. Trying to ignore the flashes of color, the snatches of laughter.

Trying not to picture Dora in her bath on the dark back porch.

Did Emmet watch her? He hated to think what that would do to a man with a weak heart.

Mosquitoes droned against the screens. Lightning flashed in the distance. A few thousand yards away, a hungry surf gnawed at the fragile barrier island. All sights and sounds an island man heard without actually listening.

Earlier tonight, as she had most evenings since he had started his nightly checker games with Emmet, Dora had declined to join them. Emmet had offered him a glass of Sal's blackberry wine. Dora had offered him nothing but a polite good-evening before disappearing with a stack of towels.

God, was she going to take her bath with him right there in the same house? Shifting uncomfortably to accommodate his lusty reaction, he wondered if she was doing it deliberately—keeping him so stirred up he couldn't think straight.

"You're not paying attention, son. That was your own man you just took off the board."

Near the thriving town of Washington, a few miles upriver from Bath, two women boarded the *Bessie Mae & Annie*. Hours later, huddled in the cramped cabin, they stared out across the dark waters of the Pamlico River, each hoping the life she was head toward was better than the one she had left behind.

Lula Russart, a tall, pretty woman with dark hair, dark eyes and a longish nose, said nervously, "I'm glad you waited to come out with me. I can't understand half of what these people down here are saying."

"I don't reckon they understand you none too good, neither, you talk so fast," Mattie Blades replied.

Lula shrugged. "Don't reckon. That's lazy talk,

Mattie. Don't you even have schools down here in the South?''

"I went all the way through the fourth grade,'' the plump little redhead said defensively. "I didn't never hear nobody say there was nothing wrong with sayin' *don't reckon.*''

The older woman rolled her eyes and sighed. An unemployed actress from Rochester, Lula had come south to marry her lover, a traveling salesman she had met some four months earlier while working as a waitress between acting jobs. It had taken her nearly a month to track him down, for he wasn't at the address he'd given her. She had finally located him living on a farm with a woman who claimed to be his wife. After a brief exchange in which her lover swore piously that he'd never set eyes on her before, she had asked his wife if he happened to have a strawberry mark on his left buttock.

The woman had gasped and turned on her lying, philandering husband. Lula, knowing when to cut her losses, had turned and walked the three miles back to town.

Pregnant, nearly penniless, without family or friends, she'd been studying the newspaper in search of employment when a certain advertisement had caught her eye.

"It won't be so bad, long's we stick together,'' Mattie Blades said diffidently. The two women had met on the dock, waiting for the boat out to St. Brides. "They say the place is so small you can walk from one end to t'other in no more 'n an hour.''

"Perish the thought.''

"What does that mean?'' Mattie shifted the pillow slip that held her few belongings to the other hand.

She had yet to release her grip since boarding the small freighter.

"It means I'd have done better to stay in town and offer lessons in elocution," Lula said dryly.

"Lessons in what?"

"Oh, never mind. Come on, dear, the attendant wants us to follow him to the cabin. Gawd, what a tacky little boat! I'm probably going to be deathly sick."

"I don't never get sick. My mama used to say I could swaller nails and spit out carpet tacks."

Lula eyed her companion in horror as the two women carefully descended the few steps into the cramped and airless cabin. Lula looked around, thanking God that none of her fellow thespians could see how far she had sunk. Every one of them had warned her against falling for good-looking, slow-talking traveling salesmen.

Grey waved the other men back as the boat came alongside. Two women, not one, were huddled in the lea of the cabin. The men had been curious to get a look at the newcomers, knowing that if a woman didn't suit her intended groom and if she passed muster with St. Bride, she'd be given the choice of choosing another man or returning on the next boat out.

Now, instead of one woman, they had two to choose from. Whoop-de-do, big celebration, he thought dourly, watching as the men began to spit out plugs of tobacco and roll down their sleeves.

Whether or not all the men had marriage in mind, Grey had his doubts, but it was his duty to look after every woman he brought out until either a match took hold or he could get her safely off the island.

God help him if either of these two had yellow curls, green eyes and the kind of body that set a man on fire. Dora had set the standard, and now too many of his men were expecting another Dora Sutton to step off the boat and fall into their sweaty arms.

Almy Dole had trimmed his beard. A couple of the men had put on shirts that, while hardly clean, didn't reek quite so much of sweat and fish.

Grey had set out for the waterfront as soon as he'd seen Dozier drop his main to come alongside the wharf, fearing his female passenger might take one look at the rough, all-male assembly and lose her courage. A total of seven women had come out since he'd placed his first advertisement. Of those seven, one had stayed but died the year following her arrival. Three others had married and stayed for a few months, taking their bridegrooms with them when they left. Two had taken one look at the prospects, shut themselves into the cabin and stayed there until Dozier had unloaded, taken on inbound cargo and hoisted sail again.

And then there was the Sutton woman. He didn't know how to factor her into the equation. She was still here, but damned if he could figure out whether she was an asset or a liability. The premise behind his plan was that married couples lent stability, and that stability encouraged more of the same.

There was nothing at all stabilizing about Emmet's bride. Married or not, she still bothered the hell out of him, and if she bothered him, then there was no telling what effect she had on the younger, more impressionable men.

One thing he'd learned from the Sutton experience, though, was not to allow a woman to get a foothold until he had looked her over and reached a decision as to her suitability.

"Good afternoon, ladies," he greeted as the two women disembarked. "Welcome to St. Brides Island." He introduced himself, allowed them a moment to stretch and to look around, then suggested they come with him to the place where they'd be staying. Scowling at the gaggle of men, who were standing at a respectful distance but eyeing the women avidly, he went on to explain the arrangements. "You'll be staying at our parsonage while you get your bearings. The preacher's not in residence, so his bed's available. I'll have another one sent over."

Grey usually allowed a week for the women to get acquainted with the men he'd picked out for them—Clarence and James, in this instance. "Naturally, your meals will be sent down every day. I'd not expect you to cook for yourselves. Preacher Filmore doesn't leave many supplies on hand on account of mice."

He winced at the slip. Women couldn't abide rodents. He remembered how Evelyn had shrieked like a scalded cat once when a mouse had run across the room.

Neither of the two women looked like Dora. For that, he gave silent thanks. The elder of the pair stood her ground and began to argue. "What about a boardinghouse? I'm sure we would both be more comfortable."

"Sorry. This is about the best we can do at the moment. One of these days we intend to remedy that, but it takes time."

"We. Who is this *we?* Do you represent a company?"

Grey waited a few moments to answer. He was beginning to get the measure of the pair. The tall dark one was obviously a Yankee. Sounded like a schoolteacher, judging from the prim way she spoke, but there was a hint of color on her face that nature hadn't painted there. And if he remembered correctly, her handwriting hadn't been all that polished.

Probably not a schoolteacher, then. In his two-and-a-half years at Princeton, Grey had heard folks who could talk faster than a whip snake could glide, without dropping a single syllable.

Curious, he mused. Why would a woman like Lula Russart be interested in an arranged marriage in a place like this?

He turned to the other one. About five feet tall, rust-red hair skinned back in braids, round body, round face, even more freckles than Clarence. From the way she was standing with her legs crossed, the poor girl needed a privy. "We'll talk once we get you settled in, shall we? It's just a few minutes walk from here. Think you can make it?"

He'd meant the question for the younger woman, but it was the northerner who answered. "You mean we're expected to *walk?* And carry our own *luggage?*"

Lady, if you had a carriage at your disposal and a porter to handle your bags, chances are you wouldn't even be here, Grey thought. "Ma'am, it would take more time to whistle up a pony and hitch a cart than it will to walk. I think your friend would like to, uh— lie down."

Lula Russart had said in her letter that she'd worked in a shirt factory since she was twelve, come South to marry and changed her mind. He hadn't pressed for details of the years unaccounted for and she hadn't offered. He didn't have so many takers he could afford to pass up any possibility.

The younger of the pair, Mattie Blades, who professed to be an orphan, hadn't spoken since they'd arrived on shore. Now taking a deep breath, she said shyly, "I kin cook and make sausage and render lard and milk cows. I'm a dab hand at doin' most ever'thing, an' my papa always said I was a real good learner."

Lula Russart rolled her eyes. "Yes, dear, I'm sure you'll prove most useful."

Grey, gathering up a battered valise and a cardboard trunk, wondered how the devil he had ended up with this mismatched pair. Seeing the stickers on the trunk, he had a feeling the Russart woman might be an actress. It would explain her careful elocution and the light touch of cosmetics. What it wouldn't explain was what the hell she was doing here, ready to marry some rough waterman, sight unseen.

Mattie Blades refused to turn loose of her pillow sack, and so Grey led the way, wondering if it was too late to simply cede the island back to the state and go to sea for the next fifty-odd years. It would be a hell of a lot simpler than trying to play Cupid to a bunch of men who didn't always appreciate his efforts.

Halfway to the parsonage he caught sight of Dora Meeks hurrying along the road carrying what looked suspiciously like a platter of food. With a grim sense of fatalism, he shifted the trunk to his other shoulder and said, "Come along, ladies, you're about to meet your nearest neighbor."

Chapter Eight

Completely ignoring Grey, Dora set about making the two women feel welcome. She could well remember how she had felt, arriving alone, not knowing a single soul and not even being met at the boat. "I live right up the road," she said. At least he'd had the courtesy to meet this pair. "You're welcome to come by to see us anytime. We're always there."

"I don't suppose you have much choice," said the tall, skinny woman with a disdainful look at the barren landscape.

Dora wondered if she could possibly be an actress. Surely Grey wouldn't consider an actress "suitable." She was almost certain she had never seen this particular woman, yet there was something about the quality of her voice, the way she seemed to strike a pose, imbuing the simplest utterance with drama, that was unusual.

"Yes, well…I'm sure you'll find plenty to do once you settle in," she hurried to say. "Mr. St. Bride will be a marvelous help. I don't know what I would have done without him when I first arrived."

Her smile, Grey told himself later, had been about

as sweet as a kick in the gut. He'd considered warning the newcomers about Dora's cooking but in the end he'd simply walked away, after promising to come by later with a few friends. In other words, introduce them to the men they were intended for.

Damned witchety woman, he swore feelingly, striding back down to the landing. The men, just as he'd suspected, were still standing idle, gossiping like a bunch of old ladies. Shipping out on the next freighter bound for Australia was beginning to sound better and better.

"I guess it doesn't look very good, does it?" Dora gazed down at the plain cake she'd brought, a doleful expression on her face. "I'm just learning how to cook, and sometimes I manage to get it to come out right, but then, just as often, something like this happens."

"Slammed a door, I reck'n," said the small redhead, whose name was Mattie. She had come in the front door, headed straight out the back door, and returned a few minutes later, a look of vast relief on her face. Dora had taken to her right away, possibly because something about the girl reminded her of Bertie, her former maid, although the two women didn't look at all alike.

At her questioning look, Mattie went on to explain the effects of sudden noise on a rising cake. "I ain't had me a sad cake since I was eight years old," she said with shy pride. "Course, I only know one kind—molasses cake. But it's real good," she added earnestly.

The older woman, meanwhile was prowling about the tiny parsonage, a look of dissatisfaction on her face. Dora wanted to reassure her, but in all honesty, there wasn't much she could say other than, *You're here now—either go back to where you came from or make the best of it.*

She had a feeling neither woman could go back, any more than she herself had been able to. And now, here she was, married to a wise, kind and sensible man who asked nothing more of her than her companionship. Every day brought a new accomplishment. She was beginning to make friends with some of the men who lived here, and now she would have women friends, too.

"Well," she said brightly, patting the regal woman on the arm. She wished she had thought to do something to brighten up the place before they arrived. "I suppose you'd like to lie down and rest until you feel steadier on your feet. I know how wobbly being on a boat all day can make a body feel."

Stalking across the room, a matter of only a few feet, Lula opened a door and peered at the narrow bed. Narrow and stripped of linens, it was hardly inviting. She said, "Humph!"

"James and Clarence should be along most anytime now. I'm sure they'll be bringing everything you need." In other words, another bed and a supply of linens.

There was nothing Dora could do about the accommodations. Both the bedrooms in her house were taken. They would simply have to work things out between them. Looking around at the unadorned walls, the single chair and table and the small potbellied stove in the corner, she couldn't imagine anyone actually living there.

But of course, no one did. Unless there was a wedding or a funeral, the Reverend Almond Filmore spent only a few days each month in residence. According to Emmet, there was far more sinning on the other two islands that required his attention.

"I brought you some coffee beans—I'm sure there's a grinder here somewhere. And if you need anything more, I'm just up the road in that house with the fence around it."

Mattie opened the cupboard and said, "There's two jars of 'maters and a tin of 'vaporated milk."

"Oh, well then—you'll be just fine until someone brings your supper. And your beds. As I said, they should be along soon, and someone's already opened the place up so that it doesn't even smell musty."

The someone, of course, would be Grey, who had also promised to send down their meals while they were here. Pity, she thought as she let herself out the door, that he couldn't have been as hospitable the day she had arrived.

From her windows, Dora watched the comings and goings all afternoon. First Mouse, that brute of a housekeeper who looked after Grey, passed by with a large covered basket. No sooner had he left than Grey and the two potential bridegrooms, James Calvin and Clarence, arrived. Each man drove a pony cart that held a wooden bed with a bare ticking-covered mattress. She did hope they'd remembered to bring bed linens. Emmet had barely enough for two beds.

What on earth, Dora wondered, would they have done had it been raining?

Clarence was wearing a bright green plaid shirt buttoned up to the neck, with what appeared to be brand-new blue denim trousers. His slicked-back hair looked redder than ever in the late afternoon sunlight.

"Mattie and Clarence? Just imagine what their children will look like," she said to Emmet. She had hurried home to describe both women in great detail. "Maybe it's the other way around. Lula and Clarence, They're both tall. I think Lula might be an actress," she said while setting out a simple supper of biscuits, boiled eggs and stewed apples. "She's pretty enough. At least, she would be if she let herself smile."

"Sakes alive, an actress," mused Emmet.

They discussed the possibility that an actress might actually settle right here on St. Bride. Dora didn't bother to mention that among her own set back in Bath, actresses were considered barely respectable.

"The other one—Mattie—she's not really pretty, but I think she'll do just fine once she settles in. I liked her. She reminded me of—of someone I once knew."

The men, Dora noticed, didn't stay long at the parsonage. Grey left first, then a few minutes later, Clarence and James. She was tempted to jump up from the table and run right over to find out what had happened. Where'd they'd found room to set up the beds. If they'd got along together—if it had been love at first sight...

Well, hardly that. "Mercy, I'm getting to be as bad as St. Bride when it comes to wanting to meddle in other folks' business." She let the window curtain fall back in place. She'd made the things with her own hands, using material from one of Sal's old dresses. Instead of being upset at the reminder, Emmet had seemed pleased when she'd asked his permission before cutting into the limp yellow calico. "I do hope they stay, though,'' she said as she began to clear away the dishes. ''It's about time for your nightly game. Why don't you get out the board while I make a fresh pot of coffee?''

''I believe I'll lie down for a spell. I'm feelin' a mite rheumatic. Must be a change coming on. When Grey stops by, tell him I'll play him two games tomorrow.'' He flexed his stiff fingers and winced.

Hiding her concern, she kissed her husband on the cheek, offered to rub his joints with liniment—he declined her offer, as he always did—and told him to call her if he needed the slightest thing.

Then she turned her thoughts back to the two newcomers. She would need to make a list of things to tell them tomorrow when she went by to wish them good morning. Such as…

She tried and failed to think of a single thing that would apply to two women who might or might not be staying. Close the windows at night in case it rains?

Don't let the screen door stand open, else the house will fill with mosquitoes and goodness knows what else?

At any rate, it would only be neighborly to show an interest in how the first meeting had gone, she told herself as she moved restlessly from room to room.

Some twenty minutes later, Grey rapped on the door and let himself in. If she'd been parading around in her nightgown, it wouldn't have made a speck of difference. The man acted as if he owned every stick and stone on the island.

''Emmet's gone to bed. His fingers were bothering him.'' At the swift narrowing of his eyes, she said defensively, ''He promised to play you two games tomorrow.''

"He's not sick again, is he?"

"Not at all, but his joints ache when there's a change in the weather. I noticed a few clouds just before sunset."

"Squall line headed up from the sou'west. Shall I send Mouse down with some liniment?"

"Thank you, but we have liniment." They were both still standing. He had let himself in, but she hadn't invited him to sit. Still, his concern seemed genuine. She would give the man that much—he did appear to care for the people who lived here.

All but the one woman who had defied him by not leaving when he'd ordered her off his island, she reminded herself. Standing almost toe to toe, speaking softly so as not to disturb the man sleeping in the room just beyond, Dora was aware of a familiar constriction in her throat—a tightness in her chest. It was the oddest thing—the way she reacted to a man she didn't particularly approve of, much less like.

No small detail of his appearance escaped her. Not the sun-bleached streaks in his dark brown hair, nor the darker rims around his deep blue eyes. The high, sharp cheekbones that were so at odds with the dimple in his chin.

She'd once heard such a dimple called God's thumbprint. Which might explain why he felt called upon to lord it over every two-legged and four-legged creature on his island.

"Seen enough?" Grey asked, his earlier concern having given away to amusement.

"I beg your pardon?"

"That's what you said the day you arrived. Haughty as anything, weren't you? And look at you now," he murmured. "Cobwebs in your hair—"

She slapped a hand to her head. "The henhouse. I was gathering eggs for supper earlier."

"Flour on your ear." Grinning now, he reached out and brushed her left ear with his fingers. "How the mighty have fallen."

Jaw clenched, she bit back all the questions she'd wanted to ask about the women and how they'd gotten along with Clarence and James. "Emmet will be expecting you tomorrow evening after supper."

"I'll be here," Grey said softly.

Why did it sound more like a threat than a promise?

Dora saw him out, closed the door behind him, then leaned against it and sighed. She really had to stop letting him affect her this way. A single touch—a single teasing remark, and her heart started racing until she all but forgot to breathe. It was as if a stranger suddenly invaded her body, making her feel all sorts of uncomfortable sensations.

"Oh, go to bed, silly, it's only the weather!"

It was indeed the weather. Sometime after midnight she found herself sitting bolt upright in her bed, her heart in her throat as she listened for whatever had wakened her.

Pitch-dark. Not a breath of air. The drone of mosquitoes beating against the window screen was the only sound until suddenly, the night burst open in a series of blue flashes, followed immediately by a rolling explosion.

She was out of bed and across the room almost instantly, racing to see if Emmet was all right. Something like that could scare a healthy person to death, never mind an elderly man with a weak heart.

She burst into his room just as lightning came again.

Emmet was sitting up, a smile on his weathered face. "Got us a real rip-snorter, ain't we?"

Feeling for matches, Dora lit the lamp on the dresser. "Are you all right?"

"Right as rain," he said just as a torrent struck the side of the house. She managed to slam the window shut before too much had blown in, then hurried to close the window in her own room. Back again, she asked, "But what about your aches? Don't you need me to rub something with liniment?"

Emmet settled back onto his pillow and drew the cotton spread up over his chest. "Funny thing—old bones acts up somethin' fierce before a storm gets here, but once she hits, they settle back down again. Go to bed, Doree. I thank you kindly for your concern."

"You'll call if you need me?"

"That I will. Now you go on and get your beauty sleep. You'll be wantin' to go lollygaggin' with your two new friends come morning."

This time her breakfast turned out perfectly. Knowing that Mouse would have provided breakfast for the newcomers, Dora bundled up a napkin full of her biscuits and set out to visit. The washing could wait. The rain had ended, but the clouds hadn't entirely moved offshore.

Besides, Emmet still had one clean shirt left, even if it did bear the faint print of a flatiron on one shoulder.

"Hello-oo," she sang out as she passed the church and made her way to the parsonage just behind it. "Is it too early to come calling?"

Mattie met her at the door, "Come on in Miz Meeks. Lula, she's sick to her belly."

Through the open bedroom door, Dora could see that one of the beds had been jammed up against the preacher's cot. The older woman was clutching a chamber pot, glaring at Mattie and their visitor alike.

"I was seasick, too," Dora commiserated, setting her bundle on the table. "It takes a while, but you should be getting over it by now."

Still holding the pot, Lula stood and crossed the room to close the door without saying a word. Dora couldn't much blame her. How well she remembered feeling so sick that even death would have been a welcome reprieve.

"That Mouse man brought us some pancakes and molasses. Lula didn't want none, so I ate hers, too. He's real nice, ain't he?"

"Mouse? I suppose—I mean, I never actually thought about him. As a person, I mean." In the cramped parlor, Mattie sat on the edge of the bed and Dora took the only chair. One of the women could have slept on the preacher's cot, but evidently, until the men decided on who would be marrying whom, the beds were important. Staking a claim, she thought, remembering the beautiful engagement ring she had worn so briefly.

Looking around, she thought a more dismal room would be hard to find. Not a single personal touch, not so much as a wall calendar. "Well, how did you like James?" she asked brightly.

"Who? Oh, you mean Mr. Calvin. He don't have much to say fer himself, does he? Why do they call him by both his names?"

"I believe there was another James here for a while.

As for being shy, I'm sure he'll get over it. And what about Clarence?''

The younger woman brightened noticeably. ''My, he's smart some, ain't he? Did you know he memorized ever' state in the Union and the capitals an' all? He said 'em all fer us last night, right out, without readin' 'em off or nothing.''

Oh my, how utterly fascinating, Dora thought, torn between pity and amusement. It occurred to her that with a little help, the child could be almost pretty. There was nothing at all wrong with her features, even if her mouth was a tad large and her short little nose did turn up. There was nothing wrong with freckles— she was even getting a few of her own.

''Tell me, Mattie—and don't mind my meddling, please, it's only because I haven't had another woman to talk to in so long. But did you ever think of wearing your hair in a different style?''

''Style?''

''Bring me your comb,'' Dora said, and rising, she walked around, studying the younger woman from all angles.

By the time a pale, drawn Lula emerged from the bedroom, Miss Mattie Blades was wearing a new and far more flattering hairstyle. And Dora was wearing a satisfied smirk. ''There, I'd like to see any man resist her now, wouldn't you, Miss Russart?''

''It's called a puppy-door,'' Mattie said eagerly. ''How does it look? I've not never worn nothing but braids.''

Lula grimaced, settled gingerly onto a chair and stared at the toes of her scuffed black high-tops.

Dora started to correct the excited girl and changed her mind. ''Where's your looking glass, Mattie?''

The girl's face fell. ''I don't have one. Papa 'llowed

as how they was the devil's handiwork, but I used to look in the pond sometimes."

"Oh, my dear," Dora said, "there's nothing wrong with—with seeing that your clothes are buttoned up right, and that takes a looking glass. I'm sure your papa only meant that one shouldn't be vain."

"Yes'm, I 'speck that's what he meant."

"Then come along, I have a looking glass at home. Miss Russart, would you like to come with us?" It seemed only polite to ask, although the poor woman looked as if she would like nothing better than to go back to bed.

Lula waved them out the door. "I don't suppose the old fart has a decent brandy around. No, don't bother," she added when Dora turned back as if to search. "I've already looked."

The morning passed surprisingly pleasantly. Emmet seemed taken with young Mattie. It was he who got most of her story from her. That her father had drowned in Millers Pond when a cypress tree he was sawing fell on him, holding him down. And that after the burial her mother had packed them up, Mattie and her seven younger brothers and sisters, and gone to live with Uncle Blackie. And that there wasn't enough space for ten people in two small rooms.

Somehow, Dora suspected there might be more to the story than Mattie was telling, but then, she had her own secrets. If asked, she would have advised the child to put the past behind her and go forward. Otherwise, the past would weigh her down like a millstone. Or a cypress tree.

The courtship took place incrementally, as both men worked hard during the day. James had stopped work on the shad boat he was building and started hauling lumber to the small oak grove down near Shallow Gut where his one-room bachelor's cabin was located.

Lula was still looking drawn, but at least she was able to sit outside with Clarence for an hour after the supper Mouse had provided. From the cottage just up the road, Dora and Emmet watched the goings and comings and discussed the possibilities.

"You know what I'd like to do?" Dora asked her husband, who sat with his Bible on his lap. Not opened—he could no longer see the words, but a comforting presence, nevertheless.

"Try your hand at stewing that old gander?" he teased.

The creature had escaped the pen and chased her again this morning, hissing and pecking at her heels. Emmet and Salty had chased him off, then managed to herd him into his pen again.

"Have a dinner party and invite both couples—and St. Bride, I suppose. I could serve cucumber sandwiches and crabmeat salad and tiny crayfish patties for a first course, and then—"

Emmet started chuckling and then Dora laughed, too. "I know, I know—but you'll have to admit, I can bake a biscuit fit for a king now."

"That you can, Doree. Sal would be right proud of you."

The laughter faded. Dora sighed, Emmet laid aside his Bible, reached out and patted her on the hand and said something about mending the goose pen. When he went outside, Dora finished cleaning up in the kitchen, then went to her room and began looking at her clothes with an eye to what could possibly be made over to fit Mattie.

Not that she was enough of a seamstress to take on any such task, but perhaps with the three of them working on it, they could come up with a decent wedding gown, at any rate. Lula had a trunk full of clothes, while poor Mattie had a nightgown made of flour sacks, a change of drawers and a checkered woolen shawl.

"Oh, this," she crowed softly, pouncing on white Swiss muslin with an overshirt and bloused waist. "And this—" She tossed out a knee-length slip with a cut-work hem and a drawstring waist.

Before long the pile grew, and she was wondering if Lula felt well enough to tackle the project. Actresses wore costumes. Costumes surely must need an occasional adjustment. If the troupe was large enough to have its own seamstress, then the actresses would not have to bother, but Dora had a feeling Lula's group had been one of the smaller ones, where tasks were shared by all.

Of course, she might not be an actress. Perhaps everyone in New York spoke with the same elegant inflection.

In any case, Mattie would need something pretty to be married in, and with an entire unused trousseau to work with, they should be able to put together something both suitable and flattering.

"I can't believe how much I've missed having someone to talk clothes with," she said later the next day. The three women were sitting in the tiny parsonage in a clutter of muslin, sateen and dotted Swiss. Lula was indeed a wizard with a needle, although Dora couldn't say much for her disposition.

Mattie was enthralled. ''I've not never seen so many pretty frocks. It's like if one of them store winders was to open up and swaller me whole.''

Lula rolled her eyes. Dora bit back a smile. Of the two women, she much preferred the young, unaffected Mattie, yet something about the older woman drew her gaze again and again.

What was it that made her hands fall idle from time to time while she stared into space? Sadness? Fear? Actress or no, no woman could hide her own feelings forever.

Chapter Nine

The clouds were back. It was that season of the year, according to Emmet, when squalls rolled in across the sound almost daily. "Storm breedin' weather. Come August, you'll be awishing for a break in the heat."

They had finished supper, and as Grey was expected soon for their nightly game, Dora found an excuse to leave. Bundling up her latest triumph in a napkin, she said, "I'm just going to run down to the parsonage and leave these ginger wafers before Clarence and James Calvin get there. They'll go well with a nice glass of cold tea."

"Proud some, ain't ye, woman?" Emmet's eyes held the old twinkle tonight. Squall or not, he didn't seem to be aching any more than usual. "Don't get caught out in the rain."

"I won't melt," she teased, wishing she had known him when he was a young man. Not that their paths would have crossed in all likelihood. Emmet had spent almost his entire life working out of St. Brides Island, while the Suttons had lived in Beaufort County, a few miles from Bath, for generations. Though she'd visited frequently with her friends in town, her father had invariably warned her to stay away from the waterfront, where the rougher elements of society lay in wait to take advantage of innocent young maidens.

Oh, Papa, if only you knew...

"I brought you something," she called out through the screened door of the parsonage a few minutes later. "I thought you might want to serve refreshments when the gentlemen come to call."

Mattie invited her inside. "Lula felt poorly again this morning," she confided in a whisper, waggling her colorless eyebrows alarmingly. "Ginger cakes? Ginger's good fer a upset belly."

"I thought surely she'd be over her upset by now. Could she have eaten something tainted on the way out?"

The dark-haired northerner sent her a baleful smile from her chair by the window. "Hardly. I'll be all right, it just takes...time."

"Perhaps the ginger will help. Isn't it lucky I didn't burn this batch?" Dora was concerned but reluctant to meddle. St. Bride had already appointed himself to the position of meddler-in-chief.

When Mattie begged her to come and "set a spell," she excused herself with a vague gesture toward the darkening sky. "I'd better get on back in time to close the windows before it rains."

The first flurry of rain struck just as she leaped up onto the porch. Grey was there, but Emmet was nowhere in sight. "Close the windows in here while I get the others, will you?" she said breathlessly. As a greeting, it was hardly polite, but it gave her an excuse to escape. Meeting him outside was bad enough. Shut up together in a small room, he seemed to absorb all the air, making it all but impossible for her to breathe.

Hurrying through the house, she slammed shut all the windows, struggling with those that had a tendency to stick. Her dress was speckled from the rain, her face was damp and her hair had long since freed itself from the neat pompadour she had arranged that morning. Coming to the door that opened onto the back porch, she paused to watch lightning streak across the blackened sky.

"Impressive, isn't it?" Grey spoke from behind her. With the sound of rain thundering down on the roof she hadn't heard his approach.

"Oh! You scared me!" Which had to be the reason her heart had jammed in her throat—why she couldn't seem to tear her eyes from his face.

"It'll pass directly over Portsmouth. We'll miss all but the edge."

Plucking at the bodice of her thin cotton dress, she said breathlessly, "If this is an edge, I'd hate to get caught in the middle."

"Emmet says to tell you good night. We played half a game, but he was growing tired. You must be working him too hard."

"The pen—the end where the goose stays? He insisted on mending it today. I never realized it before, but tying net is a lot like tatting, or making lace."

During the entire brief exchange, Dora's gaze never left his face. It was as if she were mesmerized. Even though the days were much longer now, once the storm had moved in, there was scarcely enough light left to see by without lighting a lamp.

"I'll be leaving as soon as the rain slacks off," he said, his deep voice causing goose bumps to break out all over her body. Wordlessly she nodded, still unable to drag her eyes away.

Grey said something else, but mesmerized by the movement of his lips when he spoke, she forgot to listen. Odd...she had never noticed a man's mouth before. How a sharply chiseled lower lip could look both soft and firm.

"What?" she asked belatedly.

Instead of repeating whatever it was he'd said, Grey lifted his hand and slowly brushed his knuckles down the side of her face. Then, reaching past her, he shut the door. In the unnatural gloom, she stared up at him, her face burning as if he'd touched her with a hot branding iron.

"Dora, Dora," he said, sounding oddly regretful. And then he turned and left her. She watched him stride through the house and let himself out. Watched as he came into sight on the road outside.

How was it possible, she wondered, for a man she didn't even like to affect her this way? Moving like a sleepwalker toward the window, she followed his progress as he headed up the ridge, leaning into the driving rain. His shirt was plastered to his body, the muscles of his long legs clearly delineated by clinging denim. And if he had the slightest idea, Dora told herself, what she was thinking at this moment, the reputation she had worked so hard to rebuild would be utterly ruined.

Not until much later, long after the rain had slacked off and Grey had left—long after Emmet was snoring behind his closed door, did it occur to her to wonder what it was he'd said there in the kitchen.

Probably something as innocuous as "Close the damned door!" Irritated with herself for overreacting to a man she hardly knew and didn't particularly like, she stayed up reading for another hour. There was little to choose from. A book on celestial navigation, Emmet's Bible and Sal's book of recipes. By the time she felt as if she might possibly be able to fall asleep, the clouds had moved on and the stars were glittering like handfuls of diamonds scattered on a bed of black velvet. She opened the windows, peered through the darkness to see if there was a light on in the parsonage, and wondered what excuse she could find to rush over in the morning to see how the double courtship was coming along.

Lying awake, watching a sliver of moon emerge from behind an iridescent cloud, she thought about the women she had grown up with—Selma Blunt, Missy Taylor and Frances King. And Bertie, who had proved to be the truest friend of all. She thought of her father, seeing him for perhaps the first time as a man who, though he'd descended from a long line of successful farmers, had dreams and ambitions of his own. She thought briefly about all those heroic women who had packed up home and family and set out across the country in covered wagons not too many years ago.

Was what she had done so very different? In either case, there was no point in looking back.

Just before dawn, it began to rain again. A gentle rain this time, and later Dora would wonder what had caused her to wake up. "The windows," she murmured. She had opened them again before she'd gone to bed. But it wasn't blowing. Just a light drizzle. She lay there frowning, feeling uneasy for no discernible reason.

After several minutes she arose and closed the windows on the southwest side of the house, in case the wind should spring up again. She opened Emmet's door and tiptoed across the dark room to close the window beside his bed.

Suddenly she felt as if a vast hollow had opened up inside her. Even with the gentle sound of the rain, it was quiet. *Too* quiet.

"Emmet? Em—?" she whispered. Turning she leaned over and touched his face. It was cool. "The window," she murmured, thinking perhaps the rain had blown in on him before she could close it. Or it might have turned cooler in the night and he'd gotten chilled. He was always joking about his body's old furnace no longer working the way it had when he was a young man, claiming that on the hottest day in July he had trouble working up a sweat.

But it wasn't the rain, and it wasn't a sudden drop in temperature. "Emmet!" she whispered urgently. Grabbing him by the shoulders, she shook him hard. And then, "Emmet, wake up!" she screamed.

"Oh, God, oh, God, please, no!"

Without bothering to find her slippers or throw on a robe, she flew out the front door and burst through the gate, screaming, "Grey! Grey, come quick, something's happened to Emmet!"

Grey met her at the door. Shirtless and barefoot, he was fastening his trousers when she hurled herself at him, screaming for him to come quick, come *now,* that something was wrong with Emmet.

"Calm down, tell me what's happened. Has he fallen again?"

But even as he spoke, Grey suspected it was more than that. The old man had been oddly quiet last night. Not unhappy—not even feeling the usual aches and pains. A man had a right to his own private thoughts, and so Grey had left Meeks to his own reflections.

"He's—he's not breathing!" Dora had thrown herself at him, giving him no choice but to hold her while she sobbed. "Please, oh please send for somebody to help him!"

"Dora, I'll do what I can," he said quietly, knowing that if the man had stopped breathing, the best doctor in the world couldn't help him.

But she was pulling on his arm, insisting that he come with her. "Please hurry! Make him breathe!"

He didn't bother with shoes or shirt. Nor, he noticed, had she. Her feet would be shredded, if they weren't already. Crushed shells were fine for a cart, not so fine for tender bare feet.

She was still sobbing when they reached the cottage. "There's no light on," he said.

"I didn't have time."

"How did you know—?" he asked. By then he was inside, striding across to Emmet's bedroom, the room where he'd once envisioned the bride and groom sharing a bed.

Dora lit the lamp and Grey examined the man who lay flat on his back, arms arranged neatly at his side, his face already set in the waxy mask of death. Straightening up again, he said gently, "He couldn't have suffered, else you'd have heard something."

She was still standing stiffly on the other side of the bed, silent tears rolling down her face, when he pulled the light quilt up over Emmet's face. "It's not fair," she whispered. "First Papa and now…"

"Go in the other room, I'll make coffee. Unless you'd rather have tea?"

She shook her head. Sleep had mashed her hair on one side so that it stood up like a cockscomb. Grey thought she had never looked more desirable—or more vulnerable—than she did standing there in a damp cotton nightgown, her bare feet covered in wet sand and bits of shell.

With an oddly touching air of dignity, she said, "I'll stay with Emmet. You can go home now."

But of course, he did no such thing. Rummaging in the kitchen, he came up with a bottle of blackberry wine. Brandy would have done better, but this would have to serve for now. Enough of the stuff might eventually take the edge off her pain.

More shock than pain, perhaps, although he reluctantly admitted that she'd been good for the old man. Over the past few months Emmet had seemed to take on a new vigor. At first Grey had attributed it to renewed passion, but seeing them together, he'd detected nothing of that sort. It was more as if they were close friends. Father and daughter. Nurse and patient. Whatever their relationship, he had to admit she'd been good for him.

What now? he wondered.

Dora insisted on remaining with Emmet's body once Mouse had done the necessary. She drew a chair up to the foot of the bed and there she sat, stubbornly refusing to move except for trips to the privy.

Clarence sent for Preacher Filmore. Almy Dole began working on a cypress marker bearing the name and date, which would serve until a more permanent gravestone could be brought out from the mainland. And James Calvin set about building a coffin from clear maple he'd been hoarding for a set of chairs he'd designed.

Mouse brought food and, after explaining the circumstances to the two newcomers, Grey led them over to sit with Dora until after the burial service. With the weather as warm as it was, it would have to be done as soon as the preacher could get here.

Ever practical, Grey reminded himself to inquire as to the status of the courtship. He liked to give couples a week to get acquainted, but in this case, with Filmore coming to bury Emmet, he might hurry things along. Two weddings and a funeral. Might as well kill two birds with one stone.

He winced at his own indelicacy. God, sometimes he thought living alone with only rough male companions had eroded away any manners he might have picked up in his few years away at school. He'd been a misfit, even then. The book learning had appealed to him vastly, but most of the social customs he'd seen as pointless to downright destructive.

Dora felt the presence of the two women immediately. How remarkable, she thought, that the mere sound of women's voices murmuring in another room could be so comforting.

Mattie took over the kitchen. Mouse had brought food enough for an army and, together, the two of them put it out on a makeshift table set up in the front parlor.

Lula had located a black taffeta ribbon—removed it from one of Dora's hats, probably. She made an arrangement for the front door, then went about closing curtains and arranging chairs, including those Mouse had brought from St. Bride's house.

"Miz Dora, you'd best have something to eat now," the large houseman said, peering into the gloomy bedroom where Dora kept vigil. Lula had insisted that all the curtains be closed, even though Dora would have preferred them open.

So, she suspected, would Emmet.

But then, Emmet was with his Sal now. He would hardly care what she did with his windows.

'Thank you, Mouse. If you'll leave it in the kitchen, I'll take something after a while.''

The gentle giant came and stood over her, his presence oddly comforting. She couldn't imagine why, because she'd scarcely even spoken to the man in all the time she'd been here. Biting back a smile, she recalled the first time she'd laid eyes on him. She'd been terrified. With his eye patch and his bald dome, he looked entirely too much like the villain in one of her childhood storybooks.

"Let me sit with Mr. Emmet now. I got some messages I'd like to pass along to friends.''

Messages?

Of course. Messages.

Numbly Dora rose and let Mouse take her place. As she walked stiffly from the room, it occurred to her for the first time that death could be a peaceful conclusion. An end—perhaps even a beginning...?

With her father, there had been only shock, bewilderment and crushing sorrow, followed swiftly by resentment and disillusionment. At the time, she'd been too busy coming to terms with the sudden loss of everything meaningful in her life to think about what it meant to die. Not to be here. Far too busy to consider the philosophical meaning of death.

The loss of her mother had been gradual. Elida Dixon Sutton had gone to visit her sister in Richmond. She had come back after a month, stayed a week, then left again. This time she'd stayed away for six months, come home, packed her trunks and left again. Shortly after that, her father had told her that her mother had died of the influenza.

As one of Dora's dearest friends, only eight years old at the time, had also died in the same epidemic, Dora had merged the two losses in her mind. She'd been too young, perhaps, to dwell on the meaning of death. She remembered feeling angry with her mother, and picturing her sitting on a cloud playing a golden harp.

Men began arriving soon after that, singly, in pairs and small groups. She was aware of Grey hovering in the background, and couldn't decide whether she resented his presence or welcomed it. The one thing she wasn't, was indifferent.

"Em, he was a good hand at whittling before his hands seized up on him," said John Luther. "He made this whistle for my youngest boy." He held out a small wooden whistle shaped like a bird. "Dudley and me, we'd like you to have it."

Dora's hand closed over the smooth, rounded form as tears filled her eyes. That was the way it went all day—men coming by to speak a few words about Emmet Meeks, their longtime friend and her short-time husband. Struck all over by the way they had accepted her without question right from the first, she was forced to slip outside onto the back porch to cry.

Grey found her there. Without touching her physically, he seemed to surround her with his presence. "I've been watching you, Dora. You haven't eaten anything all day. Keep it up and you won't last through the funeral."

She gestured wildly, her eyes glittering with tears.

"How can I possibly eat? I couldn't force down a bite! Oh, why does death have to be so—so—"

"So what, Dora? So painful?" Grey reminded himself that she had lost her first husband, too—and apparently, her father. She was too small, too young, far too fragile to endure so much loss. His hands hovered over her shoulders. "You've only been married a few months. Death happens to us all. We're born, we live, we die. That's the way of it, king and commoner alike. Some believe we go on from there—some don't. Emmet was one of the ones who did, so I wouldn't waste time fretting over him. I expect he's settled in to wherever he's gone by now—probably busy telling Sal all about his little pink and gold bride."

"His what?" She blinked up at him through matted lashes.

Grey wasn't about to tell her that the term had slipped out—that he never saw her without picturing her as she'd appeared that first day in her limp pink gown, with her gilded curls flying around her head. Hobbling up the road in those ridiculous pink slippers.

"Come inside now, Dora," he said quietly, taking her arm. Her flesh was cool to the touch and incredibly smooth. "You're going to eat a slice of pone bread and drink a cup of coffee. By then the preacher will be here and we'll get on with the service. I had the men dig a grave out beside Sal. It's good high ground. Tide won't reach it except in a bad storm."

He waited for an argument, and when none was forthcoming, he led her back into the house. Pausing outside the room where she slept, he tucked a curl behind her ear and said, "Go in and wash your face now. You might want to pin up your hair again. It looks fine to me, but ladies set store by that sort of thing.''

For half a minute, he didn't know if she was going to laugh or cry or hit him. ''Whatever it is you want me to eat, could you have Mattie bring it to me on the back porch? I don't feel up to being with people quite yet.''

Chapter Ten

The circuit preacher arrived late that afternoon. As the last time Dora had seen Reverend Almond Filmore had been at her wedding, she broke down and cried again. "I'm so sorry," she sobbed again and again. "I was just remembering the l-last time—"

Mattie took her by the arm and led her onto the back porch. It happened to look out over the chicken pen and the fig trees beyond, and there, just as Grey had said, was the new grave, all ready and waiting. So she began to bawl all over again.

"Jest you cry it all out, honey. It don't do to let it fester inside." The plump little redhead, her proud pompadour slightly askew, gathered her up and patted her on the back. Finally pulling away, Dora managed a wet, shaky laugh. "I've never cried so much in all my life as I have this past six months—well, I mean since...you know...."

Something in Mattie's bright blue eyes told her that she understood more than Dora was ready to confide. The one thing Dora had learned since her entire world had been overturned was that wisdom was not confined to the privileged class. Life, she had discovered, had a way of teaching lessons that those cocooned in too much wealth seldom learned until it was too late.

The service went on and on and on. The preacher, his long face more lugubrious than ever, droned endlessly until Dora wanted to scream. When he was finally done, he began to sing "Nearer My God to Thee," each word a dirge in itself. One after another, the men picked up and began to sing, moving a note or two ahead, as if urging him to follow their beat. Dora would have laughed if it hadn't seemed so wildly inappropriate. Reverend Filmore was not an unintelligent man—he might even be considered attractive by some—but invariably, he set his congregation to fidgeting before he was halfway through a service.

Dora had attended but one sermon since she'd been there. She'd been squirming on her hard plank bench by the time he reached the tenth commandment. Emmet, leaning against the wall, had been dozing beside her. The reverend made it all the way through the list of things not to be coveted. Thy neighbor's wife, his manservant, his maidservant, his ox, his A-A-A-" There he had paused for so long the entire congregation of some dozen or so men had shouted in unison, "Ass!"

She'd had to stuff her handkerchief in her mouth to keep from giggling. Thinking about it even now brought a watery smile that soon faded as the hymn dragged to an end.

There was a scattering of mumbled "Amen," and in the uncertain silence that followed, Lula began to sing. Standing across the open grave between Mattie and Mouse, she lifted her head, closed her eyes and began singing the "Battle Hymn of the Republic," chorus and verse alike, in a beautiful contralto voice.

To say that those gathered there were stunned would be an understatement. The selection was inappropriate at the very least in this bastion of the Confederacy. Emmet would have been a young man during the War Between the States. And yet, the words seemed somehow fitting.

When the last note faded away, if there was a dry eye among them, Dora missed it. But then, her own eyes were overflowing again.

"Handful of sand," Mattie prompted in a loud whisper.

It was Grey who led her closer to the grave, held her arm while she bent and gathered up a handful of sand to scatter on Emmet's casket; Grey who stood beside her until the mourners had paid their last respects and filed away.

It was Grey who handed her a wildflower—small, pink and somewhat wilted—to drop into the open grave.

And it was Grey she turned to when, drained of tears, she simply needed to be held. When his warmth, his strength, the subtle male scent of him began to seep through her misery to affect her in unexpected ways, she drew herself from his arms and said quietly, "Thank you. I'm all right now. I'll be fine."

He watched her go into the house—she could feel his gaze burning through the back of her yellow-sprigged gown. She had deliberately worn yellow and not black because Emmet had liked her in pretty colors. He had told her more than once that black was for old women, and so she wore the yellow for him, regardless of any disapproving looks from the likes of St. Bride.

Somehow, she managed to get through the rest of

the day. Mattie and Lula would stay on, of course, sharing Emmet's room, even though the grooms-to-be were sleeping on pallets in their respective bachelor cabins, waiting for the brides to make up their minds.

Mattie and Mouse had rearranged Emmet's furniture again, and someone—Mattie, she suspected—had brought in a jar of the pink wildflowers and set it beside the washbowl and ewer in her bedroom. Dora made a mental note to order flower seeds the next time the boat came in and plant them on both graves.

The sun had already set by the time she sought out Lula, who had dragged a chair onto the back porch. "Are you feeling better now? You must have had a touch of the stomach influenza. These things go around sometime. Be thankful it was no worse."

The look Lula sent her made her feel as if she had committed a faux pas, but for the life of her, she didn't see how.

So she tried again. "How are you and Clarence getting on? He must have been astonished when you started singing today. I've never heard such a beautiful voice."

"It's good. Just not good enough." Lula shrugged off the compliment. "I was an actress, you know." Dora nodded and murmured something about having thought as much, and the other woman went on as if she hadn't spoken. "I was fifteen when I left the shirt factory and went with Perretti's Theatre Musicale. We played all over Upstate New York. I worked up to second lead, but audiences want short, plump blondes, not tall, skinny brunettes. So did Roberto Perretti," she added with a bitter twist of a smile.

"I'm short and blond, and I can't sing a note." Actually, she had an acceptable voice, but she couldn't carry a tune. "I can't tell you how many times I've wished I were tall. And your dark hair is perfectly beautiful. I'm sure Clarence thinks so, too."

"Clarence." Lula sighed, twisting her elegant, long-fingered hands together. "He's a nice young man. A bit less exciting than wet bread, but thoroughly decent."

To Dora's ears, "Decent" sounded more like a criticism than a compliment. "Then the two of you are getting along all right?"

Again that bitter smile. "He calls me ma'am. Yes, ma'am, no, ma'am. Can you imagine sleeping with a man who calls you ma'am?"

Dora barely kept from gaping. She couldn't imagine sleeping with a man at all. She had never actually slept with Henry. In a moment of weakness she had done the marriage act with him, and found it to be highly overrated. Instead of comforting, much less exciting, it had been painful, messy and embarrassing. And that had been only the beginning.

"Yes, well…he does seem to be a fairly serious man." What could she say? "I don't suppose you could call him handsome, but he has a pleasant face and a really lovely smile. And as you said, I'm sure he's thoroughly decent."

Lula looked at her through eyes that seemed too old. Large, dark and lustrous, they seemed almost sad. "He's twenty-two years old. Do you know how old I am?"

Dora could only shake her head. She herself was twenty-three. She knew Mattie was seventeen. Lula looked much older, but looks could be deceiving.

"I'll be thirty-two in September. Shortly after that, I'll become a mother, and Clarence deserves better than that.'' Tilting her head, she smiled, but it was a mocking smile, one edged with bitterness. ''Don't you agree?''

It took a moment to sink in. When it did, Dora said softly, ''Oh, my, of course.''

''Don't tell me you hadn't guessed. My God, the way I've been vomiting every morning, eating everything in sight and weeping bucketsful at the drop of a hat? Did you think I was crying over your Emmet? Sorry, but I never even met the man, remember?''

''Yes, well…no. That is—'' Dora absorbed the truth, turned it around in her mind a few times, and then announced her decision. ''You'll have to stay with me, of course. At least for now. Mattie can go on and marry James Calvin, and you and I will get ready for the baby. For now, we'll just go on as we are, and make plans for the future.''

''You don't have to do this. I can always find someplace to go, someone to…''

''The baby's father?''

At first Dora thought she wasn't going to answer, but then she shrugged and said, ''Hardly. I fell in love with a smooth-talking Southern gentleman—'' The description was an epithet in itself. ''When I found out I was carrying his baby, I wrote to the address he'd given me and came south to marry him. You can probably guess the rest.''

Dora nodded wisely, not wanting to appear quite as naïve as she actually was. Dear Lord, to think such a thing could have happened to her! She had never even given it a thought, having been so wrapped up in all that was going on at the time. The loss of her father, her home—the defection of her friends. The desperation she'd felt when she finally realized that she had little money, no close relatives, no prospects at all for supporting herself. If it had even occurred to her that there might be a baby on the way, she might have walked right out into the Pamlico River and kept on walking.

Well, of course she would never have done that. Not with a baby to think of.

"What happened?"

"What do you think? The cad was already married, and his wife accused me of lying about the two-timing bastard and threatened to call the sheriff."

"What did you do?"

Lula smiled, making her look momentarily much younger. "Threw a brick at him and hiked back to town. I was going to drown my sorrows in gin, but gin always makes me sick, and I was sick enough without any help. Then I saw Mr. St. Bride's advertisement, and you know the rest."

Dora remained silent for several moments. The sky had gone completely dark by now, except for the evening star. Nodding decisively, she said, "Then here's what we'll do." Making plans even as she spoke, she declared, "Clarence can take back his bed, at least until you make up your mind. You can move in with me and we'll start a—a boardinghouse for the brides Grey intends to bring out. It's no wonder so many of them turn around and leave after taking one look at this place. There's not even a tearoom here, much less a decent place to stay. The parsonage is about as welcoming as a—well, you know what I mean. It's all right for a single man, I suppose, but I can't imagine a woman staying there for any length of time. There's not even a painting on the wall. No pretty cushions, no curtains—mercy, not even a rug on the floor."

Lula sent her a mocking look, eyebrows that looked as if they were penciled in—and might be, for all Dora knew—raised high in skepticism. "So it's all settled, just like that? The two of us are going to operate a boardinghouse? My dear, you're entirely too gullible. You don't know me at all. For all you know, I could have been lying about everything. I could be wanted for murder, hiding out here until the trail cools off."

"Well, you're not, of course. I might not be from New York, but even I know better than that."

Lula burst out laughing, and so Dora smiled, too, not entirely certain why. "You do sound like an actress, though. Who else would even think of saying such a ridiculous thing? Now, shall we go tell Mattie?"

"Why?"

"Why not? She's going to marry James while the preacher's still here. Well, never mind—we don't really need her. I don't suppose you can cook, can you?"

"No, but if I can memorize a script, I should be able to deal with a recipe."

Dora fell quiet, thinking how strange it was that on the very day she had buried her husband, she should have come up with such a marvelous plan for the future. A door closed, another door opened.

The house was empty when they went back inside, but there was a single lamp burning. The food had been put away, the dishes washed, and someone—Mouse, probably—had removed the chairs and the makeshift table.

"Suddenly," Dora said, "I am exhausted. I think I could sleep for a week."

"If you don't mind, I think I'll get something to eat. I'm famished."

And so it began, as simply as that. Lying awake, sleep the furthest thing from her mind, Dora set her mind free to roam, to make mental lists of all that would have to be done before they could open Mrs. Meek's Boardinghouse for Genteel Ladies.

Too much. The sign alone would cover half the picket fence. A simple sign reading Rooms?

Hardly. They had a total of two bedrooms. Perhaps something could be done to the back porch. Then, too, there was the attic.

She fell asleep with the vague thought that once Mattie married James Calvin, she could talk him into adding another room onto the back of the house. She couldn't pay him, but she could offer him his meals in exchange.

And why, pray tell, would the man need anyone else to cook for him when he had Mattie?

That was a complication. Of the three women, Mattie was by far the best cook, but she wouldn't be here, she'd be keeping house for her husband. Which meant that until either Dora or Lula mastered the art, they might need to hire her as chef.

There again was the problem of money. If the brides who came out to the island were no more affluent than Dora had been, they wouldn't even be able to pay for a bed, much less meals.

Around and around went her thoughts. What had seemed such a perfect plan at first was rife with flaws on closer examination.

All right, Dora, think! It's the men who have money.

It always came back to money. Perhaps Lula could think of a solution. Dora was beginning to suspect she might have inherited her father's lack of financial skills.

Restlessly she flopped over onto her stomach, punched up her pillow and snorted. Then she reared up and plucked away a feather that was sticking her in the cheek. At least she knew better than to fall for any pie-in-the-sky schemes. She fully intended to take what she possessed and, with a lot of hard work, turn it into a modest success—something that would support her and Lula and the child.

The baby. As she was never apt to have one of her own, she could be a sort of honorary aunt to Lula's child. If it was a little girl, they might even name her Sal—Sally Lou, if Lula didn't have another name all picked out.

It occurred to her that St. Bride was not going to like the idea of someone beside himself making plans for his private island. He might even tell her she had no right to turn her house into a business. But if it was her house—and Emmet had assured her that he had made a new will, witnessed by John Luther, leaving her everything—then there was nothing Grey could do about it.

The next morning over breakfast, the three women sat around the table while Lula and Dora filled Mattie in on their hastily conceived plan to open a boarding-house for the brides of St. Brides.

''Lor' he'p us, ain't that sump'in? Reckon there's room fer me?''

''You'll be married as soon as James Calvin can add a room onto his house. We'll need to hire him to close in the back porch of this one for us.''

Mattie's face fell as far as a round face could fall. "He don't want to marry me no more 'n I want to marry him."

Lula sighed and rolled her eyes again. It was one of several theatrical mannerisms Dora had noticed.

Dora patted Mattie's plump shoulder. "Honey, it's too soon to decide yet. These things can't be forced. I'm sure James wants to marry you, he's just shy, that's all."

It was Lula who cut to the heart of the matter. "Why don't you want to marry him? That's why you came out here, wasn't it? To find a husband?"

Wordlessly the young girl nodded. She looked so miserable, so dejected, it was all Dora could do not to gather her up and comfort her, the way Mattie had comforted her just the night before.

Had it only been the night before?

"Let's not rush into any decisions," she said soothingly. "We've all been upset—everything's so new. Nobody has to decide anything before they're ready."

"Won't Mr. St. Bride send me back?"

"Over my dead body," Dora declared, and Lula pantomimed applause. "We outnumber him, for one thing. There's three of us and only one of him."

Chapter Eleven

"Mattie's beau has come calling," Lula announced, rousing Dora from a deep, dreamless sleep. She felt as if she had been miles underwater and someone had just dragged her bodily to the surface.

"'S too early," she mumbled.

"It's nearly noon," Lula observed. "Your dog wants her breakfast and Mattie says you're nearly out of flour."

"Mmm. Gimme minute." *So I can clear my head, prop open my eyes and take care of a few other essentials.*

Merciful heavens, had it all been a dream? Was she actually considering opening a boardinghouse? That had been only one of the ideas they had discussed. Someone had mentioned a bakery, then Lula had jokingly proposed starting a laundry. "From what I've observed so far, most of the men would benefit greatly."

"I doubt if they'd find it worth the bother. And knowing what I do now what doing a single load of laundry entails, I can't say that I blame them."

They were still trying to make up their minds

whether to open a bakery or a boardinghouse. And while she wasn't about to rush into anything, sooner or later they would have to decide. Mouse couldn't be expected to supply them with meals forever.

In the clear bright light of a new day, neither plan seemed quite so practical. At first Dora had first pounced on the boardinghouse notion as the perfect solution. Whenever a bride came, there was always the awkward business of bringing in a bed, a cumbersome procedure at best. Even a small boardinghouse would simplify things greatly.

"Where's Mattie?" Lula was looking somewhat better today, although her eyes were still shadowed.

"She and James went for a walk." Seen through the window, Mattie's new hairstyle looked even more precarious than it had yesterday. She also looked as if a smile would crack her face wide-open, but then, so did James Calvin.

"What do you think?" she asked Lula, tying her wrapper around her more securely. The thing she missed most of all at this moment was the huge porcelain bathtub her father had had installed just last winter. A galvanized washtub dragged into the kitchen and filled with water heated in a kettle just wasn't the same when it came to soaking away one's worries. "Any sign of a spark between them yet?"

Lula's reply was a clear indication of her opinion of romance. "Hardly. Can the man even talk? I swear I've not heard him speak more than three words. Even poor Clarence, as shy as he is, had something to say about the new tariffs and how they might affect the shipping trade. So no, to answer your question, I'd say theirs is hardly a match made in heaven."

Dora shrugged, got up from the table and began

rummaging through the icebox to see if there was anything left over from the day before worth eating. "Yes, well—it was made right here on St. Brides Island, by St. Bride, himself. That's supposed to be even better."

Lula sent her a speculative look. "Was it?"

"Was it what?"

"Better. I'm assuming he made your match."

"Hmm. I suppose in a way, he did."

Lula nodded thoughtfully. "I don't suppose he'd be interested in acquiring a wife for himself," she mused. Evidently her morning sickness had eased enough so that she could nibble a dry crust of shortbread.

"Only if he could find a woman who didn't mind being told what to say, what to do, what to wear and even what to think."

"It wasn't his conversation I had in mind," Lula said dryly, and Dora choked on a bit of cheese. "I'd better feed Salty," she said when she had cleared her throat.

"Mattie took care of the chickens. I gather she was raised on a farm."

"I got that impression, too," Dora murmured. She had made it a point not to inquire too closely, hoping her two guests would return the favor. Each had volunteered parts of their story, but Dora had an idea she had heard only the sketchiest outline. She had listened sympathetically and said as little as possible. She was, after all, a grieving widow. Widows were allowed some privacy.

Grey came by a few minutes later. Dora would have preferred to have had time to put up her hair and dress in something more suitable than a Chinese silk kimono.

"Preacher needs to move on in a day or so. Do you

think those two are anywhere near ready to tie the knot?'' He nodded toward the sandy road that led to the section known as Shallow Gut, where Mattie and James Calvin could be seen walking back.

Lula shrugged. Dora, trying to look as though she'd been up for hours, said, "Haven't you issued a royal decree and set the wedding date yet?"

Turning away from the window, he glared at her. "And you, madam—have you made plans yet?"

"Oh, do I get to make my own plans now?" she asked, all bright innocence. Why did she feel as though she had to goad him to the point of retaliation? Was it the need to see just how far he would go? Once he'd begun coming by each evening to play a game of checkers with Emmet, she had almost been lulled into feeling…accepted.

But that, of course, had been for Emmet's sake.

"You won't want to stay here alone," he said, obviously hanging on to his temper by a thread. She could always tell when he was pushed too far—a tiny muscle at the side of his jaw began to twitch.

It was twitching now.

"I won't?"

"You should start making other plans."

"Why? Are you going to find me another husband?" Compelled for reasons that escaped her, she goaded him further. "With all the single men on the island, it shouldn't be too hard to find another one— after a suitable time, of course." Oh, my, that tiny muscle was really twitching now. She might have pushed a bit too far. It didn't help to see Lula biting her lips to keep from laughing.

"We'll talk about it after you've had time to make

yourself decent," he said, barely unclenching his jaw enough to form the words. "I'll be back, madam."

The minute he slammed the screen door behind him, Lula burst into gales of laughter. "Now *there*," she said, "you have *sparks*."

"No, there you have the most arrogant, opinionated, mule-headed despot that ever walked on two legs."

"Ah, but those two legs..." Lula teased.

"Oh, for heaven's sake," Dora snapped, and flounced off to her room. If he did return, she would be ready for him, dressed for battle.

"Oh, drat—!" she muttered some twenty minutes later as she struggled to button the back of her gown. How on earth did anyone manage without a personal maid to help them get dressed?

Husbands, of course.

She could have asked Lula, but it galled her to ask for help with anything she could do for herself. It was only one of many marks of how much she had changed over the past few months. How greatly she was coming to value her newfound independence.

She had chosen to wear one of her most flattering outfits, a rose-colored taffeta that happened to be utterly unsuitable for a grieving widow. Or any other woman living on a barren, windswept, sweltering, mosquito-ridden island like St. Brides. With the help of a buttonhook, she had just managed to slip the last covered button through its loop when she heard Mattie on the front porch. Evidently James Calvin hadn't lingered. The surprising thing was that he'd taken time off at all from his work.

"Well, what do you think?" Dora asked as she emerged from her bedroom.

"Lovely, but you'll ruin it," Lula said flatly. "I defy anyone to erase sweat stains under the arms."

"I meant the house, not the dress," Dora said. Lula had just descended from the attic. "I suppose we could curtain off the attic into two rooms until we can afford a partition."

"Put on one o' them pretty cottons o' your'n, Doree. I kin wash most ever'thing, but I ain't never washed no silk."

Lula rolled her eyes. "Leave her be, Mattie. When the bodice is too stained to wear, we can cut up the skirt to make curtains for the guest room upstairs."

Dora smiled a bit sadly, remembering that the last time she'd worn the gown had been the evening Henry had asked her to marry him. She had chosen it now as a gesture of defiance, knowing that Grey would be back, which didn't even make sense. While she would admit to having been a bit frivolous, she had never thought of herself as irrational.

Grey waited as long as he could before confronting the widow Meeks again. She hadn't meant what she'd said about looking for another husband. The very thought of her marrying another man set his teeth on edge. Which was probably the reason she'd said it. Trying to goad him into losing control. She'd had plenty to say in the past about his style of management, but he was only doing what was best for his people.

"Dammit to hell and back," he swore softly, slapping a pair of work gloves against his thigh. She was up to something. He knew it as well as he knew his own name. Something was going on in that household, and unless he took the reins in his own hands, there was no telling what kind of mischief those three would hatch.

Not James's woman. She was no troublemaker. Too shy, but then, so was James. Might not be much conversation between 'em, but they'd make a sound enough match.

As for the older one, he wasn't quite as certain. Something about her made him believe she might be better suited for an older man. John Luther was too old.... He'd been widowed for nearly ten years.

But then, he was no older than Emmet had been.

By that time Grey was at the Meeks's front door. Kicking the sand off his boots, he called through the screen. "Dora? Anyone home?"

Salty heaved herself up from the sunny corner of the porch and waddled over to get her ears scratched. Grey obliged the yellow mongrel, saying, "You ladies are taking over my peaceable island, aren't you, old gal? If at least half those pups you're carrying aren't male, I'm deporting you to Ocracoke."

Dora appeared at the door, breathlessly dusting her hands together. She was wearing something more suitable—in his eyes, at least—to a ballroom. She smelled faintly of pine soap, faintly of lilacs, and before he could guard against it, he found himself reacting like a starving man at a banquet.

Like a normal, healthy male who hadn't lain with a woman in more than a year.

Dammit, she had just buried her husband! Her *second* husband!

Besides that, she'd been a thorn in his side from the first day she'd set foot on his island.

"Did you need to see me about something?" she asked, barring the door with her slight form.

"I thought you might want to, uh—that is, it occurred to me that—" Nothing occurred to him; his brain had seized up like a gearbox packed with sand. "—that you might want to add something to the order I'm fixing to give Cap'n Dozier. Nothing like a funeral to use up food supplies."

Talk about tact. He felt like smacking himself on the side of the head. "What I mean is, you might want to check over your larder and see if you're running short of any staples. That is, if you're planning on staying long enough to…"

Well, hell, St. Bride—why not put both feet in your mouth, it's big enough.

"That's thoughtful of you. I'll have to see. That is, we might be needing a few things, but nothing that can't wait for another week."

Another week. Which brought to mind another matter. There was no tactful way of bringing it up, so he just came right out and asked. "What about money? I know Em didn't keep much on hand, but he had an account with a bank over in Bath. I could advance you whatever you need."

He didn't bother to add that he had taken over the sole support of Emmet's so-called savings account. It was beginning to look as if he might be taking on the support of his widow, as well. So be it.

Evidence of the strain she'd been under was clear. There were shadows under her eyes. She looked as if she hadn't slept well, which was understandable. What wasn't so understandable was the inexplicable air of subdued excitement that surrounded her.

After their earlier conversation, he felt a growing sense of unease. She couldn't have already set her sights on another man—not this soon! "Is there, uh—

anything else I can help you with?'' he managed to ask, feeling as if some unseen force had wrested the wheel from his hands and was intent on changing the whole course of his life. For a man used to being in control, it was damned unsettling.

"Well, yes. If you would be so kind, could you send Mouse over later on today to help move some furniture around?'' She bit her lip, and Grey found himself staring at the small white teeth embedded in ripe pink flesh. "I, uh—I don't suppose he'd accept a goose in repayment would he?''

"Sal's, old gander? Set him free if you don't want him.''

"He won't leave.''

"Quit feeding him.''

"He'll come into the house and attack me.''

"Not if you starve him into submission.''

By then the tension had lessened so that she was able to smile and Grey even managed a chuckle. At least, he told himself a few moments later as he strode toward the landing, that damned gander was good for something.

Let that be a lesson to you, man—never take in something to house and feed if you don't mean to keep it around.

The best course of action would be to buy back Meeks's house, paying her fair value plus a bonus for making haste. That way she would have funds for a fresh start back on the mainland and he couldn't be accused of taking advantage of a helpless widow.

Even better, he'd be rid of her before she managed to pick out another victim and dig herself in even deeper.

Grey arrived at the warehouse to find Clarence staring morosely at the half-finished lumber shed, a note-pad in hand. "I had that last shipment of cypress stacked around back. If the wind don't switch, it'll likely be all right until we can get the shed finished. James and Almy both have been working all morning."

"I thought James had been courting. Didn't I see him and Mattie walking out together around noon?"

The redhead warehouse manager shrugged and went on making notes on a grimy pad of paper clipped to a cedar shingle. "He took an hour off. Personal business."

Grey planted his fists on his hips, looked around at the capacious, two-story warehouse he'd built after tearing down the old one. One of these days the inlet would close. New inlets were constantly opening, old ones shoaling up. There was no predicting which storm would change the entire configuration of the coast, leaving shipowners and landowners alike, not to mention all who depended on them, scrambling to deal with the changes.

Was he crazy to think it couldn't happen here? Just because the inlet had been stable for as long as he could remember?

Was he crazy to think he could build enough of a community here so that when and if the worst happened and inlet pilots were no longer needed, they could find some other means of survival?

Time would tell.

"I don't think Miss Lula likes me much," Clarence said quietly, laying aside his notes.

"Sure she does. She's just, uh—well, you know how it is with women."

"Nope. Can't say I do."

Grey scratched his head and tried to come up with a few reassuring words. The truth was, the more he saw of women—*some* women, at least—the more he realized that any man who claimed to understand them was lying through his teeth.

"Listen, if things don't work out between you two we'll just shuffle the deck and deal another hand. I've got another prospect coming out in a week or so. Maybe even two."

By suppertime, the three current residents of Mrs. Meeks's Establishment, whatever it turned out to be, had their heads together and their feet up on makeshift stools, nursing tumblers of blackberry wine, they compared notes.

"Mercy," Dora said with a tired smile. "Give three independent women their head and stand back— there's no telling what will come of it."

"I'm not sure yet if anything will," Lula retorted. "The only thing we haven't considered so far is a circus."

"Oh, my—I never even seen one of them," Mattie said reverently.

Dora kept on smiling. Lula rolled her eyes again. As they were her most striking feature, she had learned to use them to great effect. "Now, where did we leave off? If we go with the boardinghouse idea, then Mattie will take charge of the kitchen—unless and until she marries. Dora will take over getting the rooms ready and I'll keep the accounts. We'll need to watch every penny we spend so we'll know how much we have to charge."

They had laid out the three projects—boarding-house, bakery and laundry, and promptly eliminated the last. "If we go with the bakery, are you sure we need to order that much sugar and flour, Mattie? And ten pounds of raisins?"

"Yes'm, I'm sure."

"Rule number one—no more yes'ms. How can you keep that much on hand without inviting bugs? I can hardly step outside without being eaten alive."

"Skeeters and greenheads don't matter. Bay leaves'll keep the weevils out'n the flour. I'll store the raisins and the sugar in crocks and set em in a pan o' water. 'Sides, I'll be usin' up supplies faster 'n they can tote 'em across the sound. Once the men get a taste o' my raisin bread and 'lasses cake, they'll wear me out bakin' more."

"And we'll take their money and spend some on more supplies and set the rest aside for buying beds. Meanwhile, you'll bake more bread and branch out to fancy cakes and—"

"I can't bake no fancy cakes. 'Bout the fanciest I can bake is raisin bread and 'lasses cake."

"Sal has a recipe book."

"I can't read too good."

"I'll do the reading, Dora will do the plain cooking, you'll do the baking," Lula announced. "Now, if we've made up our minds, and if I can beg, borrow or steal a board and a bit of paint, I'll get busy making a sign."

Dora's head was spinning. Lula, once stirred to action, was a force to be reckoned with. Only two days ago, newly widowed and uncertain of her own future, Dora had considered the possibility of providing a place for future brides to stay until they made up their minds whether or not they wanted to marry their intended bridegroom. Lula had taken over and now things seemed to have spiraled out of control.

"The stove—I don't know if I mentioned it, but it's beginning to rust out in a few places. Emmet said it was secondhand when he got it—he said he'd planned to replace it with one of the more modern ones, but he never got around to it."

"We'll save up to replace it. It shouldn't take too long." Lula made notes on a scrap of paper. The one thing she and the young warehouseman had in common, Dora thought, amused, was that they were both prodigious note-takers.

"Lula, are you sure—" Dora began.

"Do you want to find yourself another husband?"

Dora shook her head emphatically.

"Are you ready to go back to wherever you came from—Bath, I believe?"

"Certainly not, I live here now. I have a home here."

"All right, then, allow me to refresh your memory. Who has all the money on this benighted island?"

"The men," Dora and Mattie replied in unison. It had been discussed at great length.

"And who doesn't?"

"Me," Mattie replied promptly.

"The brides," corrected Dora. "If they had a choice, why on earth would they come to a place like this?"

Lula said dryly, "I think we all know the answer to that."

"Yes, well…we're about to give them choices. With the men supporting our enterprise by buying our bakery goods, we can afford to house and feed the brides until they decide when and whom they'll marry.

No more having his lordship push us around like checkers on a board.'' Her declaration of independence thus made, Dora looked from one to the other, feeling a renewed sense of resolution.

There was a speculative gleam in Lula's dark eyes. ''What do you suppose St. Bride will have to say about our plans?''

With more determination than confidence, Dora said, ''You leave St. Bride to me.''

Chapter Twelve

It was James Calvin who provided the materials for the sign. Several lengths of pine sawed to measurement, a can of paint and a small brush. "Here you go, Mattie. You want to tell me what you three are up to?"

"I reckon you'll find out, soon's the paint dries."

Observing the pair from the backyard where she was hanging out the wash, Dora wondered what had gone wrong with the match. Neither of them seemed to bear any animosity, yet neither did they show signs of any potential attachment.

Sparks, she decided. It must be the complete lack of what Lula termed sparks. She tried to remember if what she'd once felt for Henry had been sparks. She must have thought so at the time, but looking back, she was reminded of the way she'd felt when she'd first tasted champagne. The idea had been far more exciting than the reality.

From his patched and repatched pen, the gander stretched his neck and hissed at her. "Just you wait, you sorry creature, pretty soon you're going to have a new home." Mouse could either cook the bird or take him across the inlet and set him free. A hissing, threatening gander would hardly be good for business, which meant that one way or another she had to be rid of him by the time things went much further.

"I plum forgot," Mattie called from the back door. "I'll need me some bread pans. At least six."

"I'll order twelve," Dora called back around a mouth full of clothespins. "Captain Dozier's due in this afternoon."

"Law ha' mercy, kin we afford that many?"

"It takes money to make money," she said airily, and then winced, remembering the way her father had repeated the mantra whenever he sold off more acreage to pay for his ruinous investments.

But bakery or not, once the brides began to arrive they'd be expected to provide ample meals. Perhaps for the men, as well. That way they could charge double.

Mercy, you're your father's daughter all over again!

The first sign was a work of art, complete with curlicues, bluebirds and flowers. Lula, it seemed, had doubled as the troupe's sign painter and poster maker. It was Mouse who nailed it up, his bald dome gleaming in the mid-June sunlight. Mattie didn't seem to mind at all walking up the ridge and asking the hulking houseman to come and help with any task that needed doing.

"He's big, but there ain't a mean bone in his body," she said once when Lula made some remark about his villainous looks.

They had decided to put up the bakery sign first, waiting until the brides began to arrive before adding the other one. Less than an hour after Mouse nailed up the modest seven-by-fourteen inch sign, the men began showing up to see what it was all about.

First James Calvin came to satisfy his curiosity and stayed to level the sign. In anything involving hammer, nails and wood, the man was a perfectionist.

Dora noticed that neither he nor Mattie exchanged more than a few words, yet he lingered for almost half an hour. It occurred to her that he might be interested in Lula. They were alike in some ways, both dark and quiet. Lula was a few inches taller, but that only made her more striking.

Shortly after James left, the Reverend Almond Filmore stopped by to say he'd be leaving that afternoon with Captain Dozier, in case the ladies would like to move back to the parsonage. Noticing the sign, he stepped back to admire it, then commented in his slow, thoughtful way. "My, my. A bakery. Now, that'll be right nice. S-seems a right s-sensible thing to do."

He and Lula discussed hymns for several minutes, and when she confessed to not knowing the words to very many, he offered to lend her his hymnal when he returned.

"I swanee, if I had to set an' listen to that man preach, I'd end up a heathen, sure's the world," declared Mattie, coming inside a few minutes later with a basket of eggs.

Lula took on what Dora thought of as her duchess look. "He's taking care to speak slowly and distinctly so as not to stammer. I, for one, applaud a man with the courage to go into public speaking under those circumstances."

"Is preaching considered public speaking?" asked Dora.

"He speaks, doesn't he? And in public?" Lula snapped, defending the man and making Dora rather ashamed of her impatience during the one time she'd suffered through one of his interminable services.

Not that she hadn't had fair warning. Her wedding had taken so long she'd been afraid poor Emmet would collapse before they'd even been pronounced man and wife.

Lula was on her high horse. Dora could easily picture her holding an audience enthralled with a dramatic reading followed by a song, both rendered in her clear, emotional contralto voice. Earlier that day after Salty had sneaked into the house, she had held open the door, pointed a finger and declaimed, "Out, out, damned spot!"

A puzzled Mattie had said, "She ain't got no spots. Her name's Salty."

"It's a line from Macbeth, Mattie," Dora had explained gently.

"Mac Who?"

"Lula, would you explain?"

And so the actress had briefly summarized the Shakespearean tragedy while Mattie had sat, enthralled. At the end, she'd said, "My sakes alive, I never heard o'such carryin' on. Was them real people?"

Dear Mattie. Ignorance could be irritating, maddening or endearing. In Mattie, it was the latter.

"Have either of you seen the dog lately?" she called out. "I haven't seen her since this morning." The poor creature had been increasingly restless since Emmet died, missing him, no doubt.

Dora missed him, too, far more than she would have expected considering the brief duration of their union.

"I'd better go find her before she gets into any more trouble." She peered through the front door at the handful of men gathered outside the fence, discussing the new sign.

"My, would you lookee there," Mattie said, peering through the window. "I 'speck we'll be rich like them ladies that lives over the drink house back in Little Washington."

I rather doubt it, Dora thought, touched and amused by her naive young friend. She was halfway to the gate, admiring her sign from the back side, when she caught sight of Grey headed down the ridge.

"Going somewhere?" he asked.

"Looking for my dog."

"Emmet's dog," he corrected, and then shook his head. "Sorry. Do you have a minute? What is this ridiculous sign you've hung on your fence?"

Suddenly they were alone as the other men silently tipped their hats and headed back to the landing. Dora crossed her arms, waiting for Grey to explode. The jaw muscle wasn't ticking yet, but it shouldn't be long. Ever since Mouse had nailed the thing in place she'd been expecting Grey to come storming up, demanding that she take it down. The amazing thing was that it had taken him this long.

"Just what the devil are you up to now?" he demanded.

"I think it's fairly obvious, don't you?" If he thought his added height and the breadth of his shoulders gave him the advantage, he was absolutely right. He was obviously trying to intimidate her.

"The only thing that's obvious is that you've lost your mind."

"I *beg* your—"

He held up his hand. "Don't," he said grimly. "Not again."

Dora started to order him off her property—actually, they were standing on the road in front of her gate—but before she could get more than a word out, he cut her off. "Now listen carefully before you fly off the handle again. I've got a proposition for you."

Dora's eyes narrowed. Whatever it was, she didn't want to hear it.

"I'll pay you fair market value for the house and the acre of land it stands on," he announced. Her jaw fell, and while he waited for her response, he went a step further. "I'll even include a bonus if you'll agree to vacate the premises within one week."

By the time she remembered to close her gaping mouth, Dora's fists were clenched at her side. Not even that could prevent the tremors that raced up and down her body despite the heat of the sun.

Nor did it quell her sudden fear, her doubts.

Could Grey force her out? If he did, where could she go to start over? No matter how much he paid her, money didn't last forever, even when it was invested. She, more than anyone, should know that.

"No, thank you," she said, her voice betraying her feelings by only a slight stiffness. "I believe I'll stay."

Blue eyes had never looked more arctic. "The devil you will."

Her mouth suddenly went dry, and so she merely raised her eyebrows. She'd seen it done to great effect by one of Bath's starchiest matriarchs, a woman who could put down any ruffian with a single look.

On Grey, it simply didn't work. He continued to loom over her, hands on his hips, his own dark brows lowered threateningly in a silent battle of wills.

He cast a jeering glance at her beautiful new sign with the scrolled letters proclaiming her new industry. "Who the devil is going to do the baking?"

"Mattie. I'll help."

His bark of laughter jarred her fragile composure. "Then you'd better lay in a good supply of stomach bitters."

"Mattie is a wonderful cook."

"I'm sure James Calvin will appreciate her efforts."

"She's not going to marry James Calvin."

"Did she tell you that?"

Dora dug the tip of her toe against a clump of shells, leaving a white mark on the tan leather. "Not in so many words, but it's obvious, isn't it?"

"Is it?"

Lord, the man had his gall. Standing there bold as brass, deciding who was going to marry whom. "Well, you've seen them together," she exclaimed. "Did you see a single, solitary spark?"

He stared at her as if she'd suddenly stared speaking Mandarin. "What the hell do sparks have to do with anything?"

Dora told herself that trying to reason with a man like Grey St. Bride was like trying to waltz on quicksand. Not that there was another man in the entire world like him. There wasn't enough arrogance to go around. "How can I explain anything when you keep glaring at me as if you'd like to bite my head off?"

The old Adora Sutton—a social butterfly who had frittered away twenty-three years of her frivolous life—would have never dreamed of saying such a thing. Dora Meeks was another matter. If there was one thing she had discovered about herself these past few months, it was that she was perfectly capable of pushing back whenever anyone tried to push her around.

Spurred on by sheer bravado, she said, "You might as well know, we're planning to open a boardinghouse just as soon as we can earn enough money from the bakery to send off for beds." Wasn't he scheduled to leave sometime soon on a business trip? She remembered hearing about it, thinking it would be a perfect time to set her plans into action. It had worked when she'd married Emmet.

Unfortunately, he showed no signs of leaving the island.

Lula was probably going to be upset with her for sharing their plans with the enemy, but then, Lula didn't think of Grey as the enemy. Only Dora knew how utterly ruthless he could be.

She was still waiting for a reaction. If he laughed at her, she might kick him. If he forbade her, she would simply remind him that Emmet's house was now hers and she could do with it as she pleased. She didn't need his permission.

He smiled. His shoulders suddenly seemed to grow six inches on either side—seemed to spread over her like the wings of a hawk as he leaned closer, that chilling, beautiful smile on his tanned face.

She moved back a step. She would almost rather he swore at her.

"Mrs. Meeks," Grey St. Bride said softly, his warm breath stirring over her hot cheeks. "You seem to be suffering under a slight misapprehension. At the moment, you have a roof over your head. But that's *all* you have. What happens when you run out of supplies? Who do you think is going to support you? Who's going to put up your chickens and board up your windows when the first hurricane comes roaring along the coast?'' He looked pointedly at her hands, and she tried to hide them in the folds of her skirt. They were red and rough, no longer pampered, but still far less capable than she would have liked.

''Well?'' he prompted.

Thinking of how secure she'd felt the first time she'd been told that the islanders took care of their own, she was about to repeat the words. Just in time she remembered that these were his people, not hers. One word from him and they might cut her off the same way her friends back in Bath had done.

What was that old saying—once burned, twice shy?

Cautiously she took a step back in an effort to free herself from his compelling physical presence. ''You said Emmet had a bank account. I—I could always write a bank draft and hire someone.''

Slowly he shook his head from side to side. He was still smiling, the effect so chilling she found herself rubbing her bare arms.

''Have you looked through Emmet's papers yet? Have you found his account book? His deed for the house?''

Wordlessly, she shook her head. ''There's hardly been time.''

''Time enough for you to hatch a lot of harebrained schemes.''

''There's nothing at all harebrained about my plans, damn your wicked soul!''

Eyes sparkling, he pursed his lips in disapproval. Dora found herself staring at his mouth again—the full lower lip, the chiseled upper one. The incongruous dimple in his chin. He made a slow tisking sound with tongue and teeth, then turned and simply walked away.

Walked away!

Chapter Thirteen

It was all she could do not to jump on his back and hammer him with her fists until she could beat some sense into his arrogant head. Flinging open the gate so that it clattered against her beautiful new sign, she stalked back toward the house, muttering dire threats under her breath. Not until Lula spoke from the porch did she glance up.

"Careful, or you two might set fire to the whole island."

"What?"

"Sparks," the older woman said, her dark eyes alight with amusement. "I gather his highness didn't like the idea of a bakery. Do you suppose if we called it St. Bride's Fine Pastries instead of Mrs. Meeks's Bakery he might come around?"

Feeling suddenly exhausted, Dora flopped down onto the edge of the porch. Shaking her head from side to side, she began to smile. "Oh, Lula, you're good for me. I'm so glad you came along when you did. What would I have done if I'd been all alone when Emmet died?"

Standing at the end of the porch, Lula shook the

sand from a small rug. "Hardly alone. You'd have had every man on the island flocking to your doorstep, wanting to step into Emmet's shoes before the dirt even settled on his grave."

"Hardly. Grey would have bundled me off on the next outward-bound boat before I had time to think. Without you and Mattie, I'd never have come up with the idea of a bakery."

"You could still have taken in brides."

"Which wouldn't have done me much good as we're all agreed they're not likely to have any money. I certainly didn't. You said you didn't, and I'm sure Mattie didn't. The prospective grooms might have provided beds, but I'm sure I'd have been expected to feed them."

"Yes, well…one step at a time," Lula said, giving the rug one last flap. It was impossible to keep sand from being tracked inside. Now that she was feeling more herself, Lula had taken on the housekeeping duties.

Dora sighed. "I think I was on my way to locate the dog when I was waylaid. I don't suppose she's come home yet, has she?"

Lula called in through the front window. "Mattie, is the dog on the back porch?"

A moment later Mattie called back, "I've not seen her since breakfast. Don't reckon she could get lost, though."

Dora stirred herself, saying, "I'd better go find her. Emmet loved the old thing dearly. He told me how they used to sit out by the fig trees and talk to Sal."

Three days later the stack of loaf pans they'd ordered came in. The three women celebrated with glasses of blackberry wine, and Dora made a mental note to see if Sal had a recipe for making the sweet, mildly stimulating beverage. Blackberry vines, as well as wild grapevines, ran rampant over the yaupons, bay trees and stunted live oaks.

Salty got up from the corner of the room, stretched her hind legs one at a time, then circled and flopped down again. Dora had finally located her under the front stoop of the parsonage and lured her home with a strip of bacon. Since then she had become a house dog. No one seemed to mind.

Suddenly Mattie sat up and said, "East!"

Lula looked at her as if she'd lost her mind, then shrugged and said, "South?"

"I ain't got no east for my raisin bread. It ain't like biscuits, it's riz bread."

Once they managed to get to the root of the problem—that "riz" bread required yeast and not baking powder, Dora set out to place another order with Clarence while Mattie headed up the ridge to see if Mouse could lend her some "east" cakes to get started with. The boats came and went on a frequent, if irregular, schedule, but with twelve shiny new pans just waiting to be filled, they were all eager to begin their new venture.

Alone, Lula leaned back in her chair, holding a glass of wine in one hand while the other rested lightly on her faintly rounded belly. "You're the son of a true bastard," she murmured, "but you're mine, as well. We'll manage, dear heart—your mother hasn't worked this hard and traveled this far to give up now that I've got a foothold on a future for us."

She would give him a heroic name. Something to live up to. Her father's name—she barely remembered

the man who had spent most of his life in saloons—
had been Albert. Al. Too ordinary, by far. Her cheating, silver-tongue lover had been Billy Turney. Of all
the lies he'd told her, that much, at least, had evidently
been the truth. At least she had eventually managed to
track the louse down by that name.

"Maximus. Maximus Russart? Or Octavius. Or perhaps Junius," she mused, gazing up at the water-
stained ceiling. She might as well raise him here as
anywhere. At least here in the South it probably
wouldn't snow as much. She had been blue-finger cold
too many times, both in the one-room garret they'd
called home and in the shirt factory where she and her
mother had worked until her mother had died of the
consumption, ever to want to head north again.

This would do for now. With her as manager, the
three of them would be able to get along quite well
without men. Between her father, who had supported
every rum hole and bucket shop in town, and her lying, cheating louse of an ex-lover, she'd had quite
enough of that breed.

Mouse supplied the yeast, Dora cleared the table
and set out the ingredients and Mattie set about making her first batch of raisin bread. Then, while Lula
surveyed the attic again with an eye to eventually di-
viding it into two rooms, Dora and Mattie sat in the
kitchen, waiting impatiently for the loaves to rise.
Dora read aloud from Sal's recipe book, and every few
minutes both women would pause and gaze admir-
ingly at the row of shiny tin loaf pans lined up on the
shelf on the far side of the kitchen. The scent of cinnamon permeated the air, reminding Dora that soon
they would have to start taking in money, else they'd

never be able to afford all the flour, sugar and raisins, let alone the spices.

"I reckon I'd better go git in a load of wood and fire up the oven," Mattie said eventually. Rising, she lifted a hand to steady her exaggerated "puppy-door." Dora had given her hairpins and combs and taught her to arrange the fashionable style. She'd had no luck at all in getting her to pronounce it correctly.

So be it. The child had pretty hair, now that it had been set free from those awful, skintight braids.

A short while later Dora closed the recipe book and moved to open the firebox just as Mattie came in with a basket of kindling. Both women looked at the oven door, then at the neat row of loaf pans, then strickenly at each other.

"Oh, no," wailed Dora.

Mattie's face crumpled. She began to cry, soft, pitiful sobs, and soon Dora joined her. The two women were standing in the middle of the kitchen staring at the old wood range and weeping their hearts out when Grey rapped on the front door frame and let himself inside.

"Anybody home?" he called out. Coming to a halt just inside the kitchen, he muttered, "What in God's name is going on here? Where's Lula? Is somebody hurt?"

Dora took one look at him and began to cry even harder. The very last thing she needed now was for him to witness their first failure. "Go away." She waved ineffectually toward the door.

"Not until someone tells me what the hell is happening around here. Mouse said—"

At that, Mattie howled even louder. "My bread, my poor bread!"

Grey stared at first one woman, then the other, his gaze returning to rest on Dora's wet face and wild golden curls. The woman would be the death of him yet, he swore silently. Unable to help himself, he gathered her into his arms and held her while she sobbed on his chest, soaking the shirt Mouse had just finished ironing not ten minutes ago.

And then he reached for Mattie and pulled her to him, too. What the devil—they weren't in any condition to hear what he'd come to say, anyway. It had waited this long—it could wait another few days.

Until the worst of the sobs subsided, he didn't even attempt to get to the root of the trouble. Finally, however, Mattie pulled away from his spare arm—he'd had to stretch to embrace the two of them. Dora was no bigger than a minute, but little Mattie was an armful.

"Now, does either one of you ladies want to tell me what's going on?" Seeing the kindling basket on its side by the back door, the firebox open and the neat row of pans on the shelf, he was beginning to have an inkling what it might be.

"They won't fit," Dora declared, glaring belligerently through red-rimmed eyes at the old range he had rescued from a house about to be washed away in the storm of '87 and eventually installed in Emmet's kitchen.

"The bread pans? Cook 'em two at a time," he said, ever the voice of reason.

She whacked him on the arm. "You can't do that! It says right there in Sal's book that light bread has to be cooked right away when it doubles its size. If you don't bake it then, it—it—" She turned to the expert. "Tell him what happens, Mattie."

"It goes flat. It's only got two rizins in it, and if ye don't catch it on the last rise, it won't never come up again. Mattie looked as if she'd just lost her last hope of heaven.

For perhaps the first time, Grey caught a glimmer of just what was at stake for these three women.

For one of them, at least. Mattie would marry James Calvin and the other one—Lula—would marry Clarence. Eventually. Until the two couples worked things out between them, he'd just as soon they stayed here with Dora, so long as they stayed out of mischief.

As for the widow Meeks, that was another story. No way in hell was he about to match her up with another husband. He didn't know for sure, but he had a feeling one of the reasons the other two matches were slow in coming together was that every man on the island wanted a woman who looked like Dora Meeks.

Who wouldn't? God help him, she was enough to tempt the devil himself, without even trying.

"Listen to me, now—it'll be all right. I'll send Mouse down to get your bread and take it up to my house to bake. Will that make you happy?" It was a pretty damned generous offer, to his way of thinking, but the plump little redhead with the lopsided knot on her head looked at him as if he'd lost his mind.

"But you can't tote riz dough," she wailed.

You can't tote riz dough. Uh-huh. No way was he going to admit he didn't have a clue. So he turned to Dora, whose shoulders were heaving with residual sobs. It pained him to admit it, but even with a red-tipped nose and pink-rimmed eyes, she was so damned beautiful he wanted to sweep her up, carry her to the ridge and plant her in his bed.

And join her there for the foreseeable future.

God help him, the little witch had affected his brain.

"Well, listen, ladies, I'm sorry your venture didn't work out, but that's the way it goes when you get involved in a business. It takes more than enthusiasm, it takes—"

He'd been about to say it took brains, but thought it best not to ruffle any more feathers. He had business of his own to see to. Nodding in their general direction, he backed out of the kitchen and hurried outside. He'd give Dora a couple of days to come to her senses and then he'd make her another offer on her house.

Dammit, he had to get rid of her, and the quicker the better. She was not only affecting his sleep, she was affecting his judgment.

It was Dora who came up with the solution. At her instructions, Mattie stoked the fire and then together they dumped the loaf pans, two at a time, into her largest bowl.

"We'll make up a name for them," she said. "Mattie's Baby Breads? Cinnamon and raisin biscuits?" Together they rolled and cut, rolled and cut, and each time she stamped out a circle of dough, Dora whispered inwardly, *Take that, your high-and-mightiness! It will take more than a tiny miscalculation to chase me off your blasted island.*

The fallen-angel cakes sold six-for-a-penny. They weren't particularly good, but not a word of complaint was heard from the men who flocked to the new bakery to purchase whatever the women produced. Clarence proclaimed them interesting.

James Calvin bit into one and nodded. Both men bought dozens and there were dozens more for the other customers. Some were slightly scorched on the bottoms, the raisins burned black, for the old oven heated unevenly. All were inclined to be soggy, which was why Lula had come up with the name "fallen angel."

Mouse bought three dozen. Mattie said she would have to order more baking sheets, and then she and Dora looked at the small oven, looked at each other, and laughed.

Lula told them they were giddy, which wasn't far from the truth. It had taken all day long to roll out, cut and bake the resurrected dough, two sheets at a time, and both women were exhausted.

Lula had been appointed to take the money, record it and determine just how much they could afford to spend on supplies. "We'd better raise the price. Two for a penny—perhaps even a penny apiece. They'll sell. What else is there on this godforsaken sand hill for the men to spend their money on?"

"Let's not be too reckless," Dora cautioned, having learned firsthand the dire consequences. "At least we won the battle."

"The *first* battle," Lula said dryly, and Dora didn't bother to ask her meaning. She knew.

St. Bride.

Chapter Fourteen

After supper that evening, Grey read over the letter he had written in answer to one that had come in on the mail boat just that morning. According to Jocephus, business at St. Bride & Son Shipping was thriving.

Grey, himself, could attest to that fact. His own end of the family business had reached the point where he was considering hiring another assistant for Clarence. He had his eyes on John Luther's eldest boy, a steady lad with a good head for ciphering.

Jocephus had written that he'd bought Evelyn her own carriage and pair, and that Evan, who was now in his second year at Chapel Hill, was showing more interest in girls than in his studies.

Which, as Grey had written in response, was only natural for a boy of eighteen. He would settle down in time. "If you'll remember, brother, all the St. Bride men, right down to the present generation, have shown a tendency to kick up their heels before settling down for the long haul."

Grey went on to write about the encouraging way his own plans were coming together.

…The lumberyard we're building behind the warehouse is right on schedule, with two fine carpenters heading the project and a number of apprentices learning the trade, as fishing has slowed up considerably since March. As for my own project, there are now two more women in residence with another, possibly two more, on the way. The system I devised of scattering the advertisements among three areas is starting to pay off. The last two are from the Little Washington region. The pair I'm expecting next are from your neck of the woods, one from Bethel and the other from across the river near Mackeys Ferry. Once the first two marry and this next pair arrives and settles in, I'll be placing another advertisement in Bath.

The last time I advertised in Bath, the single respondent turned out to be unsuitable. Nevertheless, she remains a resident, having married Emmet Meeks. You remember him, don't you? He was Father's hunting partner and, as it turned out, his first marriage was my first successful match.

Unfortunately, the wife I found for him died of pneumonia and now Emmet is dead, too, leaving a young widow in possession of his property. It's a complicated tale, best explained in person, so I won't go into it here.

Pausing, Grey stroked his jaw and looked out the window, his gaze falling on the two grave markers, one of marble, one a temporary slab of cypress until he could have a suitable tombstone shipped out from the mainland.

Sheets and a number of feminine unmentionables fluttered in the slight breeze from the line strung across the Meeks's backyard. Smoke poured from the chimney, indicating that the pesky female was going to go right on defying him with her so-called bakery until he took a firmer stand.

He added a postscript on the bottom of the page.

Our Reverend Filmore is still as slow and exasperating as ever. A good man, though. I'm thinking of asking him to stay on full-time once we have children to school. It strikes me that he would be up to the task. He could certainly teach the children patience. The few queries I have made lead me to believe it might not be a simple matter to find a schoolteacher willing to come out here even for a few months each year. At least Almond Filmore is literate.

And so, surprisingly, enough, are at least two of the women in current residence. Perhaps I should reevaluate my original plan and appoint one of them schoolmistress.

But enough of my musings, brother. Mouse prepared your favorite baked sheepshead for supper this evening. I do wish you were here to share it, for the man still cooks enough to feed the crew of an oceangoing freighter. My love, as ever, to you, Evelyn and Evan.

He added his signature and left the letter weighted down with a clam shell on his desk for the ink to dry.

Next he took out a folder labeled "Family Planning" and read over the carefully worded advertisement he would send out in another week or two, once the last pair of brides were settled. Timing was important. He liked to wait at least three months, as it wouldn't do to have too many prospective brides on his hands at the same time. Either he would get stuck with Filmore as his guest, or he would have to allow Dora to house the women.

God knows, the woman didn't need any encouragement. She was already beginning to think she was indispensable. The sooner the Russart female and the little redhead married and settled under their own roof, the better.

A bakery. Of all the damn fool notions, he thought, nibbling on the raisin cake Mouse had served with his supper. Give the woman an inch and she'd soon take possession of his whole island.

Salty had gone missing again. While Mattie contemplated trying her hand at a molasses cake—it would have to be sold by the slice, as they could only bake two at a time—Dora walked up the ridge to ask if Mouse had seen the old dog.

Lula reluctantly agreed to go in the other direction and inquire of the men working at the landing. It was while she was passing the tiny, one-room church with the wooden cross nailed above the door that the strangest feeling came over her. Instead of continuing to the waterfront, she turned off the road and trudged through the deep sand to the door.

The minister wasn't back yet, she was fairly certain of that. It had been years since she'd last seen the inside of a church. Not since her mother's funeral, in fact.

If her father had had one of his own, she had missed it. He had disappeared a week after her mother's death, and all she could think was, Good riddance!

The single room was utterly without charm. She

stood in the door, surveying the exposed rafters, the unpainted walls and the backless plank benches, three along each side, with a short center aisle. In place of an altar there was a tall, boxlike contraption with what looked suspiciously like a ship's wheel attached.

Pathetic, she thought. Not so much as a scarf to soften the effect. Not even a branch of greenery to brighten the bleak interior. If she'd been a set designer—which she had been on more than one occasion when Perretti couldn't afford to pay his players, much less his support staff, she would have used fronds of the palms that grew in the low-lying portions of the island. She would certainly get rid of that wheel. Whatever was it doing in a place like this? Perhaps a crocheted doily on the minister's stand, and a coat of white paint on the wall behind the pulpit. She was picturing the tall, grave-faced man delivering a sermon in his slow, sonorous voice against such a background when a soft mewing sound caught her attention.

"Salty? Dratted dog, are you hiding in here?" And then, "Oh, Lord, what next?"

The creature had taken advantage of the privacy afforded by the unused church to have her pups. Staring down at the yellow bitch and her four tiny, wriggling babies hidden behind the stand that apparently served as an altar, Lula began to chuckle.

The old dog lifted an apologetic look.

"Salty, you shameless creature—a church, of all places? The reverend will die of embarrassment if he finds you under his altar."

On her knees, Lula had to examine each of the fat, squirming puppies. "Oh, my, they're precious," she murmured. Still raw and unfinished looking, their eyes not even open yet, they were so utterly helpless one couldn't help but respond. "Three blondes and a brunette. What shall we name them?" The tired old dog licked herself, licked the pups and then licked Lula's hand. "I'm warning you, though—I'm saving the best names for my own baby."

Lula had never had a pet of any kind. Never had the slightest desire for one, as it was all she could do to look after herself and, later, her mother. She knew as well as anyone what happened to unwanted pets, though.

"Over my dead body," she vowed softly. "Lula will see that no one harms a hair on your babies' fat little bodies." Bringing the runt of the litter up to her neck, she rubbed her chin against the silken fur. "I must say, however, one would have been sufficient. Don't you think four is rather excessive?"

She cuddled a squirming pup, inhaling the pungent essence of newborn dog. It wasn't quite as repulsive as she would have thought, but then, she'd be the first to admit that her own pregnancy could have affected her senses.

"If no one objects," she announced a few minutes later, after describing the pups to Dora and Mattie, "they'll be Romeo, Juliet, Othello and Ophelia. Three are yellow and one's an odd sort of brownish black."

"Brindle," said Dora, who'd been trying to sponge the sweat stains from her rose taffeta. "My father once had a brindled terrier."

"My pa had 'im a bunch o' rabbit dogs. Many's the night I heered 'em yap-yowlin' when they treed 'em a 'possum. They'd run up most any kind o' critter they come across. Skunks was the worst."

The other two women just stared at her. Finally Lula said, "Yes. Well, I'm sure Salty knows better than to chase a skunk. There probably aren't any on the island, anyway. How would they get here? Swim? Surely no one would deliberately import such an animal.''

"I'll ask Mouse. Want him to go fetch the pups? Mr. St. Bride might want one of 'em, he ain't got no dog."

"Mr. St. Bride won't lay a finger on one of our puppies," Dora declared. "Besides, I think they're probably too young to move. Couldn't we just let them stay where they are for a few more days?"

Lula shrugged, as if it didn't matter to her, one way or another. "I suppose I could walk over every day and take Salty something to eat. Is there any of that stew left from yesterday?"

Shortly after that, Lula strolled down the road, a pail of water in one hand, a shawl over her shoulder despite the midsummer heat, and a china bowl of yesterday's cold ham stew. The other two women, who were shelling nuts for the molasses cakes, gazed after her through the kitchen window.

"Lawsy, I never seen nobody change so much in all my born days. First time I laid eyes on her she was a-waitin' for the boat to load up, an' I thought to myself, that there is one highfalutin woman! First time she started to talk I couldn't even make out what she was asayin'."

Dora got out a board and a knife and began chopping the walnuts. Thinking of all the nut cakes she had eaten without giving a single thought to the work involved in producing them, she was about to ask how Mattie had learned to bake when someone rapped on the front door facing.

"It's open," she called out, dusting her hands off in her apron.

Her apron... The last time she had worn anything resembling an apron, she'd been eight years old and Miss Daisy, her old nanny, had dressed her in a clean, starched pinafore every morning, hoping her dress would survive until lunchtime.

Then, too, whenever anyone rang the front doorbell in those days there had always been someone nearby to answer it. A maid or her father's man-of-all-work.

"Is Grey here?" James Calvin inquired, halting just inside the messy kitchen. "Something sure smells good. You fixing to bake up another batch of those whatchamacallits?" The kitchen was still redolent of yesterday's resurrected raisin bread.

"Today's special will be molasses cake," Dora corrected. "They'll be ready by suppertime. We'll have to charge a—a penny a slice, to pay for the ingredients."

Mattie nodded. "The 'gredients costs something awful. I don't 'member things costin' that much back home."

"Grey's not here," Dora said. "I haven't seen him."

"I ain't seed 'im neither," Mattie said earnestly. "He might've gone to church to see our new dogs."

James Calvin sent her an odd look. "He probably went clamming. I'll walk down to the landing, see if his skiff is gone. Smells real good, ladies."

"He's really quite nice once he gets over his shyness," Dora said when they were alone again.

"I reckon."

"Lula says you two don't strike sparks. Is that what you were hoping for, Mattie?"

"I was just ahopin' to find me a place where my uncle Blackie couldn't get to me. Once Ma an' the rest moved in with him after Pa died, there weren't no place to hide.''

Oh, God. Dora closed her eyes momentarily. To think she'd once felt sorry for herself. ''You won't ever have to worry again, not as long as I'm here. You'll always have a place with me. And Mattie—if you don't want to marry anyone, you don't have to.''

''Mr. St. Bride, he's awantin' me to marry James Calvin. It's why he let me come out here to his island.''

''You leave Grey St. Bride to me,'' said Dora, at her most militant.

Chapter Fifteen

Three days later, with the help of James Calvin and Almy Dole, a new sign was hung beside the bakery sign. This one, suitably embellished with a teacup over which hung billows of steam, announced Mrs. Meeks's Tearoom. The boardinghouse would have to wait.

Hoping she hadn't acted too hastily, Dora had deliberately timed the hanging of the new sign for when Grey had gone across the sound. He still hadn't forgiven her for opening the bakery. The last thing she needed was a reminder that this newest venture just might be a speck premature. Enthusiasm, she was discovering, was no substitute for careful planning.

It was Lula, serving in her appointed capacity as bookkeeper who, less than two hours ago, had pointed out that tea was even dearer than cinnamon. By that time the new sign was painted, the paint already dry to touch. "So far we've taken in a total of only ninety-seven cents. How is your credit?"

"Oh, dear. Do we have to think about that now? Can't we just spend the first day admiring our new sign and enjoying our expectations?"

"I'm afraid I never learned to look on the bright side. Our initial goal was to open a boardinghouse for St. Bride's women. But first we have to find some means of supplying bed and board, agreed?" Without waiting for corroboration, she went on. "We can't open a proper bakery until we can afford to buy a larger stove."

"But as long as we serve Mattie's cakes one slice at a time," Dora reasoned, "we should be able to keep up with demand. There aren't that many men on the island."

"And what will you serve to drink? You might as well know, I'm personally opposed to rum houses and gin mills. We could serve pitchers of beer or ale, but we don't have enough blackberry wine left."

"Tea?" suggested Dora, who was feeling somewhat extinguished by then. "It's supposed to be a tearoom, after all."

"Tea is rather prohibitive. If we spend all our proceeds on supplies, we'll never be able to buy beds and bedding."

"I don't know nothin' 'bout no pribitive tea, but we got us all the yaupon a body could want." It was Mattie, forced to practice country economies all her young life, who came up with the answer.

"Yaupon tea?" murmured Dora. "But of course." Dora had heard of the green tea brewed from the leaves of a local shrub. Back in the fall of 1774 the ladies of Edenton, resolving not to drink tea imported from England or wear British cloth, had dumped their oolong and darjeeling into the Chowan River in protest.

A few years later, the ladies of Boston had done the same thing. She didn't know what the Massachusetts women had sipped as a substitute, but it probably had not been yaupon tea.

Still, one made do with what was at hand. "Mattie, have you ever actually tasted it?"

"That I have. With milk and sugar, it's good as anything, only you don't want to boil it up too strong, else you'll spend the day in the privy."

"Heaven forfend," murmured Lula, obviously stepping into the role of a starchy society matron.

Leaning forward, Dora inquired eagerly, "Do you know where we can purchase enough to last us until we can afford the real thing?"

"I don't know 'bout purchasin,' but Mouse, he chops and sweats it in a big ol' barrel out behind his house. If 'n I ask 'im, he'll sweat us some."

Lula did that thing with her eyes that proclaimed she had truly landed among the provincials.

Dora bit back a smile. The thought of drawing Grey's majordomo into their affairs was irresistible. As for the tea itself, while she had never actually tasted it, she did know it was widely used by those who couldn't afford the expensive imported varieties. And at the moment, the three of them surely fell into that category.

Another thought struck her. "You don't suppose Mouse will get in trouble for helping us, do you? St. Bride might not like it."

"Mouse, he ain't skeert o' nobody, not even Mr. St. Bride."

"Oh?" murmured Lula.

Hmm, thought Dora, wondering if the large, fierce-looking man knew what a champion he had in little Mattie Blades.

* * *

Grey had arrived from his business meeting in Oriental late that morning and stayed on at the waterfront to oversee the building of drying racks in the new lumber shed. He was hot, tired and out of sorts, thanks to the third week of torrid heat and high humidity. Not to mention eight missing hogsheads of turpentine that were listed on the *Hamlet*'s manifesto and scheduled to go out on the schooner *Jamaican Lady*.

Came of hiring clerks that could barely read, much less count, he thought irritably, glancing through the letters that had come in on today's mail boat. Two for him, one for John Luther and one for...Miss Sutton?

Mrs. Sutton. That is, Mrs. Meeks. Now, who the devil would be writing to Dora after all these months?

Not your business, St. Bride.

Tiredly he mounted the rawboned gelding that had trotted over to the warehouse at his three-note whistle. Normally he would have walked home rather than wait for Sam to show up, but the horse had been grazing nearby, and besides, he needed attention.

What Grey needed most at the moment was a long, hard swim in rough, cold waters of the Atlantic. Unfortunately, the sea was as calm as a bathtub, the water lukewarm from days of relentless heat. A hard nor'easter would go a long way toward clearing the air and blowing away the hoards of bloodthirsty mosquitoes, but from the looks of the sky, it would be days, possibly weeks, before they were in for a change.

He was scowling by the time he passed the Meeks place, even before he saw the new sign. Seeing it, with the tiny teacup under a curlicue of painted steam, he halted, frowned and then began to swear.

What the devil had happened to the bakery? Three days in business and she'd gone under?

"Hell, Sam," he addressed his island-bred mount, "I could have told her it wasn't going to work."

Had told her, in fact. Hardworking watermen weren't interested in petits fours and fancy tarts. By the time a man had fished half a dozen fifty-yard nets and then come in and either sold or salted down his catch, the last thing he wanted was "lady food."

By the time an inlet pilot had waited six hours for the tide to turn, then shepherded a heavy laden schooner past the ever-shifting shoals into safe waters, all he wanted was a solid meat-and-potato meal and a bed.

"Mrs. Meeks's *Tearoom?*" he read aloud. What the devil did that fool woman think she was doing? "Dora!" he shouted, even as he was sliding down off the back of his mount. "You come out here and explain yourself, madam!"

She met him at the front door, all wide-eyed innocence. "Did you call me?" she inquired sweetly.

Grey opened the gate, swinging it so hard it slammed against the new sign and bounced back. Striding across the sandy yard to the porch, he took the three steps in a single leap, not stopping until his big, sandy boots were touching the tips of her neat tan shoes.

Dora tried to back away, but having shut the door behind her, there was no room to escape. When she tried to sidle past him, he brought his hands down on her shoulders.

"Not so fast, young woman, this time you've outsmarted yourself." Sweat glistened on his tanned, angular face.

Dora stared, torn between fear and fascination. Men with dimpled chins had no business being so ornery. The irreverent thought lodged in her mind, blocking out any shred of common sense she might have possessed.

"Now that you've played your little games, don't you think it's about time you came to your senses?"

She opened her mouth to beg his pardon—her standard face-saving response when she couldn't come up with a sensible reply and needed time to think.

And then she clamped it shut again. They had had this conversation too many times in the past.

His accusations, followed by her begging his pardon.

His demands, exacting the same inane response.

From the way he was glaring at her now, if she said it one more time he just might wring her neck.

Grey counted silently to ten, and then to twenty, the letter addressed to Dora in a childish hand folded and crammed into his hip pocket and forgotten, along with his own.

God, she was something, he marveled silently. His fingers tightened involuntarily on the fine bones of her shoulders. Touching her had been a mistake. Bringing her out to the island in the first place had been an even bigger mistake. He should have known from her response to his advertisement that she wasn't the kind of woman he needed.

She's precisely the kind of woman you need, St. Bride. How long are you going to go on lying to yourself?

The truth was, he had come to admire her grit. Hell, he even liked her, which didn't make any sense at all, considering that since the day she'd first staggered off the *Bessie Mae & Annie,* practically every move he'd made had turned out to be a mistake. A reasonably intelligent man, he had always relied on careful planning, followed by equally careful execution. Setting standards and sticking to them regardless of personal feelings, he'd learned early on, was the only way to assure success. Now his matches weren't working out—his books were a mess. Even Mouse seemed distracted.

What the devil had gone wrong?

"Would you please take your hands off me?" she said quietly. *Too* quietly. Behind the mossy green depths of her eyes, anger flashed like heat lightning.

"Not until we come to an agreement."

"I agree that you're trespassing on private property." Her bosom was heaving as she tried to escape his grip.

Not wanting to scare her, Grey started to loosen his grip. He tightened it again when he realized that, hell yes, he wanted to frighten her—wanted to scare her into giving up this foolish scheme and going back to wherever she came from so that he could get a decent night's sleep for a change.

The bakery notion had been bad enough. The damned tearoom thing was the last straw! "I'm doubling my first offer. Time's up." She smelled of cinnamon, vanilla and warm, sweet woman. Reacting to his heightened imagination, his groin began to stir.

He cleared his throat. "As I was saying, I'm willing to double my offer because I need Emmet's house."

"My house," she interrupted.

Ignoring her, he said, "That should provide more than enough to buy yourself a modest house on the mainland, with some leftover to invest. If you're careful, the proceeds should support you until you find yourself another husband.''

Once again, the thought of her marrying another man made his belly twist painfully. He told himself it was only relief. Relief that he would no longer have to fear walking past her house or glancing out his own windows and catching a glimpse of her. The dratted female was not only affecting his judgment, she was putting entirely too many misguided ideas in his head.

His carefully constructed plan for establishing a self-perpetuating settlement was already far behind schedule. It sure as hell didn't include any tempting, troublesome female who looked good enough to eat and would probably poison him if he so much as tasted her lips.

Standing toe to toe, with his hands still curved over her shoulders, Grey stared at her mouth. At her lips.

''Dora, Dora—you're a witch,'' he groaned just before his mouth came down on hers.

Startled, Dora opened her mouth and collided with his hard, hot lips. She could feel the shape of them, the short, upper curve, the soft firmness of the lower one, even as the taste of him seeped into her senses.

For endless moments she allowed herself to savor the hardness of his body, the strength of his arms around her, the warmth of his hands on her back, in her hair, on her buttocks. Senses she hadn't even known she possessed were suddenly inflamed by the taste of his mouth, the feel of his masculine body stirring eagerly against her own.

Gasping, she wrenched herself away and stared at him, her lips still moist from his kiss. ''How da—'' she gasped fiercely, when he cut her off.

''I know, I know. How dare I?'' He was breathing

hard, staring at her as if he'd never before seen a woman. "I'll tell you how I dare. I dare because nothing I've said or done all summer long—not one damned thing—has managed to get through that stubborn streak of yours. Every single, solitary move you've made since the first day you first set foot on my island has been a deliberate attempt to defy me."

Her own breathing almost back under control, Dora opened her mouth to respond, but he held up a staying hand. She stared at it—at the square, hard palm, the long, straight fingers. At the lines crossing his leathery flesh.

"Oh, look—it says right here that this one's your headline, Dora, and this is your lifeline, and this one right here is your heartline. That's the same as a loveline…and—oh, my gracious, look at this awful mark that cuts right through it, Dora! According to the book, that means before you meet your true love, you'll meet a false one. Now, you tell my fortune, all right? And make it exciting—and then Selma can tell Missy's."

"Dora?"

She blinked. "What? I mean, no thank you, I don't care to sell my house."

"Dammit, madam, will you just use your head for once?"

"I am. For the first time in my life, I'm in complete control of my life, and do you know what? I like it. I like it just fine. So no, thank you, you can keep your money. We'll be just fine."

He had kissed her. For the second time in her life, she'd been kissed by a man not because he loved her, but because he wanted something from her.

Stepping back, Grey planted his fists on his narrow

hips. Sun beat down overhead, causing sweat to spring out on his tanned face. "And what about when your two helpers are married? Do you think their husbands are going to let them get involved in any of your hare-brained notions?

"Well, as to that, I wouldn't count my chickens before they hatched," Dora snapped.

"What the devil does that mean?"

Her smile was as bland as tapioca pudding, despite the fact that every sense she possessed was still raw and quivering.

She forced herself to take a deep breath. "We'll be open for business tomorrow morning. At nine. You're welcome to come by, if you'd like a cup of tea and a slice of delicious molasses cake."

It was sheer, reckless pride that made her issue the invitation, but watching his face redden, his eyes grow dark as storm clouds, she felt a gloating satisfaction.

"Tomorrow morning, then," he said, his silken voice sliding over her nerves like a fingernail on a slate. "If I can fight my way through the crowd, ma-dam, I'll make a point of being here."

And with that, he turned and left, leaving Dora to wonder just which one of them had won the encounter, and which had lost.

Chapter Sixteen

By eight-thirty Dora was a quivering wreck. The first crisis had occurred at seven that morning when she realized there weren't enough dishes. With only three cups, one cracked mug and five plates in the house, Sal and Emmet had obviously not been given to entertaining friends for dinner.

"The parsonage," said Lula. "I'll see if there's something there we can borrow when I take Salty her breakfast. I'm sure the minister wouldn't mind."

"If you can find more than a single plate and a cup there, I'd be very much surprised," Dora said dryly. "I think he dines at Castle St. Bride when he's in residence."

"Mouse might kin spare some dishes. He's got a whole stack o' real pretty plates he don't never use."

"When were you in his kitchen?" Dora asked curiously.

"Yesterday when he gimme the tea."

Mouse, with or without his employer's permission, had given Mattie a large tin of cured leaves. They didn't resemble any tea either Lula or Dora had ever seen but, simmered according to Mattie's instructions, it made a quite acceptable brew.

"I'll set out a tin o' 'vaporated milk and some sugar," the young redhead said now. "Pity we ain't got no more chairs. I kin run next door and see if Mouse—"

"No!" Lula and Dora spoke together. They were already far too indebted to the St. Bride household. Perhaps once they got established she could hire James or Almy to build a few benches.

Grey had promised, or rather threatened, to be here for the grand opening. It was going to be embarrassing enough for him to find her serving cake on his china plates, without having him find half his furniture crammed into her small parlor.

Really, there was a bit more to this business of operating a tearoom than any of them had considered. The next time she undertook a new business, Dora vowed to plan it all out on paper first. The boardinghouse, for instance. Before she hung up another sign she intended to list everything she would need to start, right down to the last pillow slip. And then she would work out how much it would all cost, how many slices of cake and cups of tea it would take to pay for everything, and what those cost her, and how long before they could expect to recoup their expenses and start making a profit.

Unfortunately, with all their widely varied backgrounds, none of them had had any experience at starting a business. It was beginning to show.

"If the next shipment of brides happens to include one with bookkeeping skills, I vote we kidnap her before St. Bride can marry her off to one of his ruffians."

Lula adjusted the newly hung curtains, frowned and then shrugged.

"They're not really ruffians," Dora admonished. "They're just not accustomed to being around ladies. Once they clean up a bit and get over being shy, they're really quite nice."

"Oh, I know, I know. It's just—" She touched her belly, where a slight swelling was already visible.

They all knew by now of Lula's dilemma. Needing a father for her baby, she couldn't bring herself to marry a man she didn't like, and refused to marry one she did like, considering it unfair to burden him with another man's child.

Personally, Dora thought that, given a chance, either James Calvin or Clarence would make an excellent father and an understanding husband. It weren't as though this was the typical small town, where the faintest whiff of scandal could make a woman's life not worth living. The people of St. Brides might be rough, but they took care of their own.

"I'm sure it will all work out in the end," Dora murmured. Meaning Lula's dilemma, her own need to hold on to what she had and establish her right to stay. "Look at how far we've come in such a short while."

"Yes, well…the curtain is about to open on the third act," Lula reminded her.

Nine o'clock came and went. The two cakes were sliced, with two more in the oven baking. A pot of yaupon tea simmered on the back of the stove. Each of the three women had paced back and forth from kitchen to the front windows at least a dozen times.

"I wonder where everyone is. I know James Calvin and Almy know about it—and Clarence, of course. Do you think we should have put up a poster down at the warehouse to let all the others know?''

''I reckon they already know. Mouse said if a green snake farts down at Shallow Gut, ever'body at North End knows what he et fer dinner.''

Dora and Lula turned to stare at her. Lula rolled her eyes again. ''I suppose they'll come out of curiosity, if nothing more,'' she said.

Dora sighed and pulled aside the curtains again to peer out at the empty road that led directly from the landing to the large house on the ridge. She left them open, doing her best to arrange them so that they didn't droop in the middle. After using one of Sal's old skirts to make curtains for the kitchen and her own bedroom, it had been a simple enough task to split one of her petticoats into four sections and string them across the two parlor windows. It had been more of a challenge to make them look like anything but what they were. A ladies' ruffled, eyelet-embroidered batiste undergarment.

She'd have done better to use her rose taffeta, as the underarms and the waist were irreparably stained anyway. But somehow, rose taffeta curtains seemed out of character in the small, whitewashed parlor, with its simple furnishings.

''Here comes Mouse!'' Mattie whispered fiercely. ''Do I look awright? My nose ain't got too much flour on it, has it?''

When it occurred to Dora that the traces of flour had been an effort to disguise her freckles and not the results of mixing up two more cakes, she looked at Lula, who grabbed the younger woman by the arm and said, ''Come with me.''

By the time Mouse's heavy tread could be heard on

the front porch, Mattie was back, blushing fiercely under a dusting of dark rachel face powder and roughly a thousand freckles.

"I come fer a piece o'yer cake, Mattie Lou. I got money."

Mattie, for once at a loss for words, looked first at Dora, then at Lula. "Kin he have some?"

"Well of course. Welcome, Mr—er, Mouse. As it happens, you're our very first customer."

"They'll be along directly. Most ever'body works right up till dinnertime."

Mattie proudly served their first customer a slice of cake on one of the rose-sprigged china plates he'd lent them, while Lula brought him a mug of the green tea, which by now had turned bitter and black. Dora stepped outside and beat her fist softly against the milled porch support.

How *could* she have overlooked such an obvious thing? Of *course* all the men were working! It was what men *did*. Not men like Henry or her father, of course, but real men. The kind who didn't rely on rich wives or wealthy ancestors or pie-in-the-sky schemes to support them.

Besides, men preferred taverns to tearooms. Tearooms were places where women gathered to gossip and speculate on who was seeing whom, and who was in an interesting condition, all the while indulging in fancy sweets and showing off their newest outfit.

A tearoom. I'd have done better to open a tavern.

Every man on the island worked from sunup to sundown at least six days a week. After long hard hours spent fishing, or piloting ships, or loading and unloading cargo, they usually gathered in either the transient barracks or one of the rough one-room huts up at

North End to drink ale and play cards and smoke their smelly pipes. Emmet had described it all to her, claiming he'd lived the same way before St. Bride had found him a wife and built him a house.

And those men were to be her customers?

Mouse was different. He worked as a housekeeper. Besides, he hardly counted as a customer. As he'd been such a great help, they could hardly charge him for a slice of cake and a cup of his own tea.

And oh, God, there came St. Bride.

Dora slipped inside, took a moment to gather her composure, then turned brightly to the massive one-eyed gentleman who was basking under the attention of the two women as if he were accustomed to such treatment.

Consider it practice, Dora told herself. They were practicing for when the rush commenced. Meanwhile, Grey was almost at the gate. "I believe I'll go see about the dogs," she said brightly. "You obviously don't need me at the moment."

Making a hasty exit through the back door, she waited until she heard Grey's boots on the front porch before slipping through the back gate between the chicken pen and the graveyard and hurrying across the stretch of sand to the church. By the time she arrived, she'd collected scores of itchy mosquito bites and a skirt tail full of the pesky sandspurs.

"Salty, are you—omigod, you scared me to death!"

Reverend Almond Filmore rose up on his knees behind the nautical altar and nodded gravely. "Good morning, ma'am," he said in his slow, deliberate manner. "I s-suppose these are yours, s-seeing as they belong to Emmet's dog."

"I didn't realize you were here."

"I came in ahead of schedule, thinking I might be needed to perform a marriage or two. Clarence didn't mention s-setting a date, but then he was busy. Is Miss Lula—that is, Mrs. Russart—s-still here?"

So Dora sat down on the floor beside the tall, solemn-faced minister. Gathering two of the pups on her lap, she soon found herself telling him all the news. How they'd intended to open a boardinghouse for St. Bride's women, but discovered that before they could do that they would need to buy beds. And about the bakery that was supposed to buy the beds, and how it had failed when they'd discovered the oven was too small, and how that had evolved into a tearoom. "This is our first day of business," she said, attempting to make it sound like more of a triumph than it was turning out to be. "Mattie is the cook—at least, until I get better at it—and Lula is the bookkeeper. It's her job to keep track of all our expenditures and balance them against our, uh—intakings."

Which so far, were nil.

It occurred to her as they sat and played with the puppies that, for a man with so little to say and that little taking an interminable time, the minister's eyes were quite lively. It occurred to her, too, that he might even have a lively mind if only one had the patience to explore it.

"Well," she said finally when the silence had drawn out for several minutes, "I suppose we'd better see about moving Salty and her family home, else these babies are going to take over your church."

For the first time she noticed the crocheted doily draped over the altar. It could hardly disguise the fact that the thing was an uprooted helm, not a real altar, but it helped. Someone had placed buckets of wild fern on either side. Despite the fact that the fern was turning brown and the buckets were somewhat rusted, it lent a bit of relief from the room's stark rawness.

"I see you've added a few decorative touches," she observed.

While the minister gathered his thoughts to reply, she scooped up two of the pups, leaving him to take the other pair, and led the way outside, leaving Salty to follow along behind.

As luck would have it, Grey emerged from the front door of her house just as they opened the gate. Dora had hoped he'd be gone by now.

"Almond," he acknowledged.

"Morning, Grey. I thought you might be needing me, s-so I came a few days early."

Grey reached out and lifted one of the pups from Dora's arms, tipping it belly-up to determine the sex.

"Three ladies and a gentleman," said Almond Filmore, sounding amused.

"Well, hell," Grey replied plaintively.

"We settled on names. They're Romeo, Juliet, Othello and Ophelia," Dora announced, and if it sounded more like a challenge, so be it. Despite a few brief truces, war had long since been openly declared between the island's only two landowners. "I'll see that they don't stray off my property until I can find them new homes."

"You do that, madam. Word of advice—"

Dora held her breath. If he tripled his offer, she would be forced to consider it, but only if the sum was large enough so that she could take Lula and Mattie with her. They would simply have to find another place to start over. Once the baby came they could decide on what their next move would be.

"I'm listening," she said warily.

"Your figs are beginning to ripen. You'll have to get up before the mockingbirds if you want to claim your share."

And with that he strolled on down the road toward the warehouse. Staring after him, her mouth agape, Dora thought of all the things she might have said. As even the mildest comment that came to mind would have shocked the poor minister, she held her tongue.

Mouse was still there. He was nailing up curtain rods to replace the string she had stretched across the windows to hold her petticoat curtains. Mattie and Lula made over the pups, cooing and cuddling them while Dora washed her hands and served the minister the last slice of one of the two cakes. "I'll make coffee. The tea looks strong enough to tan leather."

"It don't do to drink it too strong, else it'll get yer bowels into an uproar," said Mouse. Mattie, holding a pup in one hand, a nail in the other, gazed up at him with a worshipful expression, and Dora thought, *Oh, for heaven's sake, what next?*

"Our Mattie is obviously smitten," Lula said quietly a few moments later in the kitchen. "No wonder James didn't strike any sparks. The two men are as different as night and day."

Dora shook her head slowly as she picked up cake crumbs with her finger and licked them off. "I don't know how Mouse feels, but whatever happens is bound to complicate matters. Grey will find a way to blame me if Mouse defects to set up housekeeping with a wife of his own."

"It won't happen, not if your St. Bride didn't chisel it in stone first. Can't you just see him in the role of

Moses, coming down off the ridge with his arms full of laws?''

Dora gasped, pretending to be shocked. ''Lula, hush your mouth! That's blasphemy...I think.''

Lula lifted her artfully enhanced brows, and Dora grinned. ''I think that's Captain Dozier's boat coming in now,'' the older woman observed, peering through the kitchen window. ''I hope he's brought us more flour and the chickens you ordered. Mouse tells me he has a way to make eggs last for an entire year, but I'm not sure I'd care to try it.''

The *Bessie Mae & Annie* brought a fifty-pound sack of flour, six laying hens and a woman who demanded to know the moment she stepped ashore where she could find Miss Dora Sutton.

It was Clarence who answered her. ''If you mean Dora Meeks, it's that house up there on your right. The one with a picket fence around it.''

Nodding briskly, the newcomer set out, carrying a small pasteboard suitcase.

Clarence hurried after her. ''I'd better show you the way.''

''I know a picket fence when I see one.'' The small, rather plain young woman, wearing a long-sleeved black serge dress that was unsuitable for both the place and the season, didn't so much as pause.

''My name is Clarence Burrus,'' the warehouseman said, and waited for her to introduce herself. He was having trouble keeping up with her, despite his long legs and her short ones.

''She's married to a man named Meeks? Is he a good man? He don't beat her, does he?''

Hurrying beside her, Clarence reached for her suitcase, and she allowed him to take it. "Uh, yes, she was—that is, he was. I'm pretty sure he didn't beat her. St. Bride don't hold with that kind of thing, but he's dead now, you know."

Bertola Perkins came to a complete halt, turning to fix him with a suspicious look. "St. Bride's dead?"

"Emmet Meeks."

"Oh. She's already *widowed?* Lawsamercy, it's a good thing I took a notion to come. She'll be needing me now more than ever."

By that time they had almost arrived. The reunion took place on the front porch in full view of Clarence, the preacher, Mouse and the other two women. Dora's eyes widened, then she flew outside, both arms held out, to embrace the black-clad woman.

"Oh, Bertie, is it really you?" Trust Bertie to travel in something that wouldn't show dirt. "Are you all right? Has something happened? You never answered my letter! Oh, come inside where we can talk!"

Turning, Dora confronted the curious onlookers. Lifting her chin, she said, "I'd like for you all to meet Miss Bertola Perkins. She's my—my best friend in all the world."

"I'm her maid, is what I am," the small, brown-haired young woman declared. "She never wrote, and—"

"I did, too!" Dora exclaimed.

"I took to feeling she was needing me, so I come out to see. I can go back on the same boat. I got passage money."

"You'll do nothing of the kind! Come inside, let me take your suitcase." Clarence had already set it on the porch, but now, followed by the entire contingent, he picked it up and carried it inside. Mouse began clearing away the dishes. Mattie reached up to steady her top-heavy pompadour and followed him out to the kitchen, and then out the back door.

Dora said, "Are you hungry? We have some delicious cake, and some dreadful tea. I could make fresh coffee, though."

The small maid sat, then bounced back up again. "Now don't you go thinking you're going to wait on me, Miss Dora. You set and I'll fetch."

In the end, they all sat, even Clarence, who allowed himself to be served tea and cake. After adding three spoonfuls of sugar and the last of the tinned milk to the wicked brew, he pronounced it tolerable.

All the while, his gaze never left Bertola. Amused, Dora tried to see her erstwhile maid through a man's eyes, but what she saw was simply Bertie. A woman who had been a mere child when she had first come to work at Sutton Hall, starting as a scullery maid. Neat as a pin, perky as a sparrow, Bertie had proved her true friendship by staying on without the least expectation of being paid, standing by her when everyone else in town turned against her.

"Bertie, what on earth possessed you to come out here? Don't tell me you're hoping to find a husband?"

Bertie plucked a chunk of walnut from the cake and nibbled it, then glanced around self-consciously. "That I'm not, Miss Dora. Last thing in the world I want is a man. After you left I went to work for old lady Pritchard, but she up an' died on me, so I moved over across the river near Blounts Creek and worked for two nice old ladies. I wrote to tell you, but I never heard back, so I decided to come out and see for myself if you were all right."

Dora reached over and covered her hand, chaotic

thoughts tumbling through her mind. How many times had she wondered about Bertie, fearing she might not readily find work considering the way she had stood up for her against some of the most powerful people in town. As it turned out, she had fared well. The move probably explained why Dora's letter had never reached her, but it didn't explain why Bertie's letter had gone astray.

After a while, Clarence interrupted to say he was leaving. "If there's anything I can do for you, Miz Meeks—Miss Perkins, just send word."

"You can find us some customers," Lula said dryly. "Otherwise the show will close on opening night. So far we've been open to the public more than half a day and we're twenty-seven cents richer. If you don't need me, Dora, I think I'll go over to the church to see if the reverend needs any advice on how to make his chapel look like St. Peter's Cathedral. Did I tell you how I once helped transform one end of a cow barn into a Scottish castle?"

Once the house was empty, Dora and Bertie settled in to catch up on all the news.

"Your hair needs a good thinning, Miss Dora. This salt air don't help curly hair like yours a-tall."

"I know, I know, but tell me about Selma and Missy and the others first. Do they still think I—that is, do they still believe those awful stories?"

Bertie toyed with her spoon, which Dora took as an affirmative reply. "Oh, well. I don't suppose it matters, as I'd never go back anyway." Then, brightening, she said, "I hope you plan to stay, because we need you. We have all sorts of plans—as I said in my letter, we—oh, but you never received it. Well, you're here now, so let me tell you about the boardinghouse we're planning to open as soon as we earn enough money to buy beds and bedding."

Bertie listened, asked a few pertinent questions, then said, "I wrote you what happened to Polly, but you never got it. Miss Selma turned her out." Polly, Dora recalled, had been the name of her friend Selma's personal maid. "Claimed she stole from her."

"Did she?"

Bertie shrugged. "I saw her wearing a necklace once that looked an awful lot like that green one of Miss Selma's. Ask me, the two of 'em deserves one another."

Dora could only nod. She knew for a fact that Polly was a spiteful little gossipmonger. As much as it hurt to admit it, mistress and maid were two of a kind. "Is there still talk?"

"No'm, not so much now, not since Miz Kate bought herself one of them newfangled automobiles an' run over Mr. George. Broke both his legs, made him madder'n a wet hen. Ask me, them things is the devil's own handiwork."

Dora was tempted to laugh until she remembered that no matter how many new scandals erupted, she would have only to show her face on Front Street again to set every tongue in town to flapping.

"I can't ever go back," she murmured, staring unseeingly through the open back door at the leaning chicken house, the row of fig trees and the twin tombstones beyond. Be it ever so modest, it was hers alone.

"No'm, I reckon you can't. What kind of work can I do in a place like this? Reckon I could make me a living here?"

"You're sure you don't want a husband? I have an idea you're just the kind of woman St. Bride had in mind when he advertised for women to come out with a view to settling on his island.''

Bertie snorted. "Marry one of them grisly-looking fellows I saw hanging around the docks? No siree, I've got better sense than that."

"Honestly, they're quite nice—at least the ones I've met so far. What about Clarence? Surely you can't call him grisly. I'm sure he shaves every single morning."

"Humph! As if I'd give the time o'day to any man with red hair and big ears."

Dora laughed aloud, then reached across the table and covered Bertie's small, callused hand with her own small, equally callused palm. "I'm so glad you've come. There aren't any other women here except those in my house. We'll be crowded until I can afford to furnish the attic, but if you don't mind making do with a pallet—"

"I've slept on worse. Lawsy, you're looking good, Miss Dora—except for your hair and your hands and them freckles on your nose."

"I'm afraid the freckles are here to stay. The way the sun bounces off the water, there's no escaping it. Now, let's look at you." Dora leaned back and studied the small woman in black, a teasing light in her eyes. "If we're not careful, Grey will have your name on one of his lists the minute he finds out you're here."

Chapter Seventeen

At half past four, Grey, his head aching from long hours spent toting up the accounts with various shippers and catching up on his correspondence, capped his ink bottle and closed his myriad ledgers. He'd been holed up too long, far longer than he'd intended.

Standing, he stretched his back, fisted his hands and raised them over his head, groaning as stiff muscles protested.

What he needed was exercise. Fresh air. With any luck the storm that had been racing up from the Caribbean for days would sheer off and miss them entirely. It had damned well better—from all reports, it was a bruiser, gathering strength with every passing day.

At any rate, they were in for some rain—the air already had that green smell. If he didn't waste time he might get in a swim and a good ride along the beach. The tide was out, but from the sound of it, it was already roughening up some. Big combers cracking like cannonades.

Good, he thought with satisfaction. There was nothing like pitting his strength against a stormy sea to clear a man's head. Stepping outside his office, he closed the door and paused for a moment, listening to the familiar sounds of his well-run household.

It was one of the few things that was running smoothly, he told himself ruefully. Nothing he had attempted over the summer so far—not one blamed thing—had gone according to plan. His once neat lists had so many lines drawn through them they were all but useless. It was enough to make a man feel downright discouraged.

Some forty-five minutes later, feeling physically invigorated by pitting his strength against the strong currents, if no closer to an answer to his most pressing problem, Grey was back in his office. Moving from window to window, he studied the signs, taking note of the mountainous seas, the darkening sky, the whitecaps out on the sound.

The mail boat was on her way in, making one last run. Dozier had already come and gone. Thank God he was not expecting another woman. As if any woman with a grain of sense would come out at a time like this. Even the gulls had disappeared.

It was coming, all right. Whether they got the full force or just the fringes, they were in for a bad blow. By now every man would be taking in his nets, hauling up his boats or headed offshore to anchor, drop sail and ride it out. Anything that could blow or float off would be secured. They all knew the drill. Once the tide started rising, they would all head for high ground. On St. Brides Island, that meant his house. Mouse would have his work cut out to feed them all. Thank God Dozier had brought supplies.

Grey had no doubts as to the security of his own

household. He and Mouse could batten down in less time than it took to tell about it, but Dora was another matter. She didn't strike him as the type to stand around wringing her hands, but women were...

Hell, they were women.

There was a reason why he insisted on accepting only mature, sensible women on his island. The other kind had to be taken care of. At a time like this, with a bad storm bearing down on them, the last thing he needed was a bunch of foolish screaming females hanging around his neck.

Removing the screen from his window, he leaned out to unhook the storm shutters and then paused to look down at the house at the foot of the ridge. There, he told himself, was his problem personified.

Dora Meeks.

Storm or no storm, the woman was at the root of every single thing that had gone wrong since the day she had first set foot on his island back in April. If it weren't for her meddling, both James Calvin and Clarence would be married now. Possibly even expecting the next generation of St. Bridians.

A boardinghouse. What the devil did they need with a boardinghouse? That implied transients, which was the very thing he was trying to overcome. Other than the mullet fishermen who came out for a few weeks each season, transients weren't welcome.

One of the first things he'd done when he'd taken over from his father was to destroy the old shacks around Shallow Gut and build a sound barracks up at North End, complete with an attached kitchen. The single men—and unfortunately, they were all still single—took turns with the cooking.

So now they had a bakery, he thought, annoyed.

What the devil did they need with a bakery? Not a man among them didn't know how to mix salt, corn-meal and water and fry it in bacon grease on top of a stove. Granted, it wasn't as tasty as Mouse's spoon bread or those raisin cakes he'd made the other day, but Grey hadn't heard any complaints. Not many, at any rate. No more than the usual grumbling.

And a tearoom? The woman had flat out lost her mind!

They fared well enough, the men of St. Brides. He had listed the names of the twelve most stable men, those he deemed most likely to settle down. On a sep-arate list, he placed the names and qualifications of the women who responded to his advertisements and noted the initials of the men they were more apt to suit.

A deliberate man, he never set off on any course without having a clear destination in mind. The mar-riage plan had been his crowning achievement. Granted, he might've snagged his keel on a shoal or two along the way. A few of the men had married, then followed their homesick brides back across the sound a few months later.

And then there'd been Sal, a perfect candidate, al-beit older than he would have liked. Sad for Emmet, but then, the old man had himself a comfortable home at a time in his life when he was no longer able to go out and work for a living. All in all, things had been going along just fine until Dora Sutton had sashayed off the boat, bedazzling every man at the landing and succeeded in working her spell on a poor grieving widower.

Not to mention on every other man on the island—himself included. Now, as the sole non-St. Bride landowner on his island, she was collecting his women as fast as they came ashore and turning them against him to the point where he didn't even know which of the men to ask to provide beds, much less where to put them.

What the devil was a man supposed to do?

How was he supposed to fight a woman who didn't even stand as high as his shoulders? Whose waist he could span with his two hands? A woman who looked him straight in the eye and defied him to defy her.

Grey sighed. And then he slammed shut the storm blinds, fastened them and glared at the lists he'd tacked to the wall. Lists that noted where each bride was coming from, the range of time when she could be expected to show up, her background, or as much of it as she cared to reveal, and the man she was intended for. Not a single match had gone according to plan since the day the Sutton woman had set foot on his island. Not one. His lists were so scratched up by now, they were all but useless.

Unfortunately, like a bad case of the ague, there wasn't much he could do but live with it. Wait it out. In clear sight of the house next door, where he could see her coming and going even at night once it got dark enough to light the lamps.

Curtains? Who the devil needed curtains in a place like this? Sal had never bothered with curtains. No decent woman needed curtains. All she had to do was blow out the lamp if she didn't want to be seen through her window.

"I need something to eat, that's my problem," he growled, raking aside the map he'd been working on that showed future improvements. Breakfast had been at sunup. He'd skipped dinner for a ride and a swim.

"Mouse!" he shouted through the open door of his office. "How about dishing up some of that turtle stew?"

And then, "Mouse?"

Silence.

Well, hell. The man he'd once rescued from wrongful imprisonment, nursed back to health and given the well-paid job of looking after his household had obviously deserted him. There's gratitude for you, Grey thought plaintively a few minutes later as he cut himself a slab of cheese, two thick slices of soda bread and poured a mug of cold coffee.

Hard on the heels of irritation came guilt as he thought about the years of quiet, competent service he'd been given in return. The hours of uncritical listening whenever Grey needed to sound out an idea before he set it into motion. Mouse was more than an employee, he was a good friend. If the man wanted a life of his own, he damned well deserved it.

What I really need, Grey told himself as he munched thoughtfully on the dry cheese sandwich, *is a trip to the nearest whorehouse.* When a man reached a point where he couldn't even think straight for lusting after a woman who persisted in driving him wild, it took more than racing along the beach and pitting himself against a strong surf to clear his mind.

As it happened, Mouse had gone to the landing to collect the supplies Captain Dozier had brought over and stayed while the mail boat warped alongside and dropped sail. Having loaded his handcart, he lingered to collect any mail for the island as it would likely be at least a week before the boat returned.

The woman who stepped daintily off the boat,

showing more ankle than was necessary, glanced around, her nose wrinkled as if she smelled old fish.

Which she probably did.

It was well-known that St. Bride paid passage for every bride who came out aboard the *Bessie Mae & Annie,* even though as sole owner, he wasn't obliged to pay to have his freight hauled. But as every man who had ever had dealings with him knew, St. Bride was a fair man. Never asked more of anyone that he did of himself. Far less, in fact.

This woman had come out on the mail boat. Was she a bride, or a stray? The woman who had come in earlier today had not been the one they had ordered, but a friend of Dora Meeks. Was this woman a friend of Dora's, too?

The men watched warily as, arms crossed over her meager bosom, foot tapping like a rattler giving warning, she looked them over, finally focusing on Almond Filmore, who had come to give Mouse a hand with the supplies. Eyeing the house on the crest of the dune, clearly the most impressive residence on the island, she asked, "Is that Mr. St. Bride's house?"

A bride, then. But whose? The men looked at each other nervously. She was a good-looking woman—not in Dora's class, but then, few women were.

It was Clarence who cleared his throat and replied, "Yes ma'am, but—"

"You can take me to him."

"Well, as to that…" Breathing a sigh of relief, the warehouseman saw Almond Filmore approaching to help haul supplies up to the ridge and summoned him over. "Ma'am, this is—"

Not waiting to be introduced, the woman turned and

frowned. "Are you St. Bride? I've come to see the man that's been sending off for women in the paper."

Fortunately, the reverend's mind was far quicker than his tongue. "No, ma'am, my name is Filmore. My f-f-friend here is Mouse. We'll be glad to escort you to Mr. St. Bride, though, if you'll just c-c-come with us."

Edging away, Mouse muttered, "I'd rather take my chances with a cottonmouth."

The reverend murmured something about the Lord's work.

The captain of the mail boat handed a canvas mail pouch to Clarence. "Don't know if Grey's going to want this one," he said, shaking his head. "She's got a tongue on her like a whipsaw. Looks to me like the stock over on the mainland's gone to seed."

Warily the minister took the young woman's arm as she stepped down off the dock. Mouse tied the cardboard suitcase on top of the cartload of cornmeal, flour, coffee, beans and hog meat and set off up the road, leaving the other two to follow behind.

"You mean I got to *walk?*" the woman squawked.

"It's just up the road."

She snorted impatiently. Sun glinted from her improbably blue-black hair and from the sparkling broach on her collar. "You say that's Mr. St. Bride's house?"

It was Mouse who replied. "Yes, ma'am. Built by his great-grandfather, added on to by every generation since. Stood through many a storm. We'll weather this one just fine."

"Is he married?"

"Grey? Oh, no, ma'am, not him. He's too busy."

Neither man saw the smile that spread across the

woman's narrow face. Or the look of determination that settled over her features.

It was Bertie, hanging out the daily laundry, who saw the threesome making their way up the ridge. She stared for a moment, then whispered, "Saints ha' mercy, that looks almost like—" Whirling away, she slammed inside, shouting for Miss Dora.

"What is it?" Dora asked breathlessly, emerging from the kitchen. "Did you find a snake?"

"That I did! It's Polly Clinkshaw, and she's coming right up the path, plain as day. What are we going to do? If she finds you here, her tongue won't quit wagging till the cows come home."

And just like that, Dora was plunged into the icy waters of the past. The pain of her father's death. The loss of her virtue.

The deliberate destruction of her reputation.

Carefully rolling down her sleeves and drying her hands on her skirt, Dora thought frantically. She could run, but on a barren island less than three miles long and half a mile across, how far could she go?

"Get inside, Bertie, let me handle this."

"That I won't. I'll tell her she's not wanted here and send her packing."

Lula emerged from inside, where she'd been taking up a pair of Emmet's trousers for the youngest boy of John Luther's. "What's going on?"

"We got us another woman coming," Bertie muttered grimly.

"What wretched timing. I didn't know anyone else was expected," Lula whispered.

"Expected or not, this one won't be staying, not if I have anything to do with it."

The three women hurried out to the road, unconsciously presenting a united front as the two men and a woman drew close. Polly Clinkshaw, hands on her hips, said, "Well, la-de-dah, look who we got here. They said this was where you come to when you disappeared." The statement was followed by a snort of laughter.

Bertie shoved herself in front of her former mistress. "What are you doing here, Polly?"

"Same as you are, I reckon. Pickings is getting slim over on the mainland."

Lula leaned closer to Dora, her eyes never leaving Polly Clinkshaw. "A friend of yours?" she inquired softly.

"Hardly." And to Selma's maid, Dora said. "This is a rather inconvenient time, Polly. As you can see, we're all busy getting ready for the storm."

"Good thing I come, then, ain't it? Where's this Mr. St. Bride all the women are talking about?"

"What women?"

"I got me a job up in Edenton last spring, right after Miss Selma got married. I heard all about these high-and-mighty St. Brides. There's some right there in town, and they say they're all rich as cream. They say the one that's been sending off for women is even handsomer than his brother that lives there to Edenton." She smirked and tossed her head. "Reckon I might as well aim high, long's I'm aiming."

Dora, her fingernails digging into her palms, prayed for patience. "Yes, well—another time would be much better. As you can see, things here are in something of a mess, but you might as well come inside, because this is where the women stay."

Both men breathed an audible sigh of relief. Almond nodded, and Mouse untied the suitcase and set it on onto the shell road, then grabbed the handles of his handcart and set out up the ridge.

Bertie was staring pointedly at the small glittering broach on the other woman's collar, and Lula looked from one to the other, as if wondering what her own part was in this unscripted farce.

"Shall we go inside out of the heat?" Lula had evidently decided on her role. It was that of hostess. At least it served to break the tension that had sizzled from the first moment between the two former maids.

Dora felt sick. Almost as if she'd eaten tainted meat. It had barely begun, this promising new life she'd found, and now it was over. Polly would fill Grey's ears with all the vicious rumors, and he would send her away.

She had proved herself—proved she was strong enough, and, as it turned out, far more capable than she would ever have suspected.

Mattie brought cold tea. Polly said, "Ain'cha got no ice?"

"If I had I wouldn't waste none of it in tea, I'd use it in the cool-house. Meat don't keep forever in weather like this, you know."

Mattie had obviously taken an instant aversion to the newcomer. Dora introduced the two women and then searched frantically for an excuse to disappear.

"You come a ways down in the world, ain't you, Miss Dora? This is a far cry from Sutton Hall."

Dora managed a murmur. Neither Lula nor Mattie uttered a sound. They were watching the woman as if she were a snake and they were trying to make up their minds whether or not she was venomous.

Dora, to her sorrow, knew just how venomous she could be. It had been Polly, with her mistress's help, who had taken the lead in spreading Henry's vicious falsehoods all over town. A word here, a word there, and before Dora had had the slightest clue, her reputation was in ruins.

Lula murmured, "Perhaps we should open up our own marriage bureau. The ladies and gentlemen could get acquainted over tea and cake right here in our parlor, and we could offer to provide refreshments for the wedding party. For a reasonable price, of course...."

Dora shook her head, a reluctant smile easing the lines of worry. "Lula Russart, you are utterly shameless."

"No, I'm not," the older woman declared. "I'm often ashamed of myself, but I cover it well."

Both women burst into laughter. Lula placed a hand over the slight swelling that had caused her to let out the seams of her three best skirts. "Well, of course, it's the perfect solution, only I don't think this one is going to suit St. Bride, do you?"

In less than ten minutes the enemy was at the gate.

"Dora! Where the devil are you, woman?"

Thunder rumbled, the screen door rattled in its frame, and just like fleeting shadows, Mattie and Lula melted silently away. Polly brightened until Bertie grabbed her by the arm and tugged her out onto the back porch.

"Ow! That hurt! Is that St. Bride? I come here to see him, not you!"

Dora braced herself to confront the man. "I'm right here. You don't have to yell the house down."

"Now there's an idea," said the grim-faced man filling the open doorway. Grey glanced around the deserted room and said, "Where are they?"

"If you're referring to Miss Perkins, she happens to be my guest, not one of your brides."

"And the other one?"

"Well, you should know. You sent for her, didn't you?"

Long moments passed. Grey closed his eyes and drew in a deep, steadying breath. "Could we please just drop the hostilities for a minute and sort things out? I know you'd like nothing better than to see lightning strike me where I stand, but—"

"I would prefer it not to happen in my house. I'm not sure all of us together could haul your body outside."

When a flash of lightning lit up the small room, followed closely by a blast of thunder that seemed to rattle the very rafters, Dora hugged herself and bit her lower lip.

Grey stared at her lip, remembering the way it had felt, the way she'd tasted for that one brief, wild moment. "Are you afraid of storms?" he asked, his voice betraying a long-dormant protective instinct.

"Not at all. I was just—startled."

"Here on the beach, thunder sounds closer than it is. Now, as to the women, Clarence said two came in earlier today."

They were still standing just inside the door. Dora, at her most militant, had crossed her arms over her bosom. Amused and irritated at the same time, Grey couldn't help but wonder what the woman was up to, as she was so obviously determined not to give an inch.

"You may interview Miss Clinkshaw here in my parlor, if you must. Shall we say five o'clock this evening? That's when the tearoom closes."

Grey nodded thoughtfully. "I see. Matched your

hours to the times when every man on the island would be hard at work, did you? Nice planning, Mrs. Meeks. I always say careful planning makes for easy work.''

Watching a slow flush creep up over her pale skin, he bit back the rest of what he'd been about to say. ''May I remind you that there's one hell of a big storm headed our way. Whether the women are friends of yours or brides of mine, they'll be sleeping under my roof tonight, just as you and the others will.''

Watching the stricken look darken her eyes, he thought, this is too much like shooting fish in a barrel. ''The rain bands have already started to come in.''

Her lips tightened. ''I seriously doubt if we'll melt.''

''Maybe I'm not willing to take the risk,'' he teased.

Her eyes darted toward the back door. She would far rather the two never meet, but under the circumstances, what choice did she have? ''Are you sure? About the storm, I mean?''

She was up to something, Grey thought, torn between disappointment and the odd sense of excitement he felt whenever he got into a battle of wits with this woman. ''Far be it from me to tell anyone what to do,'' he said piously.

''Good. Then you'll not mind if I ignore your request.''

''Dora,'' he said softly, wondering how long he was slated to go on fighting this woman. And losing. He'd taken one good look at her the day she'd arrived and known she was trouble. Nothing that had happened since then had changed his opinion.

Her shoulders sagged as she turned away. Opening the back door, she said, ''Polly? Mr. St. Bride is here.''

Chapter Eighteen

They waited in the kitchen while the interview was going on in the front room. Bertie was fit to be tied, wanting to pin the woman down and force her to confess that it had all been a pack of lies. Dora, feeling as if the Sword of Damocles was hanging over her head, said, "Bertie, we can't do that. You know how it started—I wasn't entirely blameless."

"Hush now, Miss Dora, I know what happened. That weren't your fault. And I know what was said, and it was all a pack of lies. Who better than me to know what kind of woman you are?"

"Yes, well…lies or not, there's nothing we can say now that won't make things worse. Lula knows—I've told her everything. Mattie, you might as well know, too. I lied about being a widow when I came out here. I wasn't—I'd never been married. The trouble is, if I admit I lied then, why should anyone believe I'm telling the truth now?" In other words, why should Grey believe her when he'd been searching ever since she arrived for a reason to send her away?

Looking as if she were about to cry, Bertie nodded. A sudden gust of wind blew a washtub off the back porch and sent it clattering across the yard. The dog began to whine, and Dora sat, silent and miserable, and waited for the end.

Lula rose to close the windows on the west side, then felt the others. Curtains sucked against the screens. Polly's voice could be heard, rising in shrill objection to whatever Grey was saying.

And then Grey appeared in the doorway, looking like a man on his way to the gallows. "Ladies, you might as well get ready to come on up to the house. The way the wind's picking up, the tide will be flooding the road before long. I'll send someone down to close up your house and help carry your things."

Dora searched his face for a clue. Did he know about her yet? Had Polly told him? If she had, what was he thinking? And if not, what was she waiting for?

"A little rain, that's all," decreed Lula. "I remember snowstorms that lasted days, with the snow so deep no one could get to the street."

According to Mattie, it was thunder squalls that were the worst. "I used to crawl under the bed, but when it come right down on us, ever'body else piled in on top and the mattress nearly 'bout squashed me flat."

Dora said nothing. Storms had never particularly bothered her. And while she didn't exactly like them, a hurricane was the least of her worries at this moment.

Bertie had immediately taken Polly in hand as they busied themselves, preparing to move up to the house on the ridge. Whatever she had said to her, Polly appeared to be on her best behavior. For the moment, at least.

Mattie cooked. "Mouse said to cook up ever'thing on hand 'cause folks is goin' to be too busy later on to cook. I'm startin' on the bakin'." Soon delicious smells permeated the house. Dora thought of the spices she had yet to pay for. She would worry about her business tomorrow. The tearoom was obviously closed for the duration.

Peering through the curtainlike bands of rain, Dora could see men scurrying around on the roof of the warehouse while others hurriedly unloaded a freight boat. Still others labored farther along the shore securing the fishing boats. The nets that had been tarred recently and spread out over a framework to dry were hurriedly gathered up onto carts and stored in the warehouse.

I should be doing something else, she told herself, but couldn't for the life of her think what it might be. Despite the warnings of a severe hurricane on the way up the coast, the rain that continued to fall was light, the winds, though gusty, were no worse than she would have expected for a bad summer thunderstorm. At home it would have meant only that she couldn't go out driving her pony cart. Or that the rose garden her mother had created in the days before she'd disappeared would be tangled, some of the more fragile specimens even beaten to the ground.

And the tennis court, she recalled with amusement, would be drenched, unusable for days, possibly weeks. There'd been a time when she would have complained as loudly as anyone else.

Another world, she mused...another life.

Grey appeared everywhere in the distance. Taller

than almost every man on the island, he would have stood out by sheer force of personality in any gathering. She tried to imagine him in Bath, strolling along Front Street in a frock coat, a silk vest, checkered trousers and a top hat—or perhaps even one of the new straw skimmers.

Tried and failed. Here, he was in his element. Here, he belonged.

And so do you, a voice whispered.

Oh, Polly, Polly, why did you have to come and ruin it all?

By the time Mouse came down the ridge with his handcart, dark clouds were sagging low enough to scrape the chimneys. The wind was now howling around the eaves, the sound water visibly higher. Already the creeks were overflowing their banks. Dora could have insisted on staying behind, but in that case the others, out of loyalty, would have stayed, too. There was no denying that St. Bride's house was much higher than her own. She refused to endanger her friends because of her own stubborn pride. However, if Polly should happen to wash out to sea, then Dora would have to try to appear suitably sorrowful.

Mouse helped close up her house, Salty followed him around, clicking back and forth to sniff her pups.

"Hush, now," Dora said, "we won't let anything happen to your babies."

When the last shutter was closed, the house was dark as a tomb and felt almost as airless. Mouse opened a window on the leeward side half an inch at the bottom.

"But I just closed that window," Dora exclaimed.

Too many people scurrying around inside a small cottage added up to confusion.

"Leave it open a crack to even the pressure. This is a tight-built house."

Mattie, washing the last of her pans, said, "I 'member when a big ol' storm knocked a tree down on our roof. It like to scared me to death. They was a hurrycane down here on the coast, and Pa said it sent off a bunch of tornadies where we lived. They was a whole bunch of trees tore off, some even pulled out o' the ground by the roots."

Dora had experienced the same thing. Most people who lived in the coastal plains had, at one time or another. Not the tornadoes, but occasionally a hurricane veered inland. "What about this tomato pudding?" she took the lid off a bowl and sniffed. "It's three days old, but I think it's still good...sort of."

"Not 'nuff sugar," Mattie declared. "Nex' time I'll make it."

Lula had crammed her clothes back into her trunk, set the trunk up on the bed and tied it to the bedpost. Dora looked in through the door, shook her head and left. She'd do well to get her own gowns up out of the way of a possible storm tide.

Bertie and Polly were somewhere—Bertie was keeping her away from Dora, but that, Dora knew, only postponed the inevitable.

"You ladies hurry up," Mouse urged, looking more than ever like a villain with his gleaming dome and his eye patch. "Tide's already across the landing road."

The preacher arrived, pale and bedraggled, and Mouse handed him a basket of pups and directed him to go on ahead and take Salty with him. The old dog was a nervous wreck.

"If you're s-s-sure I can't help here," the man said, and Dora assured him that everything was under control, and they were almost ready to leave.

Ever practical, Bertie had stripped the beds and rolled up the linens in a bundle, ready for the trek. "We'll need sheets if it don't end before dark. No point in using up yours."

After gathering up Dora's toilet articles, including her apple-blossom cologne and her hand cream that was supposed to keep hands white and supple but didn't, she'd hung her former mistress's best gowns on the hook on Emmet's bedroom wall, the skirts just above the faint horizontal mark on the wall.

It dawned on Dora as she hurriedly collected Emmet's Bible and his checkerboard and crammed them in on top of her nightgown, that the grayish line was a tide mark. In which case, she thought the floors would probably end up awash. And so she rolled up the few scatter rugs and put them on the settee.

"Maybe I'd better hitch up the wagon," Mouse said as he surveyed the pile of luggage the five women had accumulated. Food, bedding, enough clothing to outfit a platoon.

Not Polly, though. She'd done nothing but complain. Mouse was kind to her, but then Mouse, as Dora had quickly come to realize, was kind to everyone. As Mattie had once said, the gentle giant didn't have a mean bone in his body, no matter how fearsome he looked.

Mouse loaded most of the oddly assorted necessities on the cart and set out first, leaning into the wind. Mattie hurried to catch up with him, carrying baskets of food. They were followed by Bertie and Polly, who was still whining and bickering. Lula clutched her belly and Dora tucked her hand under the pregnant actress's arm, guiding her past the worst clumps of shell.

The moment they reached the partial shelter of St. Bride's porch, Grey opened the door, shoved the luggage inside out of the rain, then ushered them in after it.

The preacher appeared beside him, both arms full of puppies. "I didn't know where to put them," he said apologetically.

Dora looked at the helpless pups, then looked at the other women. It occurred to her that while she, at least, had property—someplace to go after the storm—these women had nothing.

Grey moved past the huddle of wet women and lit several lamps. Watching him, Dora realized that this was the first time she had been inside his house. Even the night Emmet had died she had only come as far as the porch, screaming at the top of her lungs.

Once inside, the women began to shake out their skirts and push at bedraggled hair with cold, wet fingers. Polly looked around, her eyes wide, and immediately plopped herself in the largest chair. "My, ain't this nice? Near 'bout as fine as Sutton Hall, ain't it, Miss Dora?"

Bertie glared at her. "Get up out of that chair, woman, your clothes is wet!"

"So's my hair. Lor-dee, that's some rain, ain't it?"

"You might want to stand out under the gutter and see if it won't wash some of them nits out o' your hair!"

Lula rolled her eyes. Dora prayed silently that Polly

hadn't already infected them all with lice. That, on top of everything else, would truly be the last straw.

Despite the tension that had her nerves drawn tighter than a drum, Dora couldn't help but admire St. Bride's house. It was even lovelier than she'd envisioned. Oriental rugs that, while faded, were still beautiful. Framed maps, a few ship paintings, a document of some sort, complete with gold seal, all against paneled walls dark with age.

"Mouse, you might want to take the food out to the kitchen," Grey suggested quietly.

Almond Filmore, having divested himself of the pups, glanced quickly at Lula, then looked away, his long face oddly flushed.

Mattie said, "Coal oil's 'bout the best thing fer cooties. Some folks uses lard, but—"

Mouse gathered up all the luggage and Grey said, "Ladies, if you'll follow me, I'll show you where you can put your things. Reverend, my library is at your disposal." He nodded to the door at the far end of the room. "I'll have Mouse make up the sofa for you." To the others, he said, "Supper should be ready in about an hour. Settle in. If you need anything in particular, just sing out. Meanwhile, I'll show you to your quarters," he said as he led the way up the wide mahogany stairs.

There were three large bedrooms and one closed door upstairs. "Help yourself to the beds, I'll have Mouse make them up."

"I can do that," Bertie put in, glaring at Polly. "And Polly'll lend a hand, won't you, Pol?"

Not surprisingly, Polly chose the largest bed and flopped across the mattress. Bertie hurried into the room and took her by the hand, dragging her up again. "We've not chose up sides yet. You just wait!"

Mattie was squirming again. A trip to the privy in this wild, blowing rain would be miserable, if not downright dangerous, so Dora stepped back, leaned over and peered under the bed for a chamber pot.

Grey, the shameless man, moved up behind her and murmured, "There's a bathroom downstairs off the kitchen. No running water, but you'll find most everything else you need."

Irritated and embarrassed, she thanked him, then edged closer so that she could whisper in Mattie's ear.

Mattie headed downstairs to the bathroom and Bertie shoved Polly down on a bentwood rocker and began a careful examination of her scalp. Finally satisfied, she stepped back and brushed her hands down her skirt. "Well, she's not got cooties, but if I was you, Pol, I'd get me some more hair dye real quick. Them brown roots is going to be showing real good in another week or two."

At least it served to halt the woman's tears. "It ain't brown, it's—the sun faded it, is all."

"That's a lie, just like all the rest of that mess you told about Miss Dora," Bertie said flatly, just as a stronger gust of wind hit the side of the house. The two women were alone at the moment, the others having gone ahead to choose bedrooms.

Lula appeared in the doorway. "I actually felt that," she whispered, her hands going instinctively to her belly.

"Only because we're on the second floor," said Dora, trying to sound as if she weren't growing as uneasy as any of the others. Shutters rattled. Wind whined around the corners. The house shook, and over all that could be heard the angry roar of a hungry sea. "I suggest we go back downstairs and see if we can help get supper on the table."

"Spoken like a general," Lula murmured, and Dora grinned.

"I try, I try."

Time lost all meaning. They slept briefly, then woke again to the constant roar of the wind. Mattie appointed herself Mouse's kitchen helper. Bertie sat beside Polly, elbowing her every time she started to speak. Whatever the threat, real or implied, it seemed to work, but Dora didn't fool herself. Sooner or later, Polly would have her say.

Lula sat near a lamp sewing on a small bit of white batiste that had recently been a petticoat, the Reverend Filmore, book in hand, seated beside her. Dora, too restless to settle, tried to think of anything she might have left undone before the last remnant of daylight faded.

Grey was nowhere to be found. Not that anyone looked, but Dora did wonder. Surely he couldn't have gone down to the landing, not in this weather. If the warehouse blew away, it blew away. Nothing he could do would prevent it. No doubt he had a list of all the things that needed doing whenever a hurricane threatened. Close this, open that. Set this up, fasten that down. The real wonder was why he hadn't simply ordered the storm to go elsewhere.

Imagine his living in a house like this, she mused, looking about her with new interest now that time hung so heavy on her hands. Imagine such a house even existing on a barren, desolate island. For a landowner with delusions of royalty, Grey didn't dress any differently from his subjects. Bathed more often than some. And shaved, of course. Several of the men didn't look as if they'd ever shaved.

The clock struck the half hour. Dora thought it must be either four or five-thirty. Or possibly six. Late in the afternoon, at any rate.

And then suddenly she leaped up out of the tapestry-covered wing chair. *My chickens,* she thought, horrified that she'd forgotten all about the poor creatures and left them in that ramshackle henhouse. By now the place would have blown apart, her poor chickens terrified, if not drowned.

"Excuse me, will you?" she murmured to Lula, who raised her eyebrows but didn't inquire. Probably thought she was going to the bathroom, which was just as well. If she told anyone what she was about to do, Bertie would try to stop her, then Mouse would insist on going in her stead, and she couldn't ask him to do more than he had already done.

At least Grey was nowhere in sight. Hiding out in his office, probably, making lists of who was going to do what once this mess was over.

Without saying a word, she wandered into the foyer, cracked the door open a bit and peered outside. The wind appeared to be coming from the other side of the house. Perhaps if she just slipped out, she could run home and be back before anyone realized she was gone.

Not until she was halfway down the road, soaked to the skin, her face stinging from the wind-driven rain, did it occur to her that she didn't know what on earth she was going to do with her hens, even if she managed to rescue them.

And then she saw the water under her house.

Through the rain and gloom, she could see that the church and parsonage were already surrounded by water.

At least the half of her yard where the fig trees and graves stood was still high and dry. Or at least, high. Nothing could remain dry with walls of rainwater blowing horizontally across the island.

"Dammit, woman, come back here!" The voice rose out of the wildness like a disembodied ghost.

She continued to run, her shoes squishing with every step.

Grey caught up with her just as she reached the gate. "What the devil do you think you're doing out here—are you crazy?"

"My chickens," she yelled, her voice picked up and carried away by the howling wind.

"Damn the chickens! If they've got any sense, they'll be—"

The rest of his words were lost. She shouted as she struggled with the front gate, "The chicken house won't stand!"

"Then let it go!"

"The gander—"

"Let him drown! Come back or I'll throw you over my shoulder and take you back!"

But Dora knew that, while the chickens might have sense enough to head for the back porch to get in out of the rain, the poor gander was doomed. His pen was covered by a length of net to keep him from flying out. The last thing Emmet had done before he died was to reinforce the net on all sides and over the top, to prevent the wretched bird from escaping to terrorize Dora.

"Oh, Emmet," she wailed. The wind snatched the words from her mouth and stole her breath.

Grey stared at her as if she'd lost her mind, then both of them turned toward the backyard. The henhouse was indeed gone. Splintered, demolished, half of it already blown away. Dora, head down, fought her way toward the back porch to see if any of her layers had taken shelter there while Grey took out his knife and slit the net covering the goose pen. "Take off, you poor old bastard, before you end up in a stew-pot."

He turned, caught sight of the small, windblown, rain-drenched woman halfway up the back steps. "Dora," he shouted. "Stop right there!"

Dora halted, turned and tried to shield her eyes from the stinging rain. Grey jogged across the backyard just as a cedar shingle sailed off the roof, nearly beheading him. He ducked, eyed the section of fence washing toward him on the tide that had already covered half the yard. "You can count 'em later, if you must." He swept her up in his arm and ran around to the front porch, seeking any shelter that wasn't covered in wet manure. The last thing he needed now was for her to skid in the mess and break a leg. "God help me," he muttered, burying his face in her drenched hair, "You're more trouble than a bushel of tomcats!"

They ended up inside the house, because Dora wouldn't leave until she had accounted for every one of her laying hens. That meant opening the back door, as shutters had been secured over the windows.

Grey lit a lamp in the kitchen, but the draft from the open door promptly sucked it out.

So they stood there in the darkness, listening as the wind shrieked outside like a thousand tortured souls.

As something clattered across the front porch. As something else slammed into the side of the house. "I think I counted at least seven," Dora whispered. Her teeth were chattering. It wasn't cold—just the opposite, so she couldn't imagine why she was shivering, but she was. "Wh-what ab-ab-about the gander?"

"Flew the coop," Grey told her. "He'll survive." Then, his voice oddly gruff, he said, "Come here. No wonder you're shivering, you're soaked to the skin."

She went into his arms, but only because she was cold, she rationalized. And because it suddenly struck her what she'd just done. Risked not only her own life, but his for a flock of chickens and one hateful old gander she'd wished dead more times than she could remember.

"Stop shaking," he ordered just as if he expected her to instantly obey. She could almost smile at that.

Almost.

"Don't you have something dry you can put on?"

"It'll just get wet again."

"Maybe not," he said. "Judging from the direction of the wind, the storm's headed directly at us. If we wait for the eye to pass over us, we should have plenty of time to get back up on the ridge before the backside whips around."

Dora stood silently and let him hold her. Later she would tell herself that it was only because it sounded so reasonable. And because there was nowhere else in the world she would rather be than in a dark kitchen, safe in the arms of this man.

So she let her face settle into this warm, wet neck. Let his breath stir against her damp skin while he brushed away the hair sticking to her cheeks with his lips.

Neither of them spoke. To speak at all would be to allow the first unwelcome edge of reason to slip in. Cocooned in a warm intimacy she had felt only once before in her life—when he had kissed her—Dora knew she was being dangerously foolish. And for once in her life, she simply didn't care.

She didn't even pretend surprise when he led her to the bedroom. It had been inevitable ever since he'd followed her down the ridge.

Since he had kissed her.

Since she had first seen that terse advertisement in the *Bath Clarion* and impulsively penned a reply.

Grey murmured something about dry clothes again, but as his fingertips brushed over the top button at the neck of her wet green muslin, neither of them was thinking of anything but what was going to happen next.

This is my choice, Dora told herself, shoving aside misgivings as quickly as they arose. *I know what I'm doing. I'm doing it only because it's what I want. I'll worry about tomorrow...*

Tomorrow.

Chapter Nineteen

Grey insisted on lighting a lamp. Dora hid her face against his chest, but he eased her away so that he could see her eyes, to read any doubts she might have. Because he knew that what he was about to do might be a mistake. He also knew it was inevitable, that it had been building almost since the first day under the guise of anger, defiance, even deliberate baiting.

Not to mention reluctant admiration. On his side, at least.

Whatever happened now, it had to be mutual. He was willing to accept the consequences, but if Dora had any last-minute doubts, then he needed to know it now, before it was too late.

Women wanted love. What they called love, he considered the most disorderly, disruptive emotion of all. In almost every case, it made men do illogical things, made weaklings of the strongest among them.

He wasn't going to lie to her—he didn't love her. How could he possibly love her? She was the most maddening woman he'd ever met in his entire life. He could go for days without speaking to her, catching only glimpses of her in the distance, yet she was there whenever he climbed into bed each night. He invariably fell asleep wondering what it would be like to explore every inch of her delectable body—to feel her shudder beneath him as she cried out her pleasure.

"Dora?" Using his thumb, he lifted her chin. The front of her gown was already open enough so that he could see the faint swell of her breasts.

"What?" she replied, sounding defensive, breathless, more than a little belligerent.

"Is this what you want?"

Rain beat hard against the shuttered windows, rattling the storm blinds. A branch—something hard—struck the outside wall. She took a deep breath, paused and said, "Yes."

"Are you sure?" His voice sounded unfamiliar to his own ears.

Wordlessly she nodded.

Grey raked his wet hair back from his brow. The last time he remembered feeling this way was when he'd been about to bed his first woman, a willing widow twice his age. At fifteen, he'd just won a marathon poker game and the woman was to be his reward. Then, as now, he'd felt tired, edgy and exhilarated. Too keyed up to think clearly.

This time there was an added element. He couldn't put a name to it, but he had a feeling he was sinking fast, and there wasn't a lifeboat in sight.

Dora turned away and continued to unbutton her bodice. Grey waited, one hand resting on his belt. He *didn't* love her. The last time he'd fallen in love, almost half a lifetime ago, it had been with a woman who clung, a woman who demanded to be smothered with affection, especially in the form of gifts.

If ever there was a non-clinging, un-smotherable

woman, it was Dora Meeks. Ironically, he'd never met anyone he wanted so much to smother, if that meant caring, sharing—sheltering her from life's sharp edges.

Irrational. Illogical, a voice whispered. *All ashore that's going ashore....*

Her gown melted soundlessly to the floor. Even with her back turned, standing there in the flickering yellow light in her damp petticoat and whatchamacallit, with wet yellow curls clinging to her vulnerable nape, she was so damned beautiful his gut ached almost as much as his groin.

"Turn around, Dora." His voice was hoarse, barely recognizable.

Slowly she turned. Her eyes, meeting his, were unreadable. Darkly shadowed. So lovely, he thought, almost wishing she hadn't shed the defensive shell she wore like a badge of honor.

A pulse throbbed at the base of her throat, the rapid rhythm echoed by his own. She whispered, "Grey?"

Like putting a match to tinder, that was all it took. Come hell or high water, Grey knew he was doomed. Keyed up emotionally, physically drained from getting ready for the storm, his guard was completely down, leaving him totally vulnerable to this wild, mindless urgency.

Her mouth, oddly cool, incredibly sweet, hit his bloodstream like a jolt of two-hundred-proof moonshine. From hunger he soared instantly to greed. Twisting his head, he parted her lips to gain entrance while his hand moved lower, cupping her hips, pressing her against his urgent need.

So small, came the fleeting thought—so defenseless.

But he knew better than that by now. She was more than a match for any man.

Her arms slipped around him, her hands warm as they moved restlessly over his back. She smelled of soap and rain and something stunningly intimate, breathtakingly personal. One last time he whispered, "Dora, are you sure?"

She nodded against his chest, and that was all it took. With one arm around her, he lowered her, damp underclothes and all, to the bed. Then, with unsteady hands, he began peeling off his own wet clothing. Her fevered gaze followed his every move. As he stepped out of his wet denims, he heard her catch her breath.

His hands grew still, but only for an instant. She'd been a widow, he reminded himself, even before she'd married Emmet. He wondered fleetingly what her first husband had been like. Whether he'd been a large man, or someone built more on her own scale.

He himself was a large man, in all respects.

"Last chance," he said with an unsuccessful attempt at jocularity in case she was harboring any second thoughts.

Her voice was a strangled whisper. "Please—I want you to make love to me."

It wasn't love, he told himself again, but it was the next best thing. Reclaiming her lips, he wove his fingers through her hair and sought to impart without words all he was feeling. He kissed her throat, following a sensitive path to the hollows below. Kissed her shoulders, her breasts, savoring the taste of her, the feel of her silken skin. Using first his lips, then his hands, he saluted each discovery as he slowly, carefully removed the last of her clothing until only one stocking remained. By the time he rolled it down so that it dangled from the tips of her toes, she was trembling, her breath shuddering audibly.

So was he. Patience had never been his long suit.

When she began to twist against him as if seeking release, he moved his hand from the back of her knee upward, along the inside of her silken thigh. At first her legs closed tightly, trapping his fingers, but then they fell apart.

Slowly, slowly, an inner voice cautioned. It nearly killed him, but he forced himself not to be in too great a rush. He wanted her with him every step of the way. For the first time in his life, a woman's pleasure was more important than his own.

Urgency fought with caution as he tasted the salt-sweet softness of her flat midriff. He paid homage to the slight swell of her belly, kissing, nibbling her there before moving lower to discover other sweet, hidden secrets.

Hearts pounding, bodies entangled, they continued to explore the wild splendor hovering just out of reach while outside, the hurricane that would one day become known as the infamous San Ciriaco, wreaked its destruction. There was no lull, no calm in the middle of the storm. On and on it raged, devastating everything in its path.

With trembling fingers, he wrapped her small hand around his hard shaft and heard the quick constriction of her breathing. For the first time it occurred to him how very vulnerable even the proudest woman could be in these circumstances. Smaller, weaker...

Subordinate.

"I felt the earth move," Dora whispered in awed tones.

"Oh, yes..." His blood racing, his heart pounding,

Grey shifted over her, unable to wait a single moment longer.

And then he realized that the house was indeed moving.

Great godamighty, we're washing away!

Dora clutched at his shoulders, her fingers slipping on the hard, slick flesh. "Grey? What is it? What's wrong?"

Whatever it was, it was not what she had feared. Polly hadn't told him—Bertie had seen to that. "Please, tell me what's happening," she pleaded when he sat up and steadied himself against the bedstead.

"Stay here."

Naked as the day she was born, Dora jumped out of bed and lurched when the floor seemed to move under her feet. "An earthquake?"

"Where's Emmet's ax?"

Emmet's ax? "In the—the shed," she whispered, determined not to panic. Whatever was happening—if the house was about to blow down around their heads, she trusted Grey to do what was best. "I have a hatchet. For kindling."

"Stay here," he ordered, but she was not about to be left in a dark house that felt as if it might collapse at any moment.

"Behind the stove. I'm coming with you!" Reaching out, her hand struck his bottom and she dug her fingers into his firm flesh, unwilling to lose contact. "Can't we light a lamp?"

"Better not."

She sensed rather than saw him when he reached the stove. Her kindling basket was on the floor behind it, the hatchet and several sticks of kindling left over from the earlier fire.

"What are you doing?" she yelped when she heard the first blow.

Dear Lord, had the man lost his mind? He was chopping up her floor!

"Open the front door," he snapped. "Hurry!"

Mindless with fear, Dora felt her way through the living room and tried the door. It was closed, not locked, yet it refused to budge. "I can't open it!" she shouted.

"Then come open the back door," Grey yelled back.

Whack! Whack! Splinter, whack!

She felt water creeping over her feet and shuddered. "Grey, are you standing in water?"

"Yes, thank God," he said, and the whacking ceased. "We've floated off the foundation. I doubt if there's been time for us to drift far, but I'd as soon settle her down before she drifts out to sea."

In the darkness, Dora sensed his nearness and moved closer. His arms came around her and he held her there as water swiftly moved up over their feet, above their ankles, and approached their knees.

"Has it occurred to you," he asked with an unexpected hint of amusement, "that we're both stark naked, and that I've just scuttled your house?"

"Is that what you've done?" she asked wonderingly. To think that just a few hours ago she was distraught, thinking Polly was about to spread her vicious lies and everything she had worked for would be lost.

It seemed as if hours had passed, but it was probably only minutes before the house struck something, stopped moving and slowly settled at a sharp angle.

"Where do you suppose we are?" she whispered.

"Probably not Mount Ararat. At a guess? Halfway up the road. Must've floated up against the ridge."

She shivered, and he drew her closer in his embrace. "It's probably safe to light a lamp now if I can locate one that hasn't tipped over. We'd better get dressed."

Dora sniffed. She didn't smell lamp oil, only the muddy, marshy smell common to the soundside at low tide. "My poor floors," she murmured. "They're going to be a mess, even without the holes you chopped."

She felt his lips against her hair as she reluctantly pulled away from his arms. Only then did she feel the chill.

Only then did she think about what had come so close to happening. Would he have made love to her if he'd known about her past?

"Wind's coming around. Either we're in for a lull, or the storm's moving offshore. At any rate, we'd better get dressed in case there's a lull and we can make a run for it."

It occurred to Grey that if he'd needed a sign that he was in grave danger of getting in over his head, he could have done with something a little less extreme.

Fully dressed, with his pants rolled up about his knees, he made the rounds, looking for structural damage. On the lee side of the house, he opened the blinds and peered out, trying to gauge how far they had drifted.

It was still raining, but the wind had a different tone. The surf sounded ominously close, but if Dora's house had floated onto the ridge, then at least the ridge was still there. His own house should be still standing.

She brought a lamp. "Can you see anything yet?"

Holding it up to the window, he made out only the light reflected off turgid water. "Tide's running strong. At a guess, I'd say it's flowing out. Can't see the stars, but I have a feeling we're facing east.''

''Is that good?''

Drawing her against his side, he was tempted to lie and tell her what she wanted to hear. That everything would be all right and the storm would soon be over, and life would go back to the way it had been before.

''We'll know more within an hour or so. Once it's light, it might be a while before you can go outside, but at least we'll have an idea of what's happened.''

''What do you mean, before I can go outside?'' She moved closer to his side, under the sheltering protection of his arm. He'd set the lamp on the table behind them, shoring it up with a stick of kindling when it threatened to slide. ''What about you?''

Knowing that this was no time to argue the point, he said, ''My legs are longer than yours. If I step in a hole, chances are my head won't go under.''

''Grey,'' she wailed, and he laughed.

It was an eerie sound, in a crooked house that was still awash with a smelly mixture of mud, salt water and any number of unseen creatures that were free to swim through the hole he had made in her kitchen floor.

Dora, her skirts knotted up about her knees, thought about her shoes. Had she left them beside the bed? If so, they might be halfway across the sound by now.

''Where are you going?'' Grey asked.

''My shoes,'' she said, as if that were a complete answer.

And as if it were the most logical thing in the world, he followed her to the bedroom and lifted her onto the bed. Shoes forgotten, he lowered and came down beside her, muddy feet and all. ''Let me hold you,'' he whispered gruffly. "I can't seem to keep my hands off you—or my thoughts."

"Grey, there's something I need to tell you."

"Shh, not now. Mouse will be along shortly. Sleep while you can, we'll talk later. I'll wager it'll be a while before either of us gets much rest once this thing ends."

Amazingly, she was asleep within minutes. Safe, warm, at peace.

Grey took a few minutes more, but he, too was exhausted after days of storm preparation. His last waking thought was that nothing had ever felt quite so right as this one small woman, in his arms.

In his heart.

Grey woke first. Kissing her softly on the brow, he peered over the edge of the bed. The water was down, but the mud was going to take an army to flush out.

Dora opened her eyes as he moved gingerly across the floor. "Is it over?"

"We'll see. I'm going to take a look outside, stay where you are."

Which, of course, was the reason Dora popped out of bed and skidded halfway across the floor on the accumulation of wet slime before Grey managed to catch her. "Oh, my mercy, this is awful!"

"Yeah, well...let's go see how awful it looks on the outside. Steady as you go, mate."

Mate. How lovely that sounded, she thought. And how unlikely, in spite of what had so nearly happened earlier.

Grey unlatched the door and shoved. Earlier, she'd said it was stuck. Easy to understand, under the circumstances. But it was not just stuck, it was wedged shut. Peering through the crack he could see a heavy timber had washed across the porch.

"What if we're trapped?" There was fear in her voice, but not as much as he might have expected. A lesser woman would probably be screaming by this time, demanding that he save her.

"Back door," he said tersely, and carefully, she padded after him. Cautiously he opened the door and together they peered out onto a changed world.

"Oh, my mercy," she breathed.

Mercy, indeed. He swore softly under his breath.

The tide was ebbing rapidly. The wind had dropped off. What he didn't know was if it had truly moved offshore or if this was only the lull. If it was the eye, and there was more to come, he could think of ways of passing the time until they were rescued.

Grey had seen storms before, often two or three hurricanes in a single season. Nothing could prepare any man for the devastation wreaked by wind and water.

"Where are we?"

"Let me get my bearings." He knew, all right. Only he didn't know quite how to tell her that, while she was still in her house, her house was now on his property.

Maybe he wouldn't tell her…not yet. First things first, he told himself, but for the first time in his life, he wasn't at all certain what the first thing was.

They stood together on her back porch, gazing out over an almost unrecognizable landscape where once had stood outbuildings, gardens, fences and, in the distance, oak trees, stock pens and—

"Do you suppose everyone is all right?" Dora whispered.

"They know the rules. Once they're up on the ridge, nobody leaves the house. The house is still standing."

Thank God.

"Oh, my. It's a lot closer now, isn't it? Where's the warehouse?"

"It's in the other direction, right..." Disbelief on his face, he moved out to the edge of the porch. "Watch your step, the floor's slippery."

Back to the beginning. It wasn't the first time he'd had to start over, but this time he'd had far more to lose. His arm tightened around her in an instinctive gesture of possession.

"My chickens are gone," she said mournfully. As was the porch roof. It now covered the graves out beyond where the fig trees had once stood. Oddly enough, the tide had cut a channel around the slight rise, leaving that one small section untouched.

Further up on the ridge his own house was still standing. It had shifted slightly on its foundation, and shingles were missing from both the sides and the roof. Tide had undercut the front porch, leaving the steps dangling.

Moving cautiously to the edge of Dora's porch, he squinted toward the northern end of the island where the barracks and the single men's cabins had once stood. A brilliant sun glittered on the standing tidewater with blinding intensity.

"John Luther's landing?" Dora murmured. "His boats?"

"I see his boat, she's fine. And his net shed made it."

"It's like another world," Dora whispered, awed as she took in the changed terrain. "Like we went to sleep in one world and woke up somewhere else."

In more ways than one, Grey thought, but set it aside. He would deal with that subject later. Right now he needed to assure himself that everyone was all right up on the ridge. "The road's passable. I'm going to take you up to the house. We probably have a houseful, so Mouse will be cooking enough for a small army." He didn't bother to add that the preacher would be standing by in case he was needed. No point in anticipating the worst.

As the last of the storm clouds blew out to sea, hundreds of tiny pink clouds drifted daintily across a sky that covered every shade from rich cobalt to turquoise, to palest green and gold. Grey had seen such skies before, after a storm swept up from the Caribbean. As if the storm gods, having had their way, decided to award the losers a consolation prize.

Dora picked her way carefully back inside, relieved to see that within the past few minutes, the tide had gone down still further. There was now only a thick coating of mud and one gaping hole.

The least of her worries. She would deal with her floors later.

Knowing that dry clothing might be needed, she brought Emmet's clothes down from the attic and crammed them into two pillow cases. Meeting Grey in the kitchen, she said, "We took the food up yesterday. Can you think of anything else?"

But Grey's mind was on other things. The church still stood, but the parsonage was gone. It would take weeks for all the standing water to subside, and long before that the mosquitoes would be thick enough to choke a hog. Displaced snakes would be turning up in unexpected places. He'd have to warn the women to watch their steps if they ventured outside.

Hoisting both pillow cases, he said, "I'll come back later and open things up to air out. First let's see how the others fared."

Dora hurried along beside him, stunned at the changes all around her. A channel some three feet deep in places zigzagged along the middle of the dune where heavy rains had coursed downhill. There was no sign of the few bachelor cabins she should have been able to see from there. Praying she was mistaken, she didn't mention it, but judging from his grim expression, Grey already knew.

"It smells peculiar," she panted, hurrying to keep up with him.

"It'll smell a damn sight worse before long," he said grimly.

Mouse came down the ridge to meet them, and Dora hurried up to where the others waited. She had to clamber up onto a box someone had placed under the steps. Not even Castle St. Bride had escaped damage, she thought, and this time there was no bitterness at all involved.

"You're all right!" Bertie cried, coming halfway down the steps to meet her. She held out a hand. When Dora would have grasped it and jumped, Grey lifted her by the waist and swung her up onto the porch.

"Rule number one—don't take foolish chances," he warned quietly. Glancing around at the others, he said, "That goes for everyone."

Catching her breath, Dora glanced at the large gathering. "Is everyone here all right?"

"We're fine, but you was gone so long we was afraid you'd drownded," said Mattie, tearfully accusing.

"Pity you didn't even have your husband's checkerboard to help while away the night," Lula said dryly.

Dora glanced at her, wondering how she knew. Because she obviously did.

The reverend said, "I prayed for you. We all did. My church is still s-s-standing, but the parsonage is gone."

The two other men came up onto the porch and Grey handed the pillow cases full of clothing to the minister. "Mouse? If you men are ready, we'd better head down to the landing. Look after the women, will you, Almond?"

"Can't I be of help?" the minister inquired, clearly preferring to go with the men rather than stay with the women.

"I appreciate it, but I'd feel better knowing you're here to look after things. Looks like the house didn't suffer too much damage, but I doubt if the women can manage the storm blinds without help. Windows'll be stuck tight. House needs to be checked over from the inside for leaks and other damage." Which Mouse, Dora knew, would have already done.

"Where's Polly?" she asked quietly, edging closer to Bertie.

"I gave her a bottle and settled her down. I reck'n she's out cold by now."

Lula moved to stand next to Almond. "I'll help you," she offered, but Almond shook his head.

"You'll do no such thing. You've been awake all night long. At a time like this, you need your rest far more than I need your help."

Lula looked at him as if he had just paid her the highest of all compliments.

By telling her he didn't need her? Dora thought,

offended on Lula's behalf. But then the truth dawned on her, and against all reason, tears suddenly blurred her vision.

Lula and Almond. The preacher and the actress. Was it possible—?

Mattie conferred hurriedly with Mouse, and then she and Bertie headed for the kitchen. For the first time, Dora noticed the wooden tray of tools sitting beside the front door. Hammer, hatchet, two handsaws and a coil of heavy rope.

On the verge of leaving, Grey turned and pinned her with a look that left her breathless and burning. "You'll be all right," he declared. It was a statement, not a question.

She would be all right, Dora repeated to herself as the hours ticked slowly by with no sign of Grey. There was more than enough to keep her busy. Meals to be prepared and served whenever the men—sometimes singly, sometimes in small groups—would come straggling up the ridge. Minor injuries to be attended.

Clarence, barefoot, his clothing wet and clinging, came to eat and reported that half the warehouse was gone, with all the cargo that had been stored there. The new lumber shed had washed away, including its entire contents.

Bertie fed him an enormous serving of stew and the last of Mouse's pone bread. "Was anyone injured?" Dora asked.

"No, ma'am, not seriously. John Luther's eldest boy broke his arm. Almy Dole got knocked over the head by a dead tree when he was trying to tie his boat off. Boat sunk. Almy's got a knot the size of a water-melon on his noggin, but he's already out there trying to haul her up onto shore. He's tough. Take more 'n a busted head to get him down.''

"And…the others? The houses?"

"Not much left standing. Bunkhouse washed clean away. James's place floated off the pilings. It come down over near where mine was.''

"Your house is gone?" Bertie's distress was so obvious that Dora looked from one to the other, wondering if she could be mistaken in her sudden suspicions.

There were things taking place on his island that Grey had never planned, she told herself later as she found dry clothes for John Luther's two boys who had come for food. How that was going to sit with the man who planned every last detail, right down to who was going to marry whom and where they were going to live, she couldn't imagine.

Two full days went by before there was time for more than the briefest exchange between the men and the women. Almond, it seemed, had not always been a minister. He had worked as a clerk and briefly studied medicine in his preministry days. It was he who resplinted Herman's broken arm and bandaged numerous minor injuries. That done, he offered to help Clarence with the warehouse inventory. Mouse, with his enormous strength, was needed everywhere. Among his first tasks was to shift the timber that blocked Dora's front door.

James Calvin and Almy, the island's two carpenters, were already busy repairing what could be repaired, demolishing the rest so as to salvage the materials. Several men, including Luther's boys, broken arm and all, fanned out with pony carts to collect the lumber that had floated away from the ruined shed and now littered the waterfront.

"Most of it's probably washed all the way up to the Cape," Grey said dryly. After a near miss with a cottonmouth, he insisted the men wear boots. At least, those who could still locate their footwear. "Take down sizes, Clarence. We'll order up whatever's needed. Dozier'll be headed out here directly bringing supplies. That is, if he's still able and the mainland didn't get mommicked too bad. God knows how the rest of the banks fared."

Late in the afternoon of the second day Grey came home, his feet dragging, face gray from exhaustion and lack of sleep. Dora wanted nothing so much as to take him into her arms and offer him the comfort of her body.

Instead, she offered him the comfort of food. Mattie had stewed the fish, crabs and turtle provided by the men along with Mouse's potatoes and onions. Dora had mixed salt and water with the last of the cornmeal and fried the cakes in bacon grease. Wordlessly Grey devoured everything put before him, then leaned back and closed his eyes.

Dora slipped into the chair across from him. For once, they were alone, the others having ventured outside now that the waters had largely subsided.

All but Polly, who chose the moment when Grey finished his meal, leaned back in his chair and closed his eyes for a moment of rest—or perhaps prayer—to take her place across the table as if she had every right. "You'll be wanting to leave when the boat comes in," Dora said quietly.

"Leave? I just got here. I haven't even had time to

look around. My, this is a nice place, Mr. St. Bride. Can I call you Grey? I reckon Dora told you all about me, didn't she?''

The woman giggled. Grey winced and opened his tired eyes. ''No, ma'am, I don't believe your name's come up in any of our conversations.'' A glimmer of a smile brightened his tired eyes as he glanced at Dora.

Dora blushed. Grey's smile widened. It had the effect of making Dora's heart swell with...with something. She'd almost managed to convince herself it wasn't love. Lust, probably. Now that she'd discovered the meaning of the word, she found it all too easy to picture him as he'd been the night of the storm—gloriously naked, thrillingly masculine. Aggressive without being at all frightening. Recalling the way excitement had coursed through her body, building in intensity until she could scarcely draw breath, she could only wonder what would have happened if the house hadn't floated off its foundation.

Polly looked from one to the other, her eyes narrowing suspiciously, just as Bertie hurried into the room and said, ''Polly, I need you upstairs.''

''I'll be up directly.''

''Now!'' Bertie said, tapping her collar emphatically.

Grey sent Dora a questioning look, but she only shook her head.

Amazing, she thought later on that afternoon, how the presence of one small woman could change the atmosphere in an entire household. As if they were all waiting for the other shoe to drop. Waiting for another storm to strike.

Out in the kitchen, she peeled potatoes for Mattie to boil while Bertie ground coffee beans. Vicious cranks, muttering under her breath all the time. Lula took her sewing into the living room, where she watched Polly prowl around, picking up first one thing, then another, examining the books and paintings—even going so far as to examine the sun-faded draperies.

Lula said, "You picked a rather awkward time to arrive, you know."

Polly managed to shrug and toss her head at the same time.

Lula said, "Don't overdo the gestures, my dear. They're hardly convincing."

Sniffing, Polly said, "I don't know what you mean." She tipped an ivory figurine onto its end and studied the bottom, as if looking for a price mark.

"I suspect you do. And you'd do well to listen to a word of advice." The dark-haired actress stabbed her needle into the pincushion and set her sewing aside. Polly opened her mouth to protest, but Lula stayed her with an imperial gesture. She was rather good at imperial gestures. "I don't know what's going on between you and Dora, but I'll tell you this much, and you'd best pay heed. If you hurt so much as a single hair on that woman's head, everyone on this island will come after you. Dora has friends here. I suspect you're not one of them."

Polly plopped down in the nearest chair and said, "Well. Aren't you the huffy one? Have I said one word against her? Have I done anything to hurt her? Lady, if I was you, I'd be real nice to me, on account of I know where the bodies is buried."

The atmosphere was thick enough to slice a moment later when Dora entered the room. Ignoring Polly, she said, "Lula, I'm not feeling well."

"I expect you overdid it, trying to look after your house during the storm." Lula's lips twitched as if she could barely repress a smile.

"I don't know what all the fuss is about, it's just a storm," Polly dismissed. "You think you're the only ones that ever went through a storm? There was a drownded horse on the corner of Water Street and Craven after that storm we had year before last. Stunk something awful. People right down the street had a boat wash right up onto their front porch, so don't talk to *me* about storms."

Straightening his stiff back, Grey wiped the sweat from his brow, then waved away a cloud of mosquitoes. Another in an endless succession of endless days. With so much to do and too few hands to accomplish it, every man on the island worked from sunup to sundown, sometimes beyond, hardly taking time to eat, much less to rest.

It was growing dark when the three men, Mouse, Almond and Grey headed back up the ridge. Grey's house was open to any man who needed it until his own property was repaired, but most of the men preferred to throw up thatch shacks or sleep aboard their boats.

A number of men had volunteered to set Dora's house back on a foundation. The trouble was that it had drifted halfway up the ridge and was no longer on Emmet's land. Not that moving a house that size was even a remote possibility. The sloping terrain was bad enough, but they simply didn't have the equipment.

One more thing he would have to deal with later. Evidently, the ramifications hadn't struck her yet.

"Do what you can to secure Dora's house," he'd told James Calvin, who headed up the team of carpenters. At least he could see that no further harm came to it until they could figure out what to do. "I'd appreciate it," he said now to Mouse and Almond, "if you'd see to clearing off the graves. Set Sal's stone up again, but don't bother with Em's. It probably floated off anyway. The one I ordered from the mainland ought to be ready once things start moving in again."

"Both signs are gone," Mouse said tiredly. The top of his bald head was badly sunburned.

"Hell, the whole damn fence is gone, beggin' your pardon, Almond."

"No need. Today I'm just a laborer. When Sunday comes, I'll be a laborer in the Lord's vineyard. Naturally I'll expect you all to attend a meeting in your living room, Grey."

"You drive a hard bargain."

"Yeah, I do, don't I?"

Mouse said, "When's Sunday?" They had reached the place where Grey's boardwalk had come to rest. In tacit agreement, the three men lifted one end and began to drag it up the sandy slope.

Grey grunted at the heavy weight. "Beats me. You know what day of the week this is, Almond?"

"Saturday?"

"Oh, hell no—I think it must be Monday."

The preacher grinned. His speech was nowhere near as hesitant as before the storm. Before he'd sweated like a mule and worked until his back was breaking and both his hands were raw. "Might as well go ahead and get it over with. Sermon tonight then, after supper. Come one, come all."

They dropped the section of boardwalk in place, only slightly askew. "You don't mind if I sleep through it," Grey said wryly.

"Just so you don't snore."

The three men entered the house, still smiling despite their bone-deep weariness. Mouse headed directly for the kitchen. Almond glanced quickly around the room as if seeking someone.

A woman in a bilious green dress rose from his favorite chair and started toward him, and Grey, pretending not to have seen her, turned away. One more unwanted parcel to be dealt with and returned to sender.

Bertie hurried into the room, looking past him almost as if she were expecting someone else. "Where's Dora?" he inquired, his tired eyes taking on a gleam of anticipation.

But it was Polly who answered, moving across the room to welcome him to his own house. "Oh, my, you look real tired. Why don't you come over here and set down and let me bring you something to drink?"

Bertie turned on her. "Polly, behave yourself!"

Chapter Twenty

It was Bertie who told him that Dora had gone upstairs to take a nap. "She's been yawning all day long. Worried sick about that poor house of hers, I guess."

She had hardly stayed awake worrying, but Grey wasn't about to go into that. "Did she eat anything today?"

"Nothing that would upset her. A mug of yaupon tea with honey."

Across the room, the woman in green watched the exchange avidly. Lula tucked her skirts aside to make room for Almond, who picked up the garment she'd been working on and complimented her on her fine stitchery.

She flushed with pleasure. "Men's clothes are much easier to alter than women's costumes, especially after years of training in a shirt factory."

Mouse emerged from the kitchen, chewing on a biscuit. "They ate all the fish stew for dinner. Mattie's got corn beef stew for supper. Tastes right good."

Thank God he had a couple of men to dilute the effects of a house full of women, Grey thought tiredly. This newcomer promised to be a pain in the butt. For one thing, he didn't much like the way she was looking him over, as if he were a piece of merchandise in a shop window.

His first impulse was to rush upstairs to be sure Dora was all right, but that might engender a few questions he wasn't yet ready to answer. So he lowered himself onto the tapestry-covered sofa, wondering if he would ever find the strength to rise again.

"This is a real nice place you got here," Polly Clinkshaw said brightly.

Bertie shot her another warning look. Something was going on there, Grey mused, but at the moment he lacked the energy to go into it.

"Thank you, Miss—uh, Crankscales."

"That's Clinkshaw, but you can call me Polly."

Damn, but he despised simpering women. "You're from Edenton, I understand." In other words, state your business and leave.

"I come from Bath, but I wor—that is, I lived in Edenton for a spell, so I heard all about you. Me and your brother's wife, we used to pass by one another regular when we was out walking. We was neighbors, you know, lived right there on the same street."

If this woman had lived on the same street with Jocephus and Evelyn, it was in the servants' quarters, he thought, but said nothing. He flexed his shoulders, then his wrists and then the fingers of both hands. Aside from an assortment of bruises and abrasions, every muscle he possessed was stiff after days of hard physical labor, both before and after the storm. Today he'd helped locate and retrieve tons of various materials, raise a few sunken boats, not to mention squaring two houses back onto their foundations with the help of a dozen men and two horses.

He waited for her to get on with whatever she had on her mind. He had just about reached the point of rudely asking her to state her business and get the hell out of his hair. He knew damned well he'd never have sent for this one. Not that she was all that bad looking, but there was something about her that set his teeth on edge.

Grey had an instinct for troublemakers. The male variety learned quickly that there was nothing for them on St. Brides Island. No grog shops, no whorehouses, no loose money to be skimmed off by a card sharpster. His men worked too hard to risk losing their earnings. They played for pennies and banked the rest. Grey had helped most of them set up bank accounts over on the mainland.

Trouble of the masculine variety, he could deal with well enough. Women, he was fast coming to realize, were another matter entirely.

In all fairness, he probably shouldn't condemn a woman just because she happened to have turned up at the wrong time. Whatever her reason, he'd give her the benefit of the doubt because there wasn't much else he could do at the moment.

Meanwhile, if one of the men took a shine to her, he would look into her background a bit further.

He watched through half-closed eyes as she wandered aimlessly around the room, picking up first one thing and then another. Looking it over, setting it down. His father's old humidor, where he kept the pocket watch that had stopped running years ago and a lock of hair some woman had once given him—he couldn't remember her name, but it had seemed heartless to throw it away.

"You got some real pretty pictures," she said

brightly, gazing up at a painting of a three-master that had gone aground up the banks a few decades earlier. It wasn't a pretty picture, wasn't even particularly well painted, but his father had bought it at an auction from the captain's widow, paying several times what it was worth. The captain, along with all hands, had gone down with the ship, and the widow had needed funds to move back to Nebraska with her family.

Still wondering again what the hell the Clinkshaw woman was doing here, what she was up to, he nodded. He was hungry, his head ached, and dammit, he wanted Dora.

Almond was dozing. He'd worked as hard as any man today. Laboring in St. Bride's vineyards, as he'd called it.

"I like pretty pictures on a wall, don't you?"

Too tired to nod, Grey simply grunted. Lula continued to stare at the woman as if she were some particularly loathsome species of insect.

Hmm, curious, Grey thought idly. Bertie didn't like her. Lula didn't like her. What about Dora and Mattie?

God, he wished Dora hadn't already turned in, he could use her to deflect the woman's attention, if nothing more.

When she came close enough so that he caught a whiff of sweat and some overpowering scent that reminded him of a muskrat in heat, Grey reluctantly opened his eyes. He managed to lever himself up from the sofa and began edging away. Normally, he would never have remained seated while a lady was still standing, but these weren't normal times.

And he was growing more and more convinced that she was no lady.

"I've knowed Dora and Bertie forever, did they tell

you?'' Her smile just missed being pretty. Stained teeth and thin lips didn't help.

"I haven't spoken to Dora lately." It had only been hours—why did it seem like years? He felt the same tightness at the back of his neck he'd felt the time he'd been cornered by a rabid dog. Crazy reaction— the woman was irritating, but hardly threatening.

"Well now, I wouldn't say I was best friends with Bertie—she can be right snippy, but everybody loves Miss Dora. Just lo-o-ves her to pieces."

From the other side of the room came a broken snort as Lula pinched Almond on the arm, then stood and marched across to where Polly had Grey cornered between the secretary and the wing chair.

"Suppertime," she announced, the militant gleam in her eyes belying her smile. "Polly, why don't we go see if we can help?"

"In the *kitchen?*"

"In the kitchen. We're a democracy here. If there's work to be done, we all pitch in until it's finished."

The younger woman opened her mouth to argue, then closed it again. "He don't look to me like he's doing much." She sniffed, nodding toward where the preacher, looking embarrassed, was blinking himself awake.

"The reverend has done his fair share," Grey informed her. Then, with a wicked grin, added, "Plans to do even more as soon as supper's over. You're in for a real treat, Miss, uh—Crankscales."

"That's Clinkshaw!"

Propped up on a heap of pillows against the head of the bed, Dora braced herself to go back downstairs. After helping to mop up leaks and hang towels out to dry, sleeplessness and worry had caught up with her by midafternoon. Bertie had made her come upstairs for a nap. Knowing she was only postponing the inevitable, she'd meekly obeyed, swallowing her guilt and crawling into the big feather bed. Even with the shutters and windows open and the door ajar, it was hot. Airless.

Dora stared into the gloom while she tried to sort out the mess she had made of her life. It wasn't enough that she'd ruined herself back home—now she was about to be ruined here, too. And this time the damage would be irreparable.

Polly might not be one of Grey's brides, but she was here all the same, and she wasn't going to disappear. Not until she'd destroyed Dora's reputation all over again. Ever since she had showed up so unexpectedly, Dora had found one excuse after another to be elsewhere. She had volunteered to place pots under the leaks in the roof and keep them emptied, as an excuse to hide in the attic.

But there was no hiding from the truth. And the truth was that her house was ruined—or if not actually ruined, at least no longer usable.

And Polly was going to find a way to make her suffer. Bertie said she'd stolen jewelry from Selma, which was why Selma had dismissed her, and that she, Bertie, could prove it.

Whether or not she could, Dora knew that before she left, Polly would manage to ruin Dora in Grey's eyes.

Grey…how could any man be so arrogant and at the same time, so overwhelmingly generous and good? All day long, whenever she'd glanced out a window in any direction, she'd seen groups of men working, and as often as not, Grey was there. Tall and proud as a grand duke, he'd been working as hard as any man on the island. He'd spent hours down near one of the private landings where several men had been working to refloat a small sunken sloop. She'd watched, impressed, as they hitched two horses to a harnesslike contraption around the hull and dragged the vessel on rolling logs up onto the shore. Afterward, the men slapped one another on the back, slapped the horses on the rumps, then stood around laughing for several minutes before they picked up buckets and began bailing.

She'd seen Grey wrap an arm around the youngest Luther boy and ruffle his hair. How could she ever have thought him coldhearted? There was such a gentle streak in him. She should have known from the way he'd been with Emmet, only then she hadn't been ready to admit she'd been wrong about the man.

"Oh, Emmet," she whispered. "Your poor garden." In the distance today she'd seen several horses and even a few cows trying to graze on the flattened marsh grass. Evidently the stock fences were down. Which meant that whatever greenery the rabbits and tide hadn't taken care of, the cattle soon would. Emmet had told her once that it was easier to get his vegetables from across the sound than to try to grow them in a place where the entire garden plot could be covered in sand after a hard blow. But he'd liked watching things grow, and so he'd persisted despite the odds.

Realizing only now that her face was wet with tears, Dora wondered how it was that in the space of a few months she could have lost everything she held dear not once, but twice. The loss she was facing now was far more devastating. The loss of friends who valued her not for who her family was and what they possessed, but for herself alone. Friendships she'd had to earn.

The loss of another home. Hardly as spacious or luxurious as her old, but all the more dear for the man who had given it to her, and for the work she had put into making it her own.

And above all, there was Grey. They had fought every step of the way, forging a reluctant mutual respect.

When had she begun to love him? When she'd watched him with Emmet, seen the genuine caring for an old man with no son of his own?

When she had grudgingly realized that what she'd mistaken for meddling was wanting the best for the people who lived on his island, for looking into the future and trying to predict what would be needed?

And providing it.

If that was meddling, then it was the very best kind of meddling. "You love him, too, don't you, Salty?" she murmured to the misshapen dog who had become a house pet since the storm.

The old bitch's toenails clicked on the floors as she slowly made her way back downstairs to her boxful of nursing pups. Grey had said it was too risky to allow her outside until the water went back down. Too many displaced snakes. She had no better sense than to chase a muskrat right into a den of cottonmouths.

"Meddlesome man," Dora whispered, her heart bursting with love. "Always knows what's best for everyone, even my dog."

Voices drifted up the stairwell. She could hear Almond's slow, sonorous tones and Mattie's eager response. Bertie chimed in from time to time, but Bertie had never been much of a talker. More of a doer. She would fit in well here, if she could be persuaded to stay.

And then there was Polly's shrill voice, followed by her distinctive high-pitched giggle. Both Dora and Selma had been given their own personal maids the same year. She could never understand how her friend could bear to have the creature always underfoot, snooping, prying—listening in on private conversations. Bertie had busied herself elsewhere when she wasn't needed to help with her mistress's hair, or her clothes, or to run personal errands.

Back then, Dora admitted, she hadn't been quite so discriminating. Life had been too easy. She'd had everything any young woman could possibly desire, with no reason to consider whether or not she deserved it until it had all been snatched away from her.

Oh, the house, leaky and battered or not, would still be hers, but the land it sat on was no longer hers, and she didn't have the money to pay for having it moved.

If it could even be moved without breaking apart. It would take more than a harness, a few logs and a pair of horses. She almost wished the house had waited to wash away until after they'd finished making love.

Did one ever finish making love? How was it possible, when every look, every touch—even the sound of a voice, could send the sweetest kind of chills throughout a body?

Now Polly would tell anyone who would listen that far from being the widow she'd professed to be, Dora Sutton had been cast off by her fiancé for being a woman of loose morals.

There was no way Dora could prove to Grey or anyone else that Henry had lied, and that Polly was lying. Because she, too, had lied. And people, she had learned to her sorrow, would rather believe the worst than to give the benefit of the doubt.

It had happened before. It would happen again, and this time Grey would be the one to hear it. And he would remember all the times when he'd told her she was unsuitable, that she didn't belong there. "Dammit, I do so belong here," she muttered, flinging back the covers.

She had thought to escape Polly's taunting looks, her barbed remarks, by pretending to be ill. Not that it had all been pretense. Her headache was real enough—and the tension that had the muscles in her back tied in knots. But those maladies weren't apt to go away as long as she had this threat hanging over her head. The only way to put an end to trouble was to confront it head-on. The last time, she had run away. This time she refused to surrender without a fight.

This time she had even more to lose.

The sermon was nearly over when Dora crept downstairs. She had taken time to brush her hair and pin it into a prim style, and to splash cold water on her face. Come what may, she was as ready as she would ever be.

Almond was standing behind the wing chair, leaning against it as if he needed the support. Which he probably did, having worked as hard as any man on the island.

"The Lord giveth," he droned in his most preacherly tones. "And the Lord taketh away."

What an odd thing to say, Dora thought. He had spoken the same words when Emmet had died.

"On the other hand, He gave us the will and the strength to hang on to whatever we can salvage."

There was a scattering of "Amen" from Mouse, Mattie and several of the other men who had joined them for supper. Grey nodded. He looked half-asleep, and it was all she could do not to rouse him and make him go to bed. He needed rest far more than he needed to be preached at.

"Folks, I reckon the Lord will understand if we cut this short tonight. Truth is, I can't think of another blessed thing to say."

This time the chorus of "Amen" was much more enthusiastic.

Mattie said, "I'll fetch coffee."

Bertie said, "I'll help."

Clarence gazed longingly after the small wrenlike woman, then sat down beside James Calvin, who was snoring softly.

Lula patted the place beside her and Almond sank down and briefly closed his eyes. "I think it's Tuesday, not Sunday—not sure. Any rate, it's done now."

"Why, Miss Dora, I thought you was sick," Polly Clinkshaw said brightly.

Here we go, Dora thought. "Why no, Polly, I'm feeling perfectly well. I've been wanting to talk to you." Oh, she had. She'd been wanting even more to strangle her.

Polly glanced at Grey, who was dozing. Dora felt an odd mixture of tenderness and vicious satisfaction as she beckoned for the woman to follow her upstairs.

By the time Mattie and Bertie returned with a tray of mugs, a pot of coffee and a basket of cold sweet potato biscuits, Grey and Almond were sound asleep, Lula was sewing, a quiet smile on her face, and Dora and Polly Clinkshaw were nowhere to be seen.

It was Mouse who heaved his enormous bulk up from the sturdiest chair to reach for the heavy tray. "Let me take that there tray from you, Matilda. You done enough for today."

Bertie looked from one to the other, shrugged, then glanced at Lula. "Where's Dora and Polly?"

"Upstairs. I haven't heard any screaming yet."

"Better plug your ears, then," said Bertie at her most militant. "I've got a thing or two to say to that woman."

Chapter Twenty-One

Grey slept in his chair until Mouse shook him awake. "You'll get a kink in your neck that way."

"Dora?" Grey asked, wanting nothing so much as to fall into bed beside her and sleep until hunger drove him out of bed.

Or hunger of another kind kept him there.

Trudging wearily up the stairs, he heard a murmur of voices coming from the bedroom at the end of the hall—and what sounded almost like sobs. But knowing that there were two, and maybe more women behind the closed door, he kept on until he came to his office, where he'd installed a cot for the duration. There on his desk was the letter he'd found earlier folded up in his back pocket, the ink almost too smeared to read.

He remembered taking it to give to Dora, but with one thing and then another, he'd forgotten. He only hoped it wasn't important.

The next morning he was out at daybreak, compelled to be everywhere, to oversee everything. To see that whatever was rebuilt, was built better than before.

That the parsonage was larger, and on higher ground. That the warehouse addition was stronger, the foundation higher, the roof fastened on securely enough that it would take more than a hundred-year storm to lift it.

That's what they were calling it now, the hurricane that had killed hundreds of people in Puerto Rico, wreaking havoc as it spun its way northward. Scores of mullet fishermen, camping out on one of the narrow barrier islands, had been lost. Grey had built the barracks that had replaced the mullet shacks on St. Brides to withstand a normal storm, with holes bored in the floor so that the tide could flow in instead of floating the entire structure off the foundations.

He had not built it to withstand a constant pounding from forty-foot waves lashing in from the inlet.

Higher ground, he thought over and over, feeling guilty because his own house had been built on the highest ground of all. But high ground was scarce, and even more transient than low ground. Another bad storm could undermine his house by blowing the sand from the ridge down onto Dora's cottage, especially where it had come to rest, halfway up the ridge.

Nothing was certain. Nothing was permanent. Only by accepting that fact could a man hope to survive in such a fragile environment.

"Eat," Mouse ordered when they dragged themselves home after burying three cows and a pony. Mouse was a man of basic needs.

Grey was a man of basic needs, too. He didn't need food, what he needed was Dora.

But it was Polly Clinkshaw who met him at the front door, holding it wide as if to welcome him to his own house. "Where's Dora?" he asked.

"Still in bed, I s'pose. Ol' lazybones, I've not seen her all morning."

Grey strode past, calling up the stairs. "Dora? We need to talk!"

Bertie hurried from the kitchen to glare at Polly, who sniffed and tossed her head. "I warned you last night," Bertie said softly.

"I didn't say nothing," the other woman retorted.

Mouse, who had followed Grey into the house, witnessed the mystifying exchange, then shrugged his massive shoulders and went in search of Mattie and food.

Upstairs, Dora sat in a chair by the window and stared out over the churning sea. The beach had changed drastically. It was closer, for one thing, the dunes flattened, all but a narrow ridge. There was a dead horse washed up some hundred yards toward the North End. It looked as if it might be pregnant, but then she thought of the heat, two days—or was it three now—of hot sun beating down, and she shuddered.

"Dora?" Grey said quietly from just inside the bedroom door. He had obviously taken time to wash and change into dry clothes, for his hair was still wet. "Are you all right?"

She tried to smile, but gave up when his eyes darkened with concern. "I should be downstairs helping with dinner," she said. "I baked the corn bread today. Have you tasted it yet? It's good. Even Mattie said so."

"I have a letter for you. Trouble is, it came several days before the storm and I forgot all about it. It, uh—got a bit wet." Embarrassed, he handed her the stained and rumpled envelope.

Instead of taking it she looked as if it might be a new form of poison. "Do you know…who it's from?"

Curious, Grey shook his head. "I made out the letter *B* in the return address, but I'm afraid the rest is too smudged to read."

And then she expelled a deep sigh. "Bertie," she said. "For a minute I was afraid…"

She was afraid? Didn't she realize yet that she had nothing to be afraid of, not so long as he was there to slay her dragons?

Taking her hand, he lifted her to her feet and led her across to the bed. When she sat, he sat beside her, and the weight of his body tipped her so that she leaned against him. The letter lay forgotten.

"Has she told you yet?"

Had who told him what? "About the corn bread? I didn't stop by the kitchen. I was worried about you. You were too quiet last night—in fact, you've been quiet ever since the storm."

Dora nibbled her lip and frowned. It wasn't the storm that worried her so. That had come and gone. The men had surveyed the destruction and were well on the way to dealing with it.

"Polly," she said with a sigh. "She knows something about me."

Grey picked up her hand and, with a callused forefinger, traced the lines across her palm. The faint scars from the many burns she had received learning to cook. "So do I. Remember when I told you that you weren't suitable?" he asked, a wry twist of a smile breaking through like a shaft of sunshine on a stormy day.

"You were right," she whispered.

"I've never been more wrong."

"But I lied to you right from the first."

The silence that followed was loud enough to shatter glass. Instead, it shattered her heart, but she had to continue. He deserved to know that he'd been right all along. "Grey, I wasn't a widow when I came out here. I'd never been married before I met—that is, before I married Emmet."

She couldn't look at him, yet she knew what he was thinking—knew it as surely as she knew her heart was breaking. They hadn't actually made love, but they had come so close he had to know—that is, he must wonder...

She took a deep breath and plunged ahead. "I was engaged. That is my father..."

So then she had to tell him about that, as well. In a way, it made the telling of what had happened that night in the summerhouse seem easier. "And so you see," she told him when she had poured out the whole ugly story—how she had not only allowed Henry to seduce her, but encouraged it—how she had found her reputation destroyed within days of losing her father, her home, her friend. "You were right about me all along."

He waited a moment, then spoke. "Why now, Dora? Why did you wait to tell me?"

"Well, because I didn't love you before. That is, I didn't know I loved you, so it didn't seem so important."

His hand tightened on hers. "Then the Clinkshaw woman has nothing to do with it?"

On the verge of saying no—of lying again—Dora said, "Well, of course she does. I would have told you—at least, I think I would. Lying is like being forced to wear shoes that are half a size too small. At first, it doesn't seem so bad. You're wearing shoes, after all—you're not barefoot. But after a while they begin to chafe and before long, you can't think of anything but how much your feet hurt. No matter how fine the rest of your clothes are, no matter how pretty your hat is, it doesn't seem to matter anymore. You know what has to be done—and so you do it.''

"Confess, you mean."

She swallowed hard, waiting for him to release her hand and walk away in disgust. Every part of her ached with regret. It was a pain that would not lessen with time. Breathing in deeply, she filled her senses one last time with the clean, saltwater smell of his clothes, the sunshine and soap scent of his skin. The essence of the man she loved with all her heart.

"I knew," he said quietly.

Her heart stopped beating for an instant. "You knew? About me? That I'd lied?"

"Dora, I'm not as unintelligent as I might appear. When something doesn't add up, I investigate. It didn't seem logical that a woman like you would settle in a place like this and marry a man like Emmet. Not that he wasn't a good man—he was a fine man, with far more to recommend him that most. But I had to know what he'd gotten himself involved in."

"Did Polly tell you? Is that what you mean by investigate?" she whispered, dread chilling her to the bones.

"Give me credit for a grain of common sense. I'd never have believed her. She's obviously a born troublemaker. She'll be given some money and sent back on the first boat out."

"But you didn't order her. That is—you didn't, did you?"

He smiled then, and the warmth of it began to thaw the dread that had frozen her inside. ''No, ma'am, that I didn't. This is no time to be taking on any more projects. We've quite a ways to go before we'll be arranging any more matches.''

We. He'd said, we. Dare she hope…?

She dared. When Grey turned to take her in his arms—when he lowered her back onto the bed, hope soared. Slowly, gently, he touched her face—her lips, her chin, the tip of her nose. And then his mouth came down on hers, and she disappeared into the glittering rainbow realm of passion. Buttons gave way, laces were dealt with by increasingly eager hands. When she lay bare before him, he groaned, ''I don't deserve you, but oh, how I want you. How I love you.…''

Her heart was beating visibly when he lowered his face to her breasts. She could tell by the way he was trembling what a price he was paying for patience, for gentleness. Breathing heavily, she said, ''If you love me, don't make me wait. I couldn't bear it if the house floated away again.''

He laughed, but it was a costly effort. And then he rolled off onto his back and lifted her up, swinging her over him. He settled her astride his thighs, slowly, slowly, until his arousal brushed against her moist heat. Closing his eyes, he swore silently.

''What are you doing?'' she whispered, her voice tense with uncertainty.

In answer, he lifted her again, resettling her so that she slowly, *slowly,* enveloped him.

A hard, shuddering sigh escaped through his clenched jaws. *Hang in there, man, make it last—make it last!*

She began to move of her own accord. Unable to

restrain himself further, he bucked, gripping her hips until they adjusted their rhythm.

At first she was awkward, as if this were her first time.

And he was desperate, as if it were his.

Together they rocked faster and faster, obsessed, pursued by a glittering avalanche of sheer feeling. When the leading edge caught up with them, flowed over them, burying them in shimmering waves of pleasure, they could only surrender to the intense, mind-shattering splendor.

Much later, in the aftermath of a storm of passion, whispered words were spoken that sealed her dreams forever.

Outside, a whippoorwill called to its mate. A night heron in search of its evening meal in the still-flooded lowlands croaked.

Downstairs, other plans were made. Other dreams soared, while overhead, a new moon rose in a cloudless sky.

Three weeks later, Reverend William Dennis Lee prepared to join three couples in holy matrimony. "Line up now, two by two so I can see what's what," he commanded. The new circuit preacher was a plain-spoken man. The attendants stood at attention. Clarence nearly tripped over James Calvin's feet as he tried to maneuver without taking his eyes off Bertie. He hadn't spoken to her yet, but everyone present knew theirs would be the next match. No point in overwhelming the new minister.

"Do you, Maurice Lennon Fitzwater, take Matilda Rebecca Blades..." He went through the brief ritual rapidly, as Almond mouthed every word along with him.

And then it was Almond and Lula's turn to be joined in marriage.

Last of all, Grey, his face unusually pale, gripped the hand of a beaming Dora, and bravely met his fate.

"I now pronounce y'all husbands and wives. Sort out the documents, sign 'em, then we'll adjourn for fried chicken."

There was a riffle of laughter as some of those closest to the door of the newly repaired church moved outside. Inside, Dora opened Emmet's Bible to make note of the events of the day. So far as she knew, it was the only Bible on the island except for those belonging to the two preachers, which hardly counted as family Bibles.

And there in Emmet's spidery hand she saw the inscriptions.

Sally Redd McCutcheon married Emmet Larkin Meeks on this day of our Lord, June eleventh, 1893.

Under that was written in the same hand, Adora Sutton Meeks married Greyson Laird St. Bride on this day of our Lord...

Dora burst into tears. Grey blotted his own eyes and carefully filled in the date.

And then the entire group left the storm-battered church to enjoy fried chicken and the rest of their lives.

* * * * *

Travel to the British Isles
and behold the romance and
adventure within the pages of these
Harlequin Historicals® novels

ON SALE JANUARY 2002
MY LADY'S TRUST
by **Julia Justiss**
(Regency England, 1812)
A society lady fakes her own death and discovers
true love with an eligible earl!

DRAGON'S DOWER
by **Catherine Archer**
(Medieval England, 1200)
Book #1 of *The Brotherhood of the Dragon* series
By the king's decree a brave knight must marry
the daughter of his fiercest foe....

ON SALE FEBRUARY 2002
HIS LADY FAIR
by **Margo Maguire**
(Medieval England, 1429)
A world-weary spy becomes embroiled in intrigue—
and forbidden passion!

 Harlequin Historicals®
Historical Romantic Adventure!

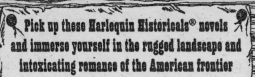

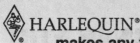

CALL THE ONES YOU LOVE OVER THE HOLIDAYS!

Save $25 off future book purchases when you buy any four Harlequin® or Silhouette® books in October, November and December 2001,

PLUS

receive a phone card good for 15 minutes of long-distance calls to anyone you want in North America!

WHAT AN INCREDIBLE DEAL!

Just fill out this form and attach 4 proofs of purchase (cash register receipts) from October, November and December 2001 books, and Harlequin Books will send you a coupon booklet worth a total savings of $25 off future purchases of Harlequin® and Silhouette® books, AND a 15-minute phone card to call the ones you love, anywhere in North America.

Please send this form, along with your cash register receipts as proofs of purchase, to:
In the USA: Harlequin Books, P.O. Box 9057, Buffalo, NY 14269-9057
In Canada: Harlequin Books, P.O. Box 622, Fort Erie, Ontario L2A 5X3
Cash register receipts must be dated no later than December 31, 2001.
Limit of 1 coupon booklet and phone card per household.
Please allow 4-6 weeks for delivery.

**I accept your offer! Enclosed are 4 proofs of purchase.
Please send me my coupon booklet
and a 15-minute phone card:**

Name: _____

Address: _____ City: _____

State/Prov.: _____ Zip/Postal Code: _____

Account Number (if available): _____

---

097 KJB DAGL
PHQ4013

Bestselling Harlequin® author

JUDITH ARNOLD

brings readers a brand-new,
longer-length novel based on her
popular miniseries *The Daddy School*

Somebody's Dad

If any two people should avoid getting
romantically involved with each other, it's
bachelor—and children-phobic!—Brett Stockton
and single mother Sharon Bartell. But neither
can resist the sparks...especially once
The Daddy School is involved.

"Ms. Arnold seasons tender passion with a dusting
of humor to keep us turning those pages."
—*Romantic Times Magazine*

Look for *Somebody's Dad*
in February 2002.

HARLEQUIN®
Makes any time special ®

*Together for the first time
in one Collector's Edition!*

New York Times bestselling authors

Barbara Delinsky

Catherine Coulter   Linda Howard

Forever Yours

**A special trade-size volume containing three
complete novels that showcase the passion,
imagination and stunning power that these
talented authors are famous for.**

Coming to your favorite retail outlet in December 2001.

HARLEQUIN®
Makes any time special ®